"Control, do you still ha___ ___ our position?"

The earpiece responded with an empty hiss. Bolan pulled the device from his ear. There was still the hope that even though he couldn't communicate Keller could still track him.

Ous stood and steadied himself against a rock. "The gunfire from the top of the gorge has stopped."

"They'll be organizing a hunting party."

"Do you think Saboor could convince our comrades to hunt me, much less the Mighty One?" Ous asked.

"No." Bolan thought about Zurisaday's mysterious bodyguards. "They'll be bringing in ringers."

Don Pendleton's Mack Bolan®

Assassin's Code

A GOLD EAGLE BOOK FROM

W⊕RLDWIDE®

TORONTO • NEW YORK • LONDON
AMSTERDAM • PARIS • SYDNEY • HAMBURG
STOCKHOLM • ATHENS • TOKYO • MILAN
MADRID • WARSAW • BUDAPEST • AUCKLAND

Recycling programs
for this product may
not exist in your area.

First edition December 2011

ISBN-13: 978-0-373-61549-0

Special thanks and acknowledgment to
Charles Rogers for his contribution to this work.

ASSASSIN'S CODE

Printed in U.S.A.

I have to bring to your notice a terrifying reality: with the development of nuclear weapons Man has acquired, for the first time in history, the technical means to destroy the whole of civilization in a single act.

—Joseph Rotblat
1908–2005

A terrifying reality is how far bad people will go to bring about Armageddon. But a few good people stand ready to defend.

—Mack Bolan

CHAPTER ONE

Helmand Province, Islamic Republic of Afghanistan

"Good Luck, sir!" the driver called. Mack Bolan, aka the Executioner, nodded as he pulled his shemagh up over the bridge of his nose and his goggles down over his eyes. He shouldered his gear bag and stepped out of the Mine Resistant Ambush Protected armored vehicle—MRAP—and into the maelstrom. Except for the watering of the Helmand River, the province was arid and when the wind blew, the dust rose. The dust storm was in its second day, and it turned the world at noon into a howling, hissing peach-colored nightmare of wind and grit.

Bolan turned his head as a wave of dust slapped him in the face. The wind plucked at his clothing as the dust sought every fold and crevice. He slammed the door shut behind him and knocked twice on the fender for thanks and luck. The MRAP 4X4 rumbled off toward the temporary airmobile depot.

The soldier leaned into the wind and walked across the village's single street to a blast-blackened native house. The wind and dust were making an earnest attempt at scrubbing the face of the house clean. What it couldn't scour away were the pockmarks in the clay from dozens of bullet strikes and the bigger craters and divots from heavy machine guns and grenade blasts.

A pair of goggled, helmeted and scarf-faced Marines

stood hunched at guard outside the door. A designated marksman on the roof was a sand-colored ghost in the gloom. The two Marines below nodded and opened what was left of the shattered, blue-painted wooden door. The wind dropped from a howl to a moan as Bolan stepped out of the storm and into a butcher's yard.

United States Assistant Attaché Henry "Hank" Millard had died hard. He had risen to the rank of commander in the United States Navy and was a Defense Language Institute Hall of Famer who spoke excellent Dari Persian and Arabic. He had been sent to the blast furnace of Helmand province to deal directly with the tribal chieftains and to woo them away from the Taliban.

Only a few threads of flesh and gristle kept his head attached to his body.

Bolan pushed up his goggles, pulled down his shemagh and set down his bag with a muffled clank. A fully armed and armored member of the Marine Military Police openly scowled at him. A man and woman in plain battle fatigues looked at Bolan suspiciously. The SIG pistols strapped to their thighs told Bolan they were most likely Naval Criminal Investigative Service agents. Of interest was an Afghan man of indeterminate middle age standing slightly off by himself. He wore a mixture of Afghan and Western dress. The pakol on his head said he was probably from the northwest. He smoked a ten-inch church-warden-style briar pipe, and every time he puffed the NCIS agents glared at him, however they seemed unwilling or unable to demand that he cease smoking at a crime scene. The man carried an M-4 rifle crooked in his elbow.

He looked disturbingly like Clint Eastwood if the actor had a broken nose, grew a salt-and-pepper beard with matching long curling hair and had skin the color and complexion of cracked saddle leather. The man gazed at Bolan in open speculation with the inscrutable yellow eyes of a wolf.

Bolan turned his attention back to the decapitated attaché. Millard had been sent in with emergency haste to keep the very delicate and contentious negotiations going after the last envoy had been killed. A lot of peacemakers were being killed. Helmand Province was critical to the war effort. The President himself had asked for Stony Man Farm's involvement, specifically Bolan's. It wasn't his usual activity, and babysitting was the soldier's least favorite job, but he knew what the stakes were in Afghanistan and he had accepted the mission. He'd been twenty-four hours too late in arriving, and it had taken orders from the Man to keep Millard's murder quiet for the ensuing twenty-four hours Bolan requested. He had twenty-four hours and counting to make something happen before the whole thing blew wide open.

The Marine MP continued to eyeball Bolan. "And just who the hell are you?"

It wasn't an unreasonable question, but the Marine just wasn't going to get a reasonable or what would qualify as a sane answer in his USMC world-view. Bolan gave the man a friendly smile anyway. "I'm your liaison, Captain Yoshida."

Yoshida wasn't impressed. "And just which branch of government are you—" the captain sought for a word "—liaising for me for, again, exactly, Mr....?" He trailed off as he scanned Bolan's plain uniform in vain for ID, rank or insignia.

"Which branch of government do you require aid or assistance from, Captain?" Bolan countered.

The captain contemplated this strange offer. The Afghan suddenly smiled in a friendly fashion and stuck out his hand. "My name is Omar Ous."

Bolan shook his hand. "Pleasure. Call me Cooper."

The NCIS agents stepped forward. The woman arranged a professional look on her face. It was a nice face, with high cheekbones, a strong chin, big brown eyes and a short ponytail pulled through the back of her fatigue cap. "Kathryn Keller, and this is Agent Neil Farkas."

Farkas was a gangling Ichabod Crane–looking individual with a slight stoop, a permanent number-four bad hair day haircut graying at the temples and an Adam's apple that would cut glass. Bolan pressed the flesh all around and then gave the assassination scene a second go-over. The soldier wasn't a detective, but his War Everlasting had taken him to firefights on every continent on Earth, and he could read a battle scene like an experienced hunter reading trail sign.

"It was an inside job," he stated.

"You think?" Keller inquired.

"Millard was done execution style. His pistol is still strapped to his thigh," Bolan continued. He looked at the four other bodies in the room. They'd all had their heads hammered apart at point-blank range with automatic weapons. "The bad guys literally just walked in and did this with complete surprise. How many servants did the attaché have?"

Captain Yoshida crossed his arms over the M-4 carbine slung across his chest. "Eight. We have two in custody. The other six disappeared. I have people—"

"The rest of the servants are dead. Don't bother."

For a moment there was no sound but the howl of the wind and the hiss of the dust outside. The motley crew of unlikely allies stood in the charnel house of death, each considering his or her own analysis. Farkas spoke first. "The man was a United States attaché, and he's three spaghetti strings of gristle short of decapitation."

Bolan nodded.

"So I got a question for you," Farkas said.

"Shoot."

Farkas gave Bolan a very questioning look. "How come this isn't all over FOX news?"

"Because I asked the President to give me twenty-four hours," Bolan replied.

That was good for several more moments of silence in the storm. Farkas shook his head. "You aren't talking about the president of Afghanistan."

"Well, I'm told he agreed to it," Bolan said.

Farkas's face went blank as machines far beyond his pay grade spun their cogs and wheels around him. "Jesus."

Keller stared. "Buddy, you're like straight out of a movie."

Yoshida examined Bolan as if he were a spider the size of Shetland pony that had suddenly dropped into their midst. "More like a comic book."

"I like him," Ous opined.

Bolan inclined his head at Ous and got down to business. "Two attachés in two months. Someone's trying to kill the peace process in Helmand Province. They want a stink. They want an uproar."

Keller's eyes widened as she started to understand what Bolan was getting at. "And we're into day two with nothing on the news."

Yoshida gave Bolan an infinitesimal nod. "And criminals can't help but come back to the scene of the crime."

"They're going to want to know what went wrong," Bolan said, nodding. "And what's happening."

Keller popped the retention strap on her holster. "You think they're going to come snooping back?"

"They're here now," Bolan stated.

Ous tapped his pipe empty against the bottom of his

boot and put the pipe in his tactical vest. He pushed off the safety of his M-4 with a click. "He is right. Now is the time of ambush. They come."

Bolan knelt beside his gear bag. "Get your men inside, Captain."

"Oh, for God's sake…" Yoshida clicked his com unit and spoke to the guards outside. "Yo! Buzz! Munoz! You got anything suspicious, any movement at all out there?"

Outside the dust hissed against the side of the house like the amplified sound of writhing serpents.

"Buzz? Munoz?" Yoshida's voice rose. "Come back!" No one came back across the tactical radio. The captain unslung his rifle and spoke to the man on the roof. "Plowman, come back!"

Nothing came back but the wind.

"God…damn it…" Yoshida unslung his carbine.

Bolan unzipped his rifle bag and took out his Beowulf entry weapon. It looked like Yoshida's M-4 carbine on steroids. The village was just outside the city of Sangin, one of only three major cities in Helmand Province and one that had seen the most brutal urban warfare of almost the entire war in Afghanistan. Bolan's Beowulf weapon was .500 caliber and was the equivalent of fully automatic buffalo rifle. His also had the unusual modification of a grenade launcher mounted beneath the barrel. He had come ready for a battle in the streets.

It seemed the battle was about to be joined.

Farkas scooped up a Joint Service Combat Shotgun leaned in the corner and Keller took a stubby black MP-5 K off the couch and pushed the selector to full-auto. Yoshida changed frequencies. "Camp Two, this is Envoy One, requesting immediate reinforcement. Come back."

Nothing came back but the same hiss.

Bolan slung a bandolier of grenades and spare mags

over his shoulder. "You're being jammed across all frequencies."

Yoshida was appalled. "When was the last time the Taliban could jam U.S. military com links?"

Bolan loaded a fragmentation round into his grenade launcher. "Puzzler, isn't it?"

Yoshida's face set in a ferocious scowl. "I'm going outside. I have to find my men. Anyone coming with me?"

"Whoever took them in this storm did it point-blank," Bolan cautioned. "They're right outside."

"Plowman's on the roof. You can't see from rooftop to rooftop, he's—"

"They're on the roof, too."

"Shit," Keller observed.

"Crap," Farkas agreed.

Ous smiled the smile of a warrior who had given himself over to violence and intended to enjoy it. "Shit-crap!"

Bolan took three steps and kicked the front door open. Shit-crap was right.

The MRAP was roaring straight toward the door. The gears ground as someone unused to driving an MRAP built a full head of steam. Luckily whoever was in charge seemed to have no idea how to use the remote-weapon station and bring the .50-caliber weapon to bear. Bolan vainly wished he'd loaded an antiarmor round, but he sent the frag grenade flying into the armor-glass windshield and lunged back. "Get back! Get back!"

The MRAP hit the house in a forty-mile-per-hour, fourteen-ton car wreck. The door, the jamb and a significant chunk of the wall came down in an eruption of shattering clay. A chunk of wall hit Yoshida in his armored chest and knocked him into the next room. Keller screamed as a section of roof fell in, Plowman's body falling on top of her. Two screaming, flailing terrorists followed as the ceiling dropped in a cascade. Bolan's Beowulf thunder-clapped twice as he gave each killer a .500-caliber sledge-hammer to the chest.

Ous's M-4 made a distinctive clack as he pushed the usually deactivated selector switch to full-auto. The glass on an MRAP was rated to stop shell splinters, the blast effect of roadside improvised explosive devices and hits from .30-caliber rifle rounds. Ous's weapon was .30 cali-ber, but the range was point-blank and he emptied his 20-round mag on full-auto. Armor glass geysered and cracked beneath the onslaught.

Bolan batted cleanup as he sent his eight remaining rounds through the driver's window and shattered it. Ar-terial spray followed the glass shrapnel. The engine died at the same time as the driver, and the vehicle stood stalled in wreckage. Armored doors clanged open and the cry of *"Allahu Akbar!"* howled above the storm as killers boiled out the back door and made for the breach on either side of the vehicle. Others came over the top.

Bolan racked open his grenade launcher and slid another frag grenade into the smoking breech. Keller rose from the rubble and human wreckage. Her submachine gun bripped as she put bursts into the portside invaders. Farkas's shot-gun boomed aft in rapid semiautomatic. Bolan raised his weapon as gears ground in the MRAP as someone tried to get the vehicle moving while crouching beneath the level of the shattered windshield.

"Fire in the hole!" The team crouched as a unit as Bolan fired his grenade through the MRAP's window and turned the insides of the vehicle into a slaughter box of buzz-sawing shrapnel. Engine activity in the MRAP ceased and desisted.

Bolan roared as he moved back and reloaded. "Move back! Farkas! Check the captain!"

Farkas pulled a fade as Bolan, Keller and Ous knelt and shot. The killers came on crying out God's name and with their AK-74s spraying as they stumbled over the rubble. Their faith made them fearless, but it didn't make them accurate or bulletproof. They fell going forward, but they fell. Bolan slammed in a fresh mag and counted a dozen dead. "Cease fire!"

The only noise was the storm beyond the shattered walls and the mechanical noise of weapons being reloaded. They had loaded the MRAP to the gills with holy warriors, but Bolan knew there had to be more in the surrounding houses and alleys. "Farkas! Sitrep!"

"Captain Yoshida's okay!" Farkas called back. "But we've got enemy gunners coming up the alley behind us! I make it a baker's dozen!"

Keller wiped blood and dust from her face and glared out into the dust storm. "Christ, there must be a platoon of them!"

"We're out of here!" Bolan shouted.

Keller looked around in confusion. "Where're we gonna go?"

Bolan clambered over the rubble on the MRAP. "The bus is leaving!"

Farkas shuffled forward, giving Yoshida a shoulder to lean on. Bolan flung open the driver's door. The interior was painted black with smoke, glinting with shrapnel gouges and swathed in blood spray. He pulled the nearly headless driver from behind the wheel. The man who had tried to replace him was torn up pretty badly from the grenade, but he was still alive. Bolan shoved him out of the way as the rest of the team began to climb in. "Can anyone drive this?"

Yoshida gave a defiant wheeze. "I'll fucking drive it out of here!"

"Do it!" Bolan moved back into the cabin. "Farkas! Stabilize the prisoner if you can! Keller! Close that back door!"

Bolan slid into the remote-weapon operator's seat. Ugly scratches scored the monitor and everything was covered with smoke and blast residue, but the screen came to life as he clicked keys. The unmanned turret and the .50-caliber machine gun it carried whirred above him as he traversed rearward. Someone outside with ill intentions noticed the move, and Keller slammed the back door shut just as bullets began whining off the hull.

Yoshida rammed the MRAP into Reverse. Clay and timbers shifted as the armored vehicle backed out of the rubble. Bullets began whining off the hull in bee swarms. Bolan tracked the remote .50-caliber gun through the gloom, silencing the enemy fire shooter by shooter. The soldier's skin crawled in anticipation of the RPG hit that would turn the cabin into a blast furnace of superheated gas and molten metal. The MRAP lurched forward as Yoshida put the hammer down. Ous leaped from armored window to armored window. "Seven o'clock! Seven o'clock high!"

The remote weapon whirled under Bolan's command, the big .50-caliber weapon tearing the three men on the rooftop into rags.

BOLAN CAUGHT THE FLASH of fire and smoke as the rocket roared past his gun camera. The rocket impacted a wall in a flash, and then the explosion and smoke was swallowed in the dust storm. Keller shook her head in mounting panic as she scanned out the portside windows. "Christ, they're everywhere!"

Yoshida roared in pain. "Shit! Shit! Shit!"

"The captain's hit!" Farkas shouted.

Bolan flicked a glance over to see the Marine captain sag, swearing, out of the driver's seat. "Shit..."

The Executioner was nearly thrown from his position as the MRAP swerved into a wall and stalled.

"Bismillah!" Ous shouted. "Rocket! Rocket!"

Bolan tracked the turret around just in time to see the rocket-propelled grenade fly straight into his crosshairs. "Everybody down!" Keller screamed. The interior lights went black as something seemed to slap the MRAP along its chassis. The turret overhead screamed as metal tore. Sparks flew from the wiring, and everything that wasn't bolted down went flying. Ous tumbled into Bolan's position and bounced off him. The Executioner's ears rang, but battle instincts took over. The vehicle was still upright. The fire-suppression system hadn't been activated, so they weren't on fire, and the hull hadn't been breached.

The remote-weapon system was gone. Bullets continued slamming into the hull. Bolan scrambled over Yoshida and Farkas. One glance told him Yoshida was in bad shape. The driver's position was a viscous swamp of blood from every man who had driven the vehicle this day.

Bolan pulled down his goggles and slid into the death seat.

The wind blasted dust through the shattered window. The soldier hit the starter button, and the engine grunted then stalled.

"They come!" Ous yelled as he looked out the rear windows.

The Executioner hit the starter again, and the Caterpillar diesel engine thundered back to life. He shoved the MRAP into Reverse and floored it. The howls of bloodlust turned to screams. Bolan was rewarded by the sound of bodies bouncing off armor.

Ous went flying as the MRAP clipped the side of a

house. Gears ground as the vehicle was cranked back into drive, then stalled. Thumps echoed hollowly from the roof as someone leaped from the rooftop and onto the MRAP. Bolan snarled as a hand appeared in the shattered driver's window and dropped a grenade in his lap. The soldier snatched the grenade and shoved it back out the window.

"Down!" Bolan flung himself below the level of the window as the frag grenade detonated on the hood and sent jagged bits of metal spitting in all directions. He rose to find someone trying to shove the muzzle of an AK through the window, and grabbed the barrel, yanking it aside. The weapon went hot in his hand as the owner fired a long burst into Bolan's armrest. Drawing his Beretta, the Executioner put a 3-round burst into the attacker's gun hand. Fingers flew apart and Bolan yanked the weapon away. He hit the starter button and the besieged MRAP coughed into life once again, but the engine didn't sound good.

People were still on the roof.

Bolan floored it once more. The MRAP roared as it accelerated. When the speedometer hit twenty, the soldier stood on the brakes. Three men went flying into the street ahead as if they had wings. Bolan stomped on the accelerator and ground the killers beneath the vehicle's massive all-terrain tires. He shoved the Beretta out the window and fired bursts at two men appearing out of an alleyway with AKs. One fell to Bolan's fire, but the other leaped back. Bullets still struck the MRAP, but they all struck the rear rather than the front, sides and roof.

Bolan burned out of the village and slowed as the storm engulfed them. "Farkas, how's Yoshida?"

"Bad."

"The prisoner?"

"Worse."

"Grab the medical kit from the locker. It's an hour back

to base, and I need you to keep them both alive. Keller, help him."

Keller put a hand on Bolan's shoulder. "Mister, you really kicked some ass."

Bolan grimaced through the dust blasting through the window. The fact was they'd been mauled, and it was thirty miles to the Marine forward base outside Sangin. "Ous, keep an eye out behind us."

CHAPTER TWO

Sangin City, Base Camp Bravo

Yoshida looked like hell.. He taken two rounds through the neck and trapezius, and a third had relieved him of his left ear. The fact that he still had a head, much less anything below that was still functioning, was a miracle. Bolan smiled down at the wounded warrior. "You look like shit, Captain."

The Marine gave Bolan a very weary smile back. "Count myself lucky to be looking like anything, Cooper."

"I'm sorry about your men."

"Thanks for hauling us out of there." Yoshida sighed. "How are Farkas and Keller?"

"Just bumps and bruises mostly."

"Yeah, that was a bumpy ride. How's the prisoner?"

"He's stable," Bolan said. "I'm about to go look in on him."

The Marine captain's eyes went icy despite the fog of painkillers. "Yeah, well, you be sure to give him my regards when you do."

"Ous is dying to give him your regards. It's been hard to hold him back," Bolan admitted. "Speaking of which, what do you know about the man?"

Yoshida sagged into his bed. "Not much. Word is he's a real bad-ass, and he's been real dark and spooky with the CIA. I hear that the Taliban has a one million afghan bounty on his head."

Bolan did a little math. At the moment one million afghans was about twenty thousand dollars U.S., plus change. Afghanistan was about as dirt poor as nations got. The Taliban putting that kind of coin on a man's head said something about Mr. Ous's reputation and activities. "Can I get you anything?"

"Bourbon," Yoshida suggested. "And the assholes who did this."

"You'll have the bourbon before Taps. You have my word on it." Bolan smiled. "The assholes will have to be after Reveille tomorrow."

Yoshida's eyes glazed over with the combination of wounds, drugs and exhaustion, and slowly closed. "Just get them…."

Bolan nodded at the wounded, sleeping Marine. "You got my word on that, too, Captain."

The Executioner strode from the regular infirmary tent into the storm and walked across the lane to another hospital tent. It was much smaller and guarded by armed Marines. Bolan nodded at the two sentries and walked in the tent. The wind flapped and shuddered the walls. There was only one patient inside. He lay on a bed with tubes sticking out of him and was heavily swathed in bandages, but he was conscious and clearly very agitated. A short, similarly agitated Marine doctor stood between the prisoner and Ous. The Hippocratic oath and naked intimidation fought for the doctor's soul, but he was a Marine and stood his ground. The doctor's head snapped around at the new intrusion. When he saw Bolan's uniform, he looked at him imploringly.

"Can you please get this man out of here?"

"Why?" Bolan asked.

"He wants to interrogate my patient!"

"I want to interrogate your patient."

The doctor waved his hands at the man on the bed and then toward heaven in mounting outrage. "You think this man is in any kind of condition for interrogation?"

Ous gazed unblinkingly at the prisoner with his disturbingly wolflike eyes. "I believe the prisoner is in an ideal condition for interrogation."

The man on the bed flinched.

The doctor was appalled. "Oh for God's sake!"

"I also believe this man speaks English," Ous added.

The prisoner flinched again. Bolan kept the smile off his face. Ous was good.

"Taliban?" Bolan asked.

The prisoner assumed a stone-faced stare at the roof of the tent.

"It was so much easier when they marched through the streets, proudly wearing their black turbans," Ous said. "But we killed so many of them they bared their heads so that they might hide in gutters like skulking dogs."

The prisoner's cheek flexed.

"Such a shocking lack of faith," Ous concluded.

Ous was literally inducing a facial tic on the prisoner.

"Taliban?" Bolan asked again.

The doctor was clearly upset. "Listen! I—"

"Dr.…?" Bolan inquired.

"What? Oh, Early. Listen, I—"

"Dr. Early, I understand the Hippocratic oath and I know this is your patient, but I need a no-bullshit assessment. When will this man be well enough to be sent to the capital?"

Dr. Early made a visible effort to control himself. "He's torn up pretty badly. I saved his left leg, but I couldn't save his left testicle. He was very lucky about the shrapnel in his abdomen. It was a miracle it didn't tear up anything vital, but a lot of his real estate is being held together by stitches. If you put him on the road to Kabul, you're going to bounce them open. Even if his stitches hold, his brains will most likely be applesauce by the time you get there. I want—hell, I demand that he not be moved for the next twenty-four hours while I monitor his concussion."

"I agree. He should only be moved by helicopter." Bolan glanced at the tent walls as they vibrated. The storm was in its third day and showed no signs letting up. "We both know that isn't going to happen today. But when you release him to me, I will absolutely guarantee his safety."

Dr. Early walked around to the other side of the bed and stared down at his patient. "More than the son of a bitch deserves, but I believe you when you say he'll get it."

"Dr. Early, if it makes you feel any better I can get—" Bolan's eyes flared as the wall of the tent lifted a few feet away from the doctor and the spherical, olive-drab shape of a U.S. M-67 hand grenade rolled to a stop at Early's feet. "Grenade!"

Dr. Early echoed the sentiment and promptly threw himself on top of it. Bolan seized the bed-frame. "Ous!"

Ous grabbed the frame at the foot of the bed and together they heaved the bed toward them and dropped prone. The prisoner screamed as his IVs tore and he toppled to the floor. The grenade detonated with a muffled whip-crack and 6.5 ounces of Composition B tried to send its lethal cloud of steel splinters through Dr. Early's body and fill the tent. It was partially successful. Medical equipment shattered and sparked. In the confines of the tent, the blast effect was like a blow to the head. The mattress bottom rippled and tufted as some splinters made it through.

Bolan was up instantly. His ears rang, but his Beretta

was in hand. Dr. Early was nothing but rags. The soldier snarled over his shoulder at Ous. "Guard the patient!"

The Executioner rolled under the tent wall. The fact that it could be lifted told him it had been doctored for the fragging. He lunged up into the storm. Fifty yards ahead the dust swallowed a running figure.

The big American broke into a dead sprint through the base's back alleys, leaping tent ropes like an Olympic hurdler. Up ahead the man became visible again. He had stopped and was leaning on a tent rope to steady himself. Apparently he thought he was safe. He lifted his goggled head and saw Bolan bearing down on him like an avenging angel. The assassin whirled and promptly tripped over the rope. He lurched back up and took three stumbling steps. He shouted despairingly over the howling of the wind. "No! Wait! You don't understand, man! No! I—" Part of Bolan's brain noted the man was speaking with a Puerto Rican accent.

The man suddenly seemed to remember the .45-caliber MEU pistol strapped to his leg.

The pistol was half out of its holster when Bolan's boot slammed up between the guy's legs. The assassin screamed like a rabbit being killed and collapsed into Bolan's embrace. The Executioner's right arm snaked under the man's chin and heaved upward as the man sagged from the testicular trauma. The big American locked his hands together and squeezed as well as lifted. The carotid artery shut off, and the more brutal trachea compression cut of his air.

Marines charged out of the dust from all directions shouting contradictory orders and waving rifles. "Freeze! Let him go! Don't move! I said drop him!" Bolan dropped the man as he went limp with unconsciousness.

"On your knees!" a Marine screamed. His bayonet was fixed. "I said, on your knees!"

Agent Keller appeared out of the dust and flashed her badge. "NCIS! Agent Keller! He's with me!"

Bolan glanced down at the motionless man at his feet. "He's the one who fragged the infirmary."

The belligerent Marine lowered his weapon. Even with the wind and dust battering him his face went slack. "Oh... my...God..."

Bolan felt the young Marine's pain. The U.S. military had seen its share of atrocities: fraggings, crimes and massacres. Rightly or wrongly, the modern United States Marine Corps considered itself above such things. The motto of the Corps was *Semper fidelis*, Always Faithful.

What this man had done was unthinkable.

The man on the ground gasped as he roused back into consciousness. "Hook him and book him," Bolan suggested.

"Right." An MP produced zip restraints. Ous appeared at Bolan's elbow.

"How's the prisoner?" Bolan asked.

"He is currently leaking clear fluids out of his eyes and ears, and his pupils are two different sizes. I fear the blast from the grenade was too much for his already beleaguered brain." Ous sighed. "You are all right?"

"I could use a cup of coffee," Bolan admitted.

Ous looked at Bolan with great seriousness. "You are a man of the West. I am sure what you require is beer."

Sangin Bazaar

BOLAN AND OUS drank beer. Islam forbade the drinking of alcohol, however across the Muslim world the laws of hospitality were some of the most powerful on Earth. A large number of Muslim men Bolan had met had come to the happy, contorted conclusion that it would be unforgivable to not offer a Westerner his dissipation, and an even worse breach of honor to make him feel uncomfortable by frowning upon his misguided ways and not partaking.

Ous did everything he could to make Bolan comfortable by keeping the bottles of beer flowing from the battered plastic cooler between them. They sat on stools in a tiny alcove curtained with a pair of rugs. Outside two enormously fat men who appeared to be twins blocked the entrance to the alcove. Their stall was piled high with oranges. Each man had an AK propped by his leg. The storm had died down, but it was still hot, windy, dusty, overcast and miserable outside. The orange trade was slow and the bazaar almost deserted.

"So," Bolan began, "you were Muj?"

Ous cracked two fresh beers and waited until Bolan had sipped from his. "I answered the call to jihad against the Soviet invaders when I was twelve. My aged father, who resides in heaven, pressed his Lee-Enfield rifle and a bandolier of fifty rounds into my hands and implored me to martyr myself in God's name. With the bayonet fixed, the rifle was taller than I was at the time. I failed to become a Holy Martyr, but I killed many, many Russians. At one point there was a ten-thousand-ruble reward out for my head."

"I understand the Taliban has a million on you at the moment," Bolan observed.

Ous shrugged modestly. "So I am told."

Bolan gave Ous a knowing look. "You were Northern Alliance?"

"For a time," Ous conceded. "I truly believed in jihad against the Soviets. God required them to be struck down. However, after liberation, I found that I had no use for the Taliban at all."

"They're—"

"They are foreign interlopers, and Wahhabist interlopers at that." Ous spit. "Destroyers of shrines."

"You're Sufi," Bolan surmised.

"Ismaili," Ous allowed.

Muhammad ibn Abd al-Wahhab had been an eighteenth-century scholar from Arabia. He considered anything but the strictest adherence to Sunni Islam and Sharia Law to be "innovations" that needed ruthless and violent crushing. The Taliban took much of their doctrine from Abd al-Wahhab's teachings and had applied it with fanatic zeal during their five-year reign of religious terror as the governing body of Afghanistan.

"The attack in the village yesterday wasn't exactly what I would call Taliban standard tactical procedure," Bolan ventured.

"Both the attack against us and the slaying of your envoy were very unorthodox." Ous puffed his pipe for a contemplative moment. "I have operated with the United States Marine Corps in the past. I found this morning's incident profoundly disturbing."

Soldiers refusing to take prisoners during the war on terror wasn't unknown. Some prisoners had been mistreated. A U.S. Marine fragging an infirmary with U.S. personnel inside was positively anomalous. Ous took another sip of beer. "What have you learned?"

There wasn't much. "Corporal Saulito Convertino, from New York City, a strict Catholic. The chaplain says he attended services every Sunday. No known radical, terrorist or criminal affiliations. Was recommended for the Bronze Star in action during the surge into Helmand."

"And his disposition now?"

"In custody, not talking to his appointed lawyer, not talking to anyone."

Ous eyes narrowed. "You said he was weeping when you apprehended him?"

"Yeah." Bolan nodded very slowly. "Yeah, he was."

"You fear he was coerced," Ous surmised.

"It's the only thing that makes sense. But he didn't owe anybody money, wasn't on drugs, the preliminary FBI investigation back in New York states his family is fine and has no idea how this could have happened."

"You believe the coercion had to be local," Ous suggested.

"We brought in the prisoner last night and he got fragged this morning. Corporal Convertino hadn't been planning this, he was activated."

"Sleeper cells," Ous said incredulously, "in the United States Marine Corps?"

"More like a mole."

"So how was he recruited, locally, as it were?"

"I can think of only one thing, Convertino was an exemplary Marine except for one thing," Bolan said.

"Oh?"

"On three separate occasions he was found AWOL, but each time the statement of charges was dropped."

"And why should this be?" Ous asked.

"Because Convertino was a scrounger."

"I am not aware of this term."

"He was good at getting things," Bolan explained. "I spoke with a few of the men on his squad. If you wanted beer or liquor in Afghanistan, he'd find a way. If you couldn't find any Marlboro, he'd get you Tajiki Kahons at half the price. U.S. and European pornography is almost impossible to sneak into Afghanistan, but if you wanted some, he could find you the Russian stuff that flows down through the northern border by the bushel basket. Every unit has a scrounger, and by all accounts Convertino was a scrounger par excellence. He was born in Puerto Rico, and they're the last bastion of bartering culture in the United States. From what I hear he had the gift of gab, everybody liked him, and he had been to the language school and spoke some Arabic."

"So why would the statement of charges be dropped if he was dealing in contraband?"

"Because he acquired contraband for his superiors," Bolan said.

"Ah, yes, I see. Truly the world is the same all over. So, you believe it was in the midst of this scrounging that he was seduced?"

"I'm thinking seduced is exactly the right word. When he was in Iraq, Convertino had the reputation of being one hell of a charming horn dog. Female soldiers and Iraqi women liked him, a lot. Here in Afghanistan the female soldiers are a lot fewer, the Afghanis are far more violent about protecting their women. What little prostitution there is takes place in the big cities, and those are few and far between. A woman in Afghanistan who has been reduced to prostitution has seen a lot of hard miles, and that's not Convertino's type. The real brothels are run by Russians and Turks, are stocked with Eastern European and Russian women and cater to rich Afghans and foreign visitors with money. Out of Convertino's league. After being transferred to Afghanistan I'm thinking Convertino was jonesing pretty hard."

"Jonesing." Ous nodded as he pondered this bit of American slang. "I believe I understand what you are saying." His eyes suddenly went wolflike. "You are saying we must find Corporal Convertino's sexy girlfriend."

"Something like that."

CHAPTER THREE

Sangin Base stockade

"Where the hell have you been?" Agent Kathryn Keller struggled to keep up with Bolan and Ous without breaking into a trot in the hallway.

"Drinking beer," Bolan replied.

"Hey!" Keller snarled.

Bolan stopped and turned. "What?"

"Well…" Keller suddenly grinned. "How come you didn't invite me?"

Bolan considered his answer and jerked his head at Ous. "He doesn't drink beer with women."

"What in God's name leads you to conclude that I do not drink beer with women?" Ous asked.

"My mistake," Bolan admitted. "Can you give me a sitrep, Keller?"

"Convertino talked."

"What'd he say?"

"Just that he admits to the murder of Dr. Early, the John Doe suspect, and the attempted murder of you and Mr. Ous."

"Anything else?"

"He's dismissed his appointed council, says he will plead guilty to all charges and requested the death penalty."

"He seems dedicated," Ous said.

"Down right self-sacrificing," Bolan agreed.

Keller looked back and forth between the two men. "What can I do to help?"

Bolan's cobalt gaze burned into Keller's eyes. "NCIS is still in charge of this case?"

"Not for much longer," Keller said. The MPs outside the cell snapped to attention and saluted the woman as she and her party approached. "And then God only knows who is going to take over. When this goes public, it's going to turn into a real dog-and-pony show."

"Then I want you to flash that NCIS badge, say 'agent in charge' and give me five minutes with the suspect," Bolan said.

Keller squeezed her eyes shut as if she had just developed a headache. She opened her eyes and grimly flashed her badge. "Keller! NCIS! Agent in charge! This man is a liaison from the Justice Department to see the prisoner!"

The ranking guard looked upon Keller with grave uncertainty. "Um...yes, ma'am?" The other unlocked the door. "Uh, sir? Just so you know, the prisoner is not currently under restraint but we are on suicide watch."

"Thank you, Private," Bolan said.

"And what shall I do?" Ous inquired.

"No one comes in or out, and I mean no one," Bolan said.

The MPs looked on in alarm as Ous took one of their folding chairs beside the door, pulled a huge Khyber knife and began cleaning his fingernails. Keller just rolled her eyes. "That's it. I'm dead."

Bolan stalked into the holding cell and slammed the door shut behind him. There was nothing inside other than a single bunk and chair. Corporal Saulito Convertino jerked erect in his chair. His eyes widened in horror at the sight of Bolan. "Oh God! No!"

Bolan's open hand cracked across Convertino's face in textbook bitch-slap perfection.

"You—"

Bolan's hand cracked across Convertino's face once, twice, three times. The Executioner didn't believe in pliers and blowtorch torture. He had been tortured himself, and all it had ever engendered within him was hatred. But crime and terror were slippery slopes that men could find themselves in against their will, sometimes finding themselves ensnared before they knew it, and Bolan could recognize a repentant sinner. Corporal Saulito Convertino's salvation was between him and his Maker, but Bolan was perfectly willing to take him behind the woodshed and hear his confession. Minor pain and intimidation worked wonders.

Bolan's blue eyes burned down on the traitor like the embodied anger of an Old Testament God of the desert with no sense of humor. Convertino was a good-looking man. His slightly hooked nose, high cheekbones, curvy lips and Kirk Douglas chin were all set in toffee-tinted skin that bespoke his Spanish, African and Taino Indian blood. His copper-colored hair was cropped into USMC regulation skull-hugging curls, and he was built like an NFL defensive end.

Tears streamed down his face as he pushed himself up to his knees.

"Where's your girlfriend?" Bolan asked.

Convertino went slack-jawed in horror.

"Your girlfriend? You know, the one who put you up to this?"

"I can't! They'll kill h—"

Bolan bodily heaved Convertino to his feet and slammed him against the wall of the cell. "What's her name?"

"Reema! Her name is Reema!"

The first admission in a situation like this usually opened the floodgates. "Tell me the whole story, Corporal."

Convertino looked up in despair. "I love her...."

"And they'll kill her if you talk?"

The Marine looked down miserably. Bolan's eyes went cold. "Did you know I was in that tent?"

"No!"

"Mr. Ous?"

Convertino blinked through his tears. "Who?"

"You know there were Marine Corps medical personnel in that tent when you fragged it?"

Convertino sagged again. "I was hoping not."

Bolan's voice was merciless. "Dr. Early threw himself on that grenade to save everyone in that tent, including myself and your target. He's going to get the Congressional Medal of Honor, presented to his widow. What do you think you deserve, Corporal?"

Convertino's voice dropped to a dead whisper. "Court martial and death by lethal injection."

"You deserve a lot worse than that. There's a special place in hell for Marines who kill their own." Convertino held his head in his hands and sobbed. "Now where's the girl and who has her?" Bolan continued.

"They'll kill her, they—"

"They already killed her!" Bolan's voice thundered in the cell. "She's the only link! The only chance she has is that a hot piece of tail is a valuable commodity and they might have sold her. That is, if she's not in on it!"

A flicker of anger kindled in Convertino's agonized eyes. "What?"

"Don't you get it? She's a whore!"

"What did you say?"

"You pussy-whipped son of a bitch! Afghan girls don't put out! And if they do, they sure as hell don't risk it for loser corporals like you! She's Taliban!" Bolan spit, turning the provocation dial all the way up to high.

"No, she loves me! She said yes. She was going to be my wife." Fresh sobs racked the conflicted young soldier. "She's pregnant with my kid."

Bolan relented, just slightly. "I don't know what's going to happen to you, Corporal. It's been a long time since the U.S. Military put anyone to death, but you're a prime candidate.

"But I'll tell you this. If you're the one who's right, and she's innocent like you say, I'll save her, if I can. I'm the only chance either one of you has."

"What do I have to do?"

"Three things," Bolan said. "One, NCIS is going to get a sketch artist on a live feed and you're going to describe Reema. Two, you are going to tell me everything, and I mean everything that happened right up to the point you pulled that pin."

Convertino nodded. "And three?"

"Three? You're busting out of here."

NCIS temporary office, Sangin Base

"No, no, no, and no." Keller looked about to explode. Farkas stared out the window at the rain with a very unhappy "Don't know, don't have an opinion" look on his face. At that time of year Helmand Province averaged about two inches of rain. Right now they were getting three and on the tail of the dust storm it turned the world from a Martian landscape to gray floods and muck.

"Oh, come on, Keller," Bolan cajoled, "What could happen?"

Agent Keller's eyes flew wide in outrage. "He fragged a goddamn Marine Corps medical station! He killed a

Navy doctor, and my suspect, and I'm personally going to see to it that the Navy reinstitutes death by firing squad! And if they don't, I'm going to shoot Corporal Convertino myself!"

Bolan shrugged. "Give him to me."

"No!"

"You can shoot him later."

"What if he escapes?" Keller asked.

Bolan smiled.

"Okay," Keller acknowledged. "Maybe he can't escape you, but what if you get your head blown off?"

"Where'll he go? A Puerto Rican Marine in Afghanistan? He's dead meat wherever he runs."

"Yeah, and our boy is borderline suicidal."

"And he wants redemption. Let him fall going forward," Bolan said.

"Damn it! You know my orders were to extend you every courtesy! Every courtesy! This? This is pushing it!"

"Give him to me."

"No!" Keller replied.

"What? You don't trust me?"

"I don't know! And stop smiling at me!"

"Give him to me," Bolan pressed.

"God have mercy on us all…"

"Good." Bolan nodded. "I'm glad we have that settled."

"What!"

Bolan switched gears. "What did the sketch artist in D.C. come up with?"

Farkas opened a laptop and clicked an icon. Bolan could almost sympathize with the corporal. "Reema" was something right out of an old Arabian Nights movie: huge dark eyes, sensuous lips, perfect cheekbones and chin. All she was missing was a see-through pink veil and a ruby in her belly button. Bolan flicked through the multiple sketches he had ordered. Reema in Western-style clothes, Reema in the traditional long pants and tunic, Reema naked, Reema with just her eyes and the bridge of her nose peering out of a veil. Bolan downloaded the sketches into his highly modified tablet computer.

"Assuming I agree to go along with this," Keller said, "which I haven't, how do you want to play it?"

"Close to the vest. Convertino is on suicide watch. He makes an attempt, and busts out on the way to the infirmary. He steals a Humvee, crashes the gate and tries to contact his woman or whoever has her."

"Or whoever has her, if anyone has her, takes him out."

"That's about it," Bolan said.

"That's just about a death sentence, not to mention that during the manhunt, not many of our guys are going to try to bring him back alive."

"He's looking at life in prison or the death penalty anyway. He wants redemption, he wants his woman safe, and if his woman was in on it, he wants payback. And he's volunteered. He's already sworn he won't resist if captured."

"You know how many things can go wrong on this?" Keller asked.

"He's being implanted with a tracking device as we speak. I had to slap him around a bit to get him intimidated, so he has enough bruises on him no one should notice. The damage should help make his case."

"You know, even if they bite, the only reason will be to kill him," Keller said.

"I know."

"How big a team do you want?"

"Just me, and I'll take Ous along in case I need to talk to any locals," Bolan replied.

"No backup? No surveillance?"

"I'll have my own surveillance, but I'd take it as a favor if you were to pick me a crack team and keep a chopper hot on the pad in case I call. If things get hot, they're going to get hot fast."

Keller gave Bolan a very frank look. "I hope to God you've got some kind of pull with the Attorney General, or we are looking to get seriously rat-screwed on this one."

"Never met the man," Bolan admitted.

Keller just stared.

"But I know his boss," Bolan stated.

Keller opened her mouth and closed it. The Attorney General of the United States served at the pleasure of the President. "Can I ask you a question?"

"You can ask."

"Who are you?"

Bolan shrugged. "I'm Batman."

"I'm not surprised at all."

He gazed at Keller speculatively. "You speak Arabic?"

"Yeah, that's why I'm here." The NCIS agent's eyes narrowed. "Why?"

"How'd you like to be a caped crusader, too?"

CHAPTER FOUR

Sangin

"Yeah, nice cape, buddy!" Agent Keller sat in the battered Toyota pickup, mildly outraged, swathed in a full burka and sandwiched between Ous and Bolan. "It suits you," the soldier said.

"Indeed, you look most fetching," Ous agreed.

"No woman looks fetching in a pup tent," Keller muttered.

Ous sighed. "You have no idea how much time and energy we men spend, our eyes attempting to burn through the burka. We gasp at the accidental flash of an ankle, but much more can be told by a moment's fall or fold of cloth, the change in drape as a woman sits or stands, the sway of it as she moves, and we yearn, burning, to catch a heartbeat's glance of approval from a pair of shining eyes. I assure you, Agent Keller, our eyes are well practiced, and were you to walk across the bazaar, garbed as you are, all eyes would be upon you."

Keller turned to Bolan. "You know you could take some charm lessons from him."

"Actually, I may be the first man in Afghanistan to have charmed a woman into a burka rather than out of one," Bolan replied.

The radio link crackled with Farkas's voice. "Batman, this is Control, do you copy?"

"Loud and clear, over."

"Mission is go."

Bolan mentally counted down the seconds. Ous sat behind the wheel looking at his watch.

"Batman!" Farkas's voice rose slightly with excitement across the link, "The rabbit has run!"

"Right on the mark," Ous observed.

Bolan could hear gunfire on the other side of the link. "Understood. Control, maintain radio silence from now on unless we initiate."

"Copy that, Batman. Over and out."

Bolan took up his phone-size tablet and switched frequencies. Aaron Kurtzman's voice came across the link from Stony Man Farm, the nation's top counterterrorist organization, half a world away in Virginia. "Batman?"

"Inside joke. You have Convertino?"

"Affirmative. I have him on satellite tracking and satellite visual. My current visual window is two hours. After that I'll have to switch to a different orbiter. I predict a ten-minute visual lag, but you'll have constant from the transmitter."

"Copy that. Give me visual." Bolan watched as his screen lit up with a gray-green scene observed from overhead by a thermal-imaging satellite. Sangin Base was a constellation of lights, and a vehicle was tearing away from it with reckless speed. There was little to do but wait. Convertino would abandon his vehicle once he had covered some distance and then use his skills as a Marine scout sniper to make his way into the city unseen.

"I might just have something for you, Batman."

"What's that?"

"The woman, Reema." Bolan's screen split. Ous and Keller leaned over to peer at it. The NCIS sketch took up one-half of the screen and the other was a photo of a woman sitting in a café. She was blonde, wearing oversize sunglasses, and someone who wasn't a professional surveillance artist had taken the shot from across the street, but there was a similarity.

"Who is she?"

"I called in a few favors and got this from Israeli Intelligence. Last year an Israeli military industrialist was suspected of leaking information. This woman was suspected of being his mistress. The day after that photo was taken the man was found in his office with his brains blown out in an apparent suicide."

"And the woman?" Bolan queried.

"Disappeared without a trace."

Bolan had guessed that. "What else?"

"Working backward, the Israelis believe a woman matching her description may be linked to the death of several prominent Israeli and Lebanese citizens, but they can't prove anything," Kurtzman stated.

"They have a name?"

"All they have is a first name."

"Lay it on me," Bolan said.

"Zurisaday."

It was a beautiful name for a beautiful woman.

"A few clues lead them to believe she might be Jordanian," Kurtzman continued. "But they're not sure."

Keller echoed Bolan's thoughts. "A beautiful name."

"It means 'over the earth' in Arabic," Kurtzman said.

Ous scowled. "It should mean 'viper.'"

"Well." Keller sat back. "Convertino got bit, and bit bad."

"It is said the righteous man cannot feel their sting." Ous gazed long upon the sketch. "Though I must admit I have yet to meet such a man."

The feed suddenly switched to the satellite imaging.

"The vehicle has stopped. Convertino's just outside the southern end of the city and proceeding in."

"We're moving," Bolan said. Ous pulled the truck out of the alley and began negotiating the winding, narrow back streets of Sangin. Bolan checked the load of 9 mm subsonic hollowpoint rounds in his machine pistol and screwed the short black tube of a sound suppressor onto the muzzle.

"Be advised the corporal has changed course."

Bolan grimaced. Convertino had first met the woman at an after-hours club that catered to Western soldiers. That was the first place he was supposed to try. Failing that he would try to establish contact with some of her friends. "Where's he headed now?"

"North and west. He's moving toward the outskirts of the bazaar."

Keller was incensed. "Son of a bitch! Does he really think there's any place to run? I say we get the chopper in the air and scoop him up. This mission is over."

Bolan was confident that he had a pretty good read on the young corporal. "He's not trying to escape."

"Well, he sure as hell isn't sticking to the plan!"

Bolan nodded. "He's still in love. He wants to see his woman one more time, and confront her alone before we pick her up and he goes to jail for the rest of his life."

"Well, that's so sweet I might just throw up." Keller shook her head in disgust. "And you knew he was going to rabbit on us in the name of love all along?"

"I knew there was a chance. It was a chance I was willing to take. We still have him, satellite eyes on and GPS tracking. The mission is still go."

"I concur," Ous said.

"We've lost visual," Kurtzman reported. "He's entered a building."

"Vector us in, Bear," Bolan said, using Kurtzman's

nickname. His screen zoomed and a route appeared in green across a grid of the city. Bolan started calling rights and lefts fast as Ous took the alleys at breakneck speed. "What's Convertino's status?"

"Signal hasn't moved."

The pickup pulled up in front of a patio. A flowering lemon tree grew in the middle, and a scattering of wrought-iron chairs and tables surrounded it. "Looks like a teahouse.

"Indeed I have taken tea here before," Ous said.

"Keller, stay here and stay in character," Bolan ordered. "And get the chopper in the air."

Keller wasn't pleased but she got it. "You got it."

Bolan and Ous spilled out of the truck with their pistols drawn. "Cover me."

Ous took a firing position over the hood of the truck as Bolan moved across the open area and kicked the door. An old man at a table looked up from a breakfast of tea and rice. A very young man nearby jumped and dropped the broom he was sweeping with. Ous came in through the door a second later and began snarling questions in Pashto. Bolan swept through the tearoom and kicked open the door to the empty kitchen.

"They see an American soldier?" Bolan called back.

"They say not."

Bolan looked out the back door. It opened onto a blind alley jammed with carts, barrels and clotheslines. He returned.

"You believe them?"

"Indeed not."

Bolan glanced around the room. The walls, floor and ceiling were all clay. He turned his gaze to the table the old man sat at and the carpet beneath it. He gently but firmly pulled the old man out of his chair and kicked over the table.

The young man screamed as he pulled an ancient Russian Tokarev pistol out of his sash. *"Allahu Ak—"* Ous cut the cry of faith short by ramming the butt of his rifle into the young man's belly. A blow to the back of the legs toppled the adolescent and sent the pistol clattering across the floor. Bolan shoved the old man into Ous's embrace and yanked the carpet aside. The revealed wooden hatch in the floor was a recent construction. Bolan took out his tactical light. "Ask him if it's booby-trapped."

Ous asked. "He says not."

"Do you believe him?"

"I told him I would send his grandson to hell a eunuch if you were blown up opening it." Bolan glanced at the old man, who was weeping. Ous shrugged fatalistically. "I give you a fifty-fifty chance."

Bolan rolled his eyes. "You're a good man, Ous."

"One tries. I will stand over by the door and cover the prisoners in case of your demise."

"Thanks."

"You are welcome."

Bolan spoke into his com link. "Control, you have my position?"

"Copy that, Batman," Farkas replied. "We're receiving the Bear's feed."

"I have two suspects, tagged and bagged in a teahouse. I think I've found a tunnel."

"Copy that. I'll have a unit scoop them up."

Bolan took out his tactical knife and snapped it open with a flick of his wrist. He probed the edges of the hatch but could find no hidden wires or leads. The soldier grabbed the handle and flung the hatch open. He aimed the muzzle of his Beretta and his tactical light into the tunnel.

"Ous, tie them up and follow me."

The big American dropped down. It was a very well-dug tunnel, lined with planks, and Bolan could almost stand up. Twenty yards along he came to a side chamber—and Convertino's corpse. The body lay facedown in a huge pool of blood. That was, if the corpse had still had a face.

Bolan eyed the corpse clinically. He had seen more decapitations than he cared to think about. One look told him the head-taking had been neither clean nor swift. It had been done with a large knife and while Convertino was still alive.

"Bismillah!" Ous exclaimed.

Bolan dropped to a knee beside Convertino's cadaver. He noted two pinprick tears in the USMC-issue PT shirt the man had escaped in. He tore the T-shirt down the young Marine's back and examined the two, bee-sting-like marks six inches apart between his shoulder blades. The corporal had been hit with a stun gun before he'd been beheaded.

Ous frowned at the gruesome scene. "What do we do now?"

Bolan rose. Convertino had bought his redemption in the hardest way possible, but he was still sticking it to the enemy. The Marine was a Trojan Horse. They might have taken his head, but the Radio Frequency Identification tracking chip had been implanted behind his ear.

"Bear, do we still have GPS on the Corporal?"

"Of course, why?"

"The corporal's body is down here in the tunnel, but his head isn't."

"Oh, damn it."

"Do you have visual on the signal?"

"No, I was assuming he was inside, but the signal is still very close to you. I'm saying it is just entering the bazaar," Kurtzman stated.

"Keller, deploy into the bazaar, in costume. Try to get ahead of us and the signal."

"Copy that."

Bolan moved down the tunnel with Ous at his back. There was no blood trail, so the soldier assumed Convertino's head was packaged for transport. The tunnel dead-ended with another hatch above, which was unbarred. Bolan listened a moment to the silence up top, then flung it open. No grenades or gunfire met the intrusion. He clambered up four iron rungs and found himself in a storeroom laden with burlap sacks of grain. He swept the room as Ous emerged. The storeroom opened into a storefront. No one was around. Bolan tucked his weapon away, pulled on a fatigue cap and a pair of sunglasses, then stepped out into the open air of the bazaar.

He took a moment to scan the early morning activity.

The Taliban had been mostly driven out of Sangin City proper; those who still lurked did so under deep cover. Still, most women in Sangin wore burkas when they left their homes, some out of tradition, many out of a very real and justified fear of reprisal. Groups of hooded women moved around buying milk, eggs and fruit and looking to see if the morning had brought any new goods in the stalls since the day before. Others carried baskets laden with lentils, coffee and grains. Most women wore black burkas, some light blue and a few other colors. They all moved in interlocking streams when they weren't poking, prodding or bartering. All over the bazaar, eyes were drawn to the Westerner.

"Bear, are you sure?"

"The tracking device is within one hundred yards of

you. That's as exact as it gets. I have eyes on the bazaar and eyes on you, but all the tracker does is put out a low-frequency signal. I have it. It's nearby, but the device isn't sophisticated enough to triangulate on an individual without some other target verification."

"Bear, give me anything."

"I can't swear to it, but my gut and dead reckoning tells me the signal seems to be on the southern end of the bazaar."

Bolan had navigated by dead reckoning many times, and he would literally and figuratively bet the Farm on Kurtzman's instincts. He moved south. "Ous, find her."

Ous scanned the packs of swaddled, shopping women and the sellers they were haggling with. "I will try!"

Bolan subvocalized into his throat mike. "Keller, get to the southern end of the bazaar and deploy."

"I'm already there."

"Control, get that chopper in the air. I may need backup or fast evac out of the bazaar."

"Bird is in the air, Batman," Farkas confirmed.

"Batman," Kurtzman said, "I can't swear to it, but I think the signal is now moving westward."

"She's meeting someone," Bolan concluded. "Making a delivery."

"And now they are here," Ous agreed.

Bolan picked up his pace. They passed through an open-air alley of rug sellers. The rain had abated, and the bazaar was swiftly filling with shoppers.

The soldier caught sight of a woman in a full-length burka. Similarly clad women surrounded her, but the one he had his eye on carried a woven basket about the size of a hatbox. She wasn't hurrying but she moved with purpose. Bolan's instincts spoke to him as he moved through the crowd to intercept her.

"What do you think of that one, Ous?" Bolan asked.

Ous's smile flashed through his beard. "You have keen eyes, indeed. She walks with purpose, and that purpose is not shopping. On any other day, were I taking tea and watching people pass, I would guess that the basket she carried was a prop, and that she went to meet her lover."

"You see our suspect's curves beneath all that fabric?"

"Nothing in life is certain except God's will and the words of the Prophet. But I would wager on it, my friend. I would wager a great deal."

Bolan was willing to back Ous's wager. He spoke quietly into his throat mike. "Bear?"

"I have eyes on you, and you're right on top of the signal."

"Keller, we're moving in," Bolan said. "Suspect is wearing a burka and carrying a basket, moving due west through the rug sellers."

"I have visual on you and Ous. Moving to intercept."

"Ous, hang back a bit. Cover me," Bolan instructed.

"Of course."

Bolan caught up to the woman and followed her for just a moment. There wasn't a speck of blood on her burka or her basket. As an American man, if he stripped the burka off the wrong woman there was likely to be a riot, if not a genuine international incident he might have to shoot his way out of. Bolan spoke very quietly. "Zurisaday."

Ous spoke in his earpiece at the same moment. "I believe some of the women around her are her escorts. You have been noticed!"

The basket fell from the woman's hands to the ground. The lid popped off, and Corporal Convertino's, gray, frozen-in-agony head rolled into the mud. A pair of heavily kohled violet eyes glared pure murder at Bolan, and a slab-sided Russian Pernach machine pistol snaked from under the burka.

Bolan's knife hand chopped the chattering weapon out of the woman's hand. The bazaar erupted into screams and chaos at the sound of the shots. His back-fist shot at the woman sent Zurisaday's eyes fluttering like slot machines. He whirled, and a second blow flattened the killer into the mud.

He turned again as a robed woman screamed and plunged a foot-long, blood-crusted Khyber knife at Bolan's chest. He caught her wrist and continued his turn, hip-tossing the shrieking killer in a windmill of limbs into a rug seller's table. The soldier caught sight of a woman five yards away cocking a stubby submachine gun.

"Ous!" Bolan called.

The Afghan strode up from behind and clouted her with his pistol.

Another woman struggled slightly to get her Russian submachine gun out of the folds of her burka. Another woman hit her from behind in a flying tackle that sent both of them sliding a good six feet through the mud. Keller rose to one knee and secured her suspect. Bolan scanned for more targets. He waited for whomever Zurisaday was meeting to declare themselves. Cries of outrage and alarm were rippling outward across the bazaar. The remaining enemy had no need to attack just yet. It would be only a matter of moments before the good citizens of Sangin, a good portion of whom owned Kalashnikov rifles, took restoring order into their own hands, and the bad guys could take that opportunity to blend in and launch their attack.

"Control! I need air! Now!"

Farkas's voice came back over the thudding sound of rotor noise. "Copy that! ETA thirty seconds!"

Bolan tore rope from an awning and bound two of the suspects. "Keller! Get the truck!"

Agent Keller ran for it. Instantly she was one more running figure in the mob wearing a burka. The woman Bolan had thrown rose groggily and he hip-tossed her next to Zurisaday for her trouble. Ous strode forward and threw his captive on the growing pile of women. He scooped a fallen submachine gun and glanced around anxiously.

"In but moments our position will become untenable!"

Bolan knelt and put Corporal Convertino's head back in the basket.

Salvation came in the form of a USMC UH-1Y Venom helicopter dropping out of the sky like a stone. The chopper hovered over the bazaar like an angry leviathan, its door guns tracking for targets. The rotor wash of its twin General Electric turboshaft engines sent awnings flying like ghosts, and grain and light goods swirling from their baskets. The locals ran crouching and clutching their hats and burkas in the vortex. Unfortunately there was no good place for the chopper to land.

The truck's horn blared over the roar. Melons exploded into shrapnel rinds as Keller clipped a stall. The lanes between stalls and stands were too narrow for the pickup, and she sent goods of all descriptions flying. Mud sprayed as she slid to a halt. Bolan and Ous tossed the bound women into the bed of the truck and jumped in. Bolan slapped the top of the cab. "Go!"

"Which way!"

There was no way to turn around. "Straight!"

The spinning tires buzz-sawed mud in all directions, and then the truck suddenly lunged forward like a racehorse out of the starting gate. Tables and tents fell in disarray, leaving a wake of commerce carnage. A bullet whined off the top of the cab, but it could have come from anywhere. Keller kept hitting the horn, and shoppers and shopkeepers leaped out of the path of the plunging pickup. Keller found the edge of the bazaar and drove under an ancient arch. The truck burst onto the streets of Sangin with the helicopter above orbiting like a guardian angel.

"Bear, you got eyes on?" Bolan queried.

"Oh copy that, Batman. It was one hell of a show. The Sangin bazaar is officially a riot area."

"What's our quickest route out of the city?"

"Head straight for the river."

"Control, you copy that?" Bolan asked.

"Copy that, Batman."

"We're going to abandon the truck in the first open area outside of town. Request evac."

"Copy that."

Bolan and Ous both dropped down among the bound, squirming women and relaxed as Keller tore through town. He looked at Zurisaday's unconscious form and the basket containing Convertino's head. The corporal was a traitor to his beloved Corps and the United States he had sworn to serve, but he had fallen going forward.

Someone was going to pay for that.

CHAPTER FIVE

The massive, tapered clubs were half the height of a man. Gholam Daei's mighty frame was stripped to the waist as he swung the sixty-five-pound clubs rhythmically around his head. A local woodworker had turned the clubs from a pair of sapling trunks to the man's specifications. Daei noticed his servant, Karim, enter the chamber, but he finished his five hundred swings before he acknowledged him. "Yes?"

Karim ushered in two men. Azimi and Khahari were brothers, and local Taliban. They goggled at the bearded, bare-chested giant who stood in front of them radiating power. Gholam gave them a benevolent smile. "What news, brothers?"

"The news is bad, brother," Azimi said.

"Oh?"

"Zurisaday has been captured."

"And what became of the women who were supposed to guard her?"

Azimi lowered his head. "Captured."

"Captured? They are living martyrs, sworn to die in their duty, sailing to paradise on an ocean of infidel blood. I find such a thing very hard to believe."

Khahari cleared his throat. "There was an American."

Gholam nodded sagely. "There usually is." His smile slowly faded. "So, this American single-handedly took

Zurisaday and her escort, while you, your brother and your men watched helplessly?"

"There was an infidel whore, shamefully hidden beneath a burka like a pious woman!" Azimi objected.

Daei raised one bushy brow in displeased question.

"And there was a gunship!" Khahari added.

Daei privately admitted to himself that in his own experience gunships could qualify as mitigating circumstances.

"And Omar Ous!" Khahari cried.

"Omar Ous, indeed?" Gholam grunted at this news.

"Indeed, brother!"

"You and your brother are aware that a fatwa has been issued against Omar Ous?"

The brothers looked down at the ground. "Yes, brother."

"And that it is your holy obligation to kill him?"

"Yes, brother."

Daei looked for the silver lining. "And what were the civilian casualties of this assault?"

"A few broken bones, as some were trampled fleeing or injured throwing themselves out of harm's way."

Daei felt his anger beginning to rise. "Tell me at least this amorous Marine is dead."

"Yes, Zurisaday herself took his head from his body."

"Well, at least that is something. Tell me the other bad news."

"The teashop owner, Abdullah, and his son Razi were both arrested. The tunnel between the tea shop and the bazaar has been compromised."

"So, during the, abduction, I gather you held back and observed?"

"Yes, brother, we held back, waiting for the crowd to attack them so that our own attack would blend in," Azimi stated.

It wasn't the worst of plans. "And then the gunship descended and drove the crowd away?"

"Yes, brother, so we observed."

"What did you observe?" Daei queried.

Azimi and Khahari both took out their cell phones. Daei took them and examined the video files. He watched the jerky film several times without comment. There were several decent shots of the American except that all Daei could make out was that the man was from the West, wearing a ball cap pulled low and sunglasses that hid his eyes. Daei switched to Khahari's phone. His device clearly showed Ous knocking down one of Zurisaday's escorts. Then the helicopter descended and turned the world into a confused maelstrom. He had some very bad footage of the pickup pulling away and Azimi taking several potshots at it.

Daei considered what he had seen.

Omar Ous was a hero among mujahideen veterans and considered a lion of the Northern Alliance. He was also ethnically Tajik. He had no use for southerners, less for Pashtuns, and considered the Taliban and their creed of Islam an abomination to be crushed. Such a man would have no compunction about shooting up the Sangin bazaar, much less gunning down female assassins in burkas. It was also well-known that he didn't like Westerners and that he considered accepting their soldiers and their assistance a necessary evil. Yet here, digitally captured, he was following the American's nearly suicidal rules of engagement.

Daei had been fully prepared, even expecting the escaping Marine to be a trap. He had been well prepared in the village, and he had believed so yet here again in the Marine forward base. It was an unprecedented, indeed, anomalous string of failures, one after the other, blowing up in his face like a string of firecrackers. They all had one thing in common.

The same, unknown, American operator.

He watched the video of the big American again, whirling among the living martyrs like a dervish. He was fairly sure he could take the man in hand-to-hand combat, and part of him yearned to lock horns with the American, lock him up and choke him out, only to have him awake, mewling and screaming to the final sensations of having his head sawed from his body with knife. For the moment he was invulnerable. He was surrounded by several thousand United States Marines, had Omar Ous to warn him of dangers Westerners normally couldn't see, and had the United States Navy and God knew whom else backing his play. The situation was quite simple. Omar Ous needed to be shown the error of his ways, and the American operator needed to be cut from the herd.

Daei's huge teeth split his black beard.

It was always good when one could kill two birds with one stone.

Sangin Base, Suspect Unit

ZURISADAY'S SKETCHES did her no justice. Even with the left side of her face swollen she was mind-emptyingly erotic. The push into Helmand Province had provided some of the heaviest fighting of the Afghanistan conflict and had provided a great number of enemy captures. The Sangin base had its own unit for processing terror suspects before shipping them out to the Kabul facilities or the United States. Zurisaday sat in a prefab holding cell complete with one-way glass. She sat staring at the glass, unblinking, with an almost reptilian hatred. Bolan had seen such looks many times before. He could feel her eyes on the other side of the glass, and he knew she could feel his. The woman was much more than a religious fanatic.

She was a sociopath.

"She said anything?" Bolan asked.

Keller looked up from a file she was amending on her laptop. "Not a peep since we brought her in."

Bolan nodded. It would take very advanced interrogation techniques and time they didn't have to get anything out of her. "What do we know about her escorts?"

"They've clammed up. Farkas suggested we leave them together for about an hour before separating them."

"And?"

"A little bit of pay dirt. They were just dumb enough to whisper to each other. They didn't say much except 'say nothing' and 'remember your duty,' but that was enough to determine that they're Afghani, Pashtun and local."

"Anything else?"

Keller clicked on the file. "They were armed with cheap-ass, copies of Russian Borz submachine guns. The knife one them attacked you with was the same knife used to murder Corporal Convertino. Zurisaday's prints were on it, as well. I'm predicting she was the one who actually did the decapitation."

Bolan looked into the unblinking, inhuman eyes on the other side of the glass. "I'll buy that."

"Yeah, but the part I don't get? You'd think the Taliban would just put some men under burkas and be done with it."

"For one, even though he was unarmed, Corporal Convertino was a U.S. Marine and a dangerous individual. If he found Zurisaday with only a couple of apparently helpless women with her, he would have let his guard down." Bolan smiled faintly. "You heard Ous. You can tell a lot about a woman by how she moves in a burka. Practiced eyes, and just about every Afghan male's eyes seem practiced, would probably spot a man beneath that garment almost instantly, and they wanted to get her and the head to an extraction point."

"Okay, you got me, but it's still kinda odd. The Taliban hardly ever uses women for anything except punching bags." She cocked her head at Bolan. "What are you thinking?"

"I'm thinking about suicide bombers in Moscow."

Keller blinked. "The Black Widows?"

"Right, women whose husbands were killed fighting the Russians in Chechnya, Dagestan and the Caucasus region republics. They get widowed, they get radicalized, and they go to Moscow and blow themselves up to rejoin their husbands as holy martyrs."

"I know who they are, but it's just not Taliban MO."

"I know. This whole thing stinks of something a whole lot more than the local Taliban."

"Like a whole lot more what?"

"Like either the local Taliban has had some kind of sea change, or there's a new player involved."

"Oh Jesus." Keller shook her head. "A new player? Like who?"

"I don't know. It wouldn't be the first time I've seen terrorists coopted by an outside party, either knowingly or unknowingly."

"Thanks. I'm going to sleep a lot better tonight."

"Where's Ous?" Bolan asked.

"He pulled a fade. He doesn't like spending the night on U.S. or coalition bases unless he absolutely has to. He's got his own safehouses and his own web of informants." Keller's eyes narrowed slightly in irritation. "None of which he's ever shown any inclination to share."

Bolan could understand. Alliances often shifted and changed in Afghanistan, and those who fought beside the Western Coalition were all too aware of the fact that they were on a timetable to leave. They were lucky Ous was playing ball at all.

Keller shrugged. "He said he'd be back at dawn."

"All right." Bolan stretched out his arms and felt his shoulders creak. "I'll see you then."

"Yo, mystery man."

Bolan turned. "Yes?"

"You got a snuggle buddy for the night?" Keller asked.

The left corner of Bolan's mouth quirked. "Snuggle buddy?"

"I'm a lone female NCIS agent on a base full of horny United States Marines."

"There's always Farkas."

"Farkas already made his move, and he's married, and I don't mess around with partners."

Bolan laid his hands on his chest guilelessly. "We're not partners?"

"You're my liaison with every branch of government, with godlike powers." Keller looked at Bolan seriously. "And Convertino fragged the infirmary. He may not be the only compromised Marine in this camp, and maybe I'd feel better with a tall dark stranger with a machine pistol watching over me tonight."

"Well, I'm sharing a tent with a couple of lieutenants."

"And I have an air-conditioned container unit to myself, and the two sergeants who shared it left their DVD collection behind when they were evicted in the name of NCIS."

"Well...I don't know."

Keller's eyes began to widen in bemused outrage. "I've had over a hundred Marines hit on me per day, I choose you, and you're gonna make me beg?"

"Beg, it's such an ugly word."

Keller's face went flat. "I have popcorn."

Bolan nodded. "I'll bring beer."

Keller clapped her hands. "Yay!"

Ous's safehouse

COLD SWEAT BROKE OUT across Omar Ous's body. He stood over his bed bare-chested. His Browning Hi-Power pistol had filled his hand without thought as he had lunged up from slumber. Ous had been a guerrilla fighter since the age of twelve. He knew he could be ambushed, and he knew he could be tricked, for much to his shame such things had happened before. Even in righteous jihad, such were the fortunes of war. He bore many scars both great and small upon his body for every mistake he had made and lived to learn from. However, without unseemly pride, Ous believed it was nearly impossible for someone to sneak up upon him, even in slumber. Like many veterans who had fought hard and lived long enough, he was attuned to that which didn't belong. The odd smell, the almost subliminal sound, or the lack of those that did belong, all spoke to him consciously and unconsciously. Wherever Ous laid his head he took precautions.

In the case of this night, in this room he had taken over a weaver's shop, Ous's precautions were as simple as a chair jammed beneath the doorknob and a length of wire sealing the window. A determined opponent could quickly breach such defenses, but not without waking the warrior slumbering within. His precautions were still in place. Apparently untampered with. Apparently a ghost had entered his room this night.

A ghost, or worse.

Ous looked down upon his pillow and what he saw strained credibility. What it represented had been reduced to old wives' tales and myth since time out of mind. Nonetheless, Ous knew that he wasn't mad. He also knew that he wasn't dreaming.

The blade that lay glittering upon his pillow was very real.

The dagger would be strange to Western eyes. It looked like the dorsal fin of some delicate, exotic fish. The blade started wide at the base and then tapered very quickly through a shallow S curve to a needlepoint. Despite its eight-inch length, the blade almost looked dainty. Nothing could have been further from the truth. The thick T-shaped spine along its back and its acute wedge shape made it utterly rigid. In ancient times it had been designed to exploit the weak points in metal armor and burst chain-mail links. East or west, the ancient, Persian Pesh Kabz was arguably the best armor-piercing dagger design ever to emerge from medieval times, and the Moghul Empire had spread them across South and Central Asia. Ous knew from personal experience that such a blade, driven with enough enthusiasm could plunge through 1980s-vintage Soviet spun fiberglass and titanium body armor to find the life beneath it. He had little doubt that it could pierce the more modern Kevlar armor if required.

Ous looked at the photograph of his wife and his two children lying beneath the blade, and he knew what was required of him.

CHAPTER SIX

Bolan's machine pistol was instantly in his hand as he sat up. Keller murmured and snuggled closer. Beer was forbidden to U.S. troops in Afghanistan, but it flowed like a river to the German coalition contingent, to the tune of 260,000 gallons a year. Like cigarettes, beer was an excellent bribe and Bolan had made sure a case or two of Bundeswehr beer was available to him to cement the love of the United States Marines. The soldier had allowed himself two bottles and allowed NCIS Agent Kathryn Keller to work her wiles on him. The woman had allowed herself four bottles and had worked her wiles on him with a vengeance. Marine Corps cots were definitely not built for two, so they had made a nest of blankets on the floor and made it exactly halfway through *Casablanca*. Bolan pushed the 93-R's selector switch to 3-round burst mode in answer to the quiet knock at the door.

"Who is it?"

"Omar Ous! Are you decent, or shall I come back?"

Bolan flicked his selector to safe. "Give me a minute."

"Of course."

Bolan pulled on a pair of boxers and a T-shirt, and tossed his Beretta onto the bare cot. Keller made a tiny noise and took the opportunity to cocoon herself in all of the covers. The container-shelter unit was literally an upgraded cargo container unit with power, AC, and because it was an officer's unit, its own portable toilet. Bolan found

Ous at the door, smiling in the pearly dawn light and holding a steaming mug of coffee.

"Good morning, my friend," Ous said.

"Good morning, did you—"

Ous struck like a snake.

A snap of his wrist sent hot coffee sleeting for Bolan's eyes. Most men would have recoiled from the attack. The Executioner dived into it. He closed his eyes as the coffee scalded across his face and hit Ous in a flying tackle down the unit's three steps. The ground was unyielding dust and gravel, but both men had taken hard falls before and it appeared Ous's revered father had taught him how to wrestle as well as shoot. As they rolled, Ous took the opportunity to drive two hard right palm heels into his target's sternum. Bolan took the shots and the opportunity to yank his adversary's pistol out of his sash. Ous's hand closed on Bolan's wrist like a vise as he attempted to drive his knee up between the American's legs. Bolan had two decades and a good twenty pounds on his opponent but Ous was as hard as nails and grimly determined as they wrestled for the pistol. Ous struggled with all of his strength to keep the muzzle away from his face. Even though he was on top, Bolan's strength and experience began to tell.

Ous seemed to produce the sinuously curving dagger out of thin air.

The dagger flashed across the top of Bolan's wrist and the pistol fell from his hand. Ous rose up to drive the dagger into the American's heart with both hands. Bolan got a foot into the man's chest and shoved him off. Ous snarled and came back instantly as Bolan rolled up to find him plunging the dagger straight for his heart.

The soldier clapped his hands. For a heartbeat the blade was trapped between the heels of Bolan's palms just inches from his chest. Before Ous could react to this incredible turn of events, Bolan snap-kicked him in the groin. Ous's face crumpled and he fell to his knees with a groan.

Bolan took the dagger from Ous's palsied hand and picked up the pistol. He pushed off the safety and squatted beside the vomiting warrior. "Well, I'm thinking you either got religion or someone got to you."

Ous looked up at Bolan through tearing eyes. "I...have never...seen...such a thing."

In Asian martial arts the move was usually called some variation of the name "catching the lightning." Few styles still taught it. At best, most considered it a desperation move and a relic left over from the days when people carried swords, and in any event a very good way to lose a hand. Bolan was adept at many fighting techniques, and he was always willing to add any new move.

"What did they threaten you with, Omar? Your family?"

"My wife...my children," Ous said. "They have them."

"Who's they?"

Ous ground his brow into the dust. "Those who put the dagger into my hand."

"Do you know where they are?"

"I believe they are still in my home. They will die if your death is not proved within forty-eight hours, or if any police or military force attempt a rescue."

Ous's eyes widened in shock as his pistol and dagger clattered to the gravel in front of his face. Bolan held out his bloody right hand to help him up. "Let's go get your family."

Kunduz Province, 20,000 feet

THE C-12 HURON ROARED across the sky. It had crossed the length of Afghanistan from south to north. Omar Ous had never jumped out of plane before. As it turned out, he had never been in a plane before and he was throwing up again. Bolan and Ous shared the cabin with a highly bemused Keller and an equally bemused jumpmaster. Neither Keller nor Farkas were jump qualified, and Bolan could only tandem jump with one amateur. By necessity it had to be Ous.

The copilot's voice came across the intercom from the cabin. "Five minutes, jumpers. Descending to jump altitude." They would be jumping high enough that no one on the ground would hear the plane or see it without night-vision and magnification but not so high they would need oxygen. Keller looked askance at Bolan and finally aired the question that had been bothering her the entire day. "So…"

"Yeah?"

"Didn't this guy try to kill you this morning?"

"That he did."

Bolan and Keller watched as the jumpmaster solicitously gave Ous a fresh bag. He had stopped vomiting and now he was hyperventilating. Ous was wide-eyed as he worked the barf bag like a bellows.

The jumpmaster gave Bolan a sidelong look. "You jumping into a hot LZ with this guy?"

"He'll be fine once he has dust beneath his boots," Bolan replied, "and with luck the LZ won't be hot until we light it up." Bolan checked the pair of Navy MP-5 SD-N sound-suppressed submachine guns a final time and then attached the weapon and his pouch of six magazines to his web gear. Ous's gaze flew around the cabin in mounting panic as Bolan clipped his weapon to his harness. He gasped as Bolan pulled night-vision goggles over the man's eyes.

"Listen, you're going to be fine," Bolan said. "Just remember what I showed you. Arch hard when we go out the door. I'll take care of everything else."

The jumpmaster assisted Bolan in buckling in Ous. The soldier could smell the fear oozing off the man. So could the jumpmaster, and he gave Bolan another look as he gave the straps and buckles a second going over. The intercom crackled. "One minute! Going dark!"

The interior cabin lights went off, and the red emergency lights came on. Bolan pulled his goggles over his eyes and adjusted the gain slightly. The jumpmaster opened the door and the wind roared into the cabin.

Keller put a hand on Bolan's armored shoulder. "Luck!"

"Thanks!"

"One minute!"

Bolan nudged Ous, and the two of them did the awkward tandem-man shuffle to the door. Ous made a terrible noise in the back of his throat.

"Remember," Bolan said. "A hard arch!"

"Get ready!" the jumpmaster shouted.

The intercom crackled for the final time. "We are on target! Jumpers away!"

"Go! Go! Go!" the jumpmaster called.

Ous's hands slammed into the door frame in mortal terror.

"Go!" the jumpmaster called.

Bolan spoke above the roar of the wind in the door and tried to take a step forward. "Ous! We gotta go!"

Ous's body went rigid.

"Go!" the jumpmaster bellowed.

Ous shuddered with horror in the door frame.

"Ous!" Bolan snarled in Ous's ear. "What's your wife's name?"

"What…"

"Your wife! Her name!" Bolan demanded.

"Yamina, my wife's name is—"

"Your children! Their names!"

"My son, his name is Esfandyar," Ous replied.

"And your daughter?"

"Afshan."

"For them, Ous! Yamina! Esfandyar! Afshan! You've gotto do this! For them! I'm with you." Bolan spoke with deadly seriousness. "God is great, Ous, and by God our cause is righteous!"

Ous squeezed his eyes shut, clenched his teeth and released the door frame. *"Allahu akbar,"* he whispered.

The jumpmaster gave Bolan a helpful slam between the shoulder blades with both hands. "See ya!"

Bolan and Ous flew out into the jet stream. Ous failed to give Bolan a hard arch and they tumbled wildly in the shrieking, streaming darkness with Ous screaming in the Tajik of his youth and flailing his limbs. Bolan idly considered choking him out. He still owed the Afghani for the six surgical stitches in his arm. Bolan let him flail a few moments more. Despite what one saw in the movies, it was almost impossible to have a conversation during free fall. The soldier waited for a few more moments as they fell like stones to the dark Earth below. When Ous momentarily ran out of breath. Bolan slapped him hard on the side of his helmet. Ous stopped his flailing. Bolan slapped the helmet once, twice, three times more.

Ous suddenly got it and managed his arch.

It was enough. Bolan extended his arms and legs to make ailerons of his limbs. It was awkward with a large man strapped to him, but the big American managed to gracefully turn the two of them over into a belly-down position. He pulled the rip cord and the big tandem chute deployed. Ous clenched like a spider about to get stepped on as their straps cinched against them with the sudden pull.

The roar of free fall disappeared. The strain was gone and their legs dangled like a carnival ride as Bolan took the toggles. He began a slow, comfortable spiraling descent over Ous's village. Ous lifted his head slightly and began peering around, taking in the world below him through the greens and grays of night-vision equipment.

"It is not an unpleasant sensation," he stated.

"No, it's not," Bolan agreed. "Which house is yours?"

Ous examined the village beneath them and pointed. "Slightly away from the main village, to the west, among the orchards, there."

It appeared a life of war hadn't treated Omar Ous too badly. His house was bigger than most. Not bad for a wanted man. Bolan took in what looked like perhaps four or five hectares of orderly, terraced rows of fruit trees and a corral and stable for horses. It appeared Ous owned a Toyota Landcruiser and an ex-Soviet era GAZ-69 utility vehicle. Bolan picked a lane in the trees about a hundred yards from the house. They were the best source of cover on the valley floor. "Get ready, lift your legs...now!"

The earth swung up beneath Bolan's boots and he flared his chute. A few cherry branches broke as the shrouds enveloped them, and the trees took the two warriors' combined weight. The crackings and snappings seemed as loud as gunshots, but no gunfire or shouts of alarm ensued. Ous became a deadweight as they lost all lift. Bolan bent his knees and they both hit the ground in a fairly professional manner. It was cherry-picking season, and a small hail of fruit fell upon them from above. Bolan instantly got him and Ous separated and out of their harnesses. Both men unclipped and checked their weapons. Bolan flicked his selector to full-auto. "On my six."

"My family—"

"I'm on point, Ous." Bolan moved through the heavily

laden trees. He dropped to a crouch behind the bole of a tree by the edge of the orchard, and Ous knelt next to him. There was a nicker from the stables and a goat ambled past, drawn by the smell of the fallen cherries. "You notice anything?"

Ous stared at his house for long moments, nearly vibrating with the need to burst in with guns blazing. "Yes, my dogs should have already greeted me or attacked you."

That was enough for Bolan. He clicked his link. "Bear, I'm calling the domicile taken. High probability of hostiles and hostages inside."

"Copy that, Striker," Kurtzman came back.

Bolan turned to Ous. "You have stairs that lead to the roof inside?"

"I do."

Bolan took out a padded grapnel and coil of rope from his pack. "Cover me. Come quickly when I give you the signal."

"Indeed."

The house was the usual Central Asian structure, a hollow cube with a courtyard inside. In Ous's case it was a cube with smaller cubes attached as outbuildings. Bolan ran across the dead ground waiting for the weapons in hiding to open up, but made it to the side of the house unscathed. Bolan tossed the foam-covered grapnel up and over the roof. The rasp of the rope on the side of the house was louder than its landing. Bolan slowly pulled up the slack and the rope went taut. The grapnel stood horizontal with two tines firmly hooped over the ceiling ledge. Bolan moved up the rope with an alacrity and precision that U.S. Army Rangers, Navy SEALs and Spider-Man would have admired. He motioned Ous to come ahead and the guerrilla fighter moved with impressive silence across the open ground. Bolan peered down into the inner courtyard. Below were the usual fountain, some potted trees and benches. On the other side of the roof Ous had a satellite dish. The tinkling of the fountain competed with the wind in the orchard for the only sounds.

The silence broke as the trapdoor to the roof opened. The intruder wore a turban wound to conceal his face like a desert wanderer. The stock of his AK was folded, and the weapon was slung as he clambered up the roof ladder.

The hatch opened to look upon the road from town rather than toward the orchards behind. Bolan took up the grapnel in one hand and the rope in the other as the sentry stepped onto the roof and peered west. Bolan gave the rope a single gyration like a man tossing a lasso and hurled the grapnel. The rope bent around the man's neck, and the soldier heaved back with all of his strength. The tine croquette hooked the sentry's throat. The veiled man gagged and clutched at the unyielding steel as Bolan reeled him in. The Executioner drove a knee into the sentry's kidney to still his struggles and tossed him off the roof by the iron around his throat.

The sentry made a low thudding noise as he hit the ground two stories below. Bolan heard a single chuff and click as Ous's sound-suppressed weapon fired once and the action cycled. A moment later the grapnel sailed up again. Bolan caught it and secured it to the roof. Ous scrambled up and the two warriors crouched by the open roof hatch, listening. From within the house a woman sobbed.

Bolan's slammed his hand down on Ous's shoulder. "Wait."

A blow cut off the sob. Ous went rigid beneath Bolan's hand. A sneering voice called out from below and then laughed.

"What did he say?" Bolan asked.

Ous's voice was tightly controlled. "From what I can

gather, the man you hurled from the roof is named Mehtar. The man below taunts Mehtar, telling him he is a prude, and that he hopes Mehtar enjoys masturbating upon my roof alone while he himself avails himself of the pleasures of my virgin daughter."

"You want to take point?"

"I do."

They pushed up their night-vision goggles, and Bolan took Ous's six as he descended into his home and beelined down a hallway. Their boots made no sound on the Persian carpet. The two men stopped at an open door. Ous's daughter, Afshan, cringed in a corner with one of her cheeks swollen. One of the veiled men crouched next to her. The teenager cried and flinched as the man ran his fingers through her lustrous dark hair. His other hand held a knife to the girl's throat as he whispered ugly, cooing endearments in a guttural voice. He had but one moment to widen his eyes in horror as Omar Ous filled the door to his daughter's bedroom.

Ous burned his entire magazine into the offender.

At that range the sound of the bullets striking flesh and clothing was louder than the coughing and clicking of the silenced weapon. The silenced MP-5 cycled like a sewing machine knitting living flesh. Spent brass fell to the thick carpet. The veiled man shuddered and shook as he took twenty-nine rounds in the chest. Ous's weapon clicked open on empty, and smoke oozed from the muzzle of the suppressor as he reloaded. He arched one eyebrow at his daughter in a question and she shook her head. Ous nodded once. His daughter nodded back and took the dead man's pistol from his sash.

Ous spoke very quietly. "This man with me is a friend. We will speak English for his benefit."

Afshan nodded.

"Where is your mother?" Ous asked.

"Downstairs."

"Where is your little brother?"

"Downstairs. They beat him and tied him up when he resisted," Afshan replied.

"Where is your grandmother?"

Afshan's eyes filled with fresh tears. "She stabbed one of the bad men. They shot her."

"Where are the servants?"

"They shot them and put their bodies in the stable."

"Where are my hounds?"

"They shot them, too, Father."

A mighty scowl passed across Ous's face. "I see."

Bolan knelt beside the girl. "How many are they?"

"Twelve or so took the house, I think. Then perhaps half of them left."

"Are they local?" Bolan asked.

Afshan blinked.

"Ah." Ous nodded and put a hand on his daughter's shoulder. "Were they men of Kunduz? Did they speak Tajik? Pashto or Dari Persian?"

"They spoke Arabic among themselves. I believe the men who stayed are southerners. The men who left were foreigners. Forgive me, but from where, I do not know."

"At least six were left upon the premises," Ous surmised.

"And between us we've taken two."

Ous rose. "Stay here, little rose."

Afshan clutched at her father and shook her head. Bolan caught her gaze and held it. "Your father and I are going to fetch your mother and your little brother. I want you to go up on the roof. Take the pistol. If we fail, shoot anyone who comes up the hatch. No matter what happens, in half an hour American soldiers will come, but do not let anyone up unless they say 'Rambo.' Do you understand?"

The barest hint of a smile tried to quirk one corner of Afshan's mouth. "The password is Rambo."

"Good, now obey your father. Go."

The Russian-made Gyruza pistol was huge in the girl's tiny hands as she ran in a whirl of skirts for the roof ladder. Ous's eyes glimmered. "She is a good girl."

"An honor to her family," Bolan agreed.

"What is the plan?"

"We rescue your wife and son," the soldier replied.

"Do you wish prisoners?"

"Not at your family's expense."

"Very good."

"Half of the raid team left and they haven't posted any sentries," Bolan said. "I think they're waiting for the phone call that I'm dead and you're dead or captured. If they do have any sentries, they're down in the village watching the road."

"An intelligent assessment, I agree."

"Where would they most likely be in the house on a low state of alert?" Bolan asked.

"If they are like this one—" Ous gestured at the riddled corpse "—and seek diversions? Most likely in my parlor. It has a television and opens into the kitchen."

"By all means, Ous, show me to your parlor."

Bolan followed the man downstairs and into the darkened courtyard. They walked across it and glanced through the window into the kitchen. The light was on, and in the summer night the kitchen window was open. Bolan could see where Ous's daughter got her good looks. Mrs. Ous was stirring something on the stove with a very unhappy look on her face. One of the veiled man sat at the kitchen table. He had uncovered his mouth and busily shoved down yellow rice with raisins and peas with his fingers. From somewhere out of sight Bolan could hear Bollywood-style music playing.

The soldier put a single silenced bullet through the eye slit of the eater's veil.

Mrs. Ous didn't notice. She only turned at the sound of the man slumping with his face in his bowl. In an incredible show of calm she walked over to the slumped man, lifted his head by his turban and noted the copious blood flooding into his food. She lowered his head back down and walked to the kitchen window. Ous spoke in English.

"Wife, where is our son?"

"Husband, our son is in the parlor with the intruders, to make sure I do not attempt anything with a kitchen knife as my mother did." Her fists clenched. "Two men are upstairs with our daughter."

"Our daughter is safe. We have killed the two men upstairs. How many remain here below?"

"Three."

"They are all in the parlor?"

"Watching television."

"Let us in."

Mrs. Ous disappeared and a door to the patio opened. Bolan followed Ous through a laundry room and into the kitchen, which opened into a Western style dining room. The dining room led to a capacious parlor. A series of sofas formed a U shape facing a large-screen TV. Three of the veiled men sat around the sofas watching a Bollywood song-and-dance number on the television with great interest. Ous's son lay on the floor hog-tied and gagged. One of the intruders was using him for an ottoman.

"Leave the one in the middle," Bolan whispered.

The Executioner and Ous gunned down the two men on the flanking couches. The last intruder stared up their smoking suppressor tubes and made a small unhappy sound.

"Take your feet off my son before I cut them off."

The man obeyed and Ous nodded at Bolan. "This one speaks English."

Ous kept the intruder covered while Bolan cut the boy free, then gave the twelve-year-old a hand up. "Esfandyar, I am a friend of your father's."

The young man rubbed his wrists. "I am very pleased to meet you, sir."

"My son," Ous said, "your mother is in the kitchen. I wish you to take her upstairs. Go to the roof, where you shall knock and say 'Rambo' lest your sister shoot you."

"Yes, Father." Esfandyar looked around at the carnage. "And you?"

The old warrior's eyes bored into the surviving intruder. "Our friend and I wish to speak with this man."

CHAPTER SEVEN

Ustad Ghulz was a very unhappy man. The United States Marines had come to Omar Ous's house, rescued his family and removed the dead. Ghulz had been taken from the parlor, bound hand and foot and thrown into the cellar until the Marines had left. He now sat tied to a chair beneath the glare of the cellar's single bare bulb. Ghulz was a fountain of useless information. He had been a hired thug most of his life. He had worked for the opium lords as a gunman and leg-breaker. When the Taliban had taken over, he had adopted the black turban and shot people and broken legs for the Taliban drug lords with fanatic zeal. When the Taliban had been driven out of the north, he had taken off his turban and shot people and broken legs for the new drug lords. Ustad Ghulz was a man who had found his niche.

Now he found himself tied to a chair in the cellar of Omar Ous, the Lion of Kunduz.

Ghulz shook like a leaf.

"Powerful men" whom he couldn't readily identify had hired Ustad and half a dozen like-minded souls. These powerful men claimed to have the Lion of Kunduz on a leash. Another half dozen men who remained veiled joined them. Other than that, they were foreign and scared him. Ghulz had no idea who they were.

"Did they act like soldiers?" Bolan tried.

"Yes!" Ghulz leaped at the question like a lifeline. "Very much like soldiers!"

"They spoke Arabic?"

"Yes! I was asked if I spoke it before I was hired! It was the tongue in which they gave us orders! But among themselves they spoke some foreign tongue!"

Ous drew the sinuously curving Pesh Kabz he had found on his pillow just twenty-four hours earlier. Ghulz flinched as Ous pointed the blade at him. "Do you know what this is, dog?"

Ghulz leaned back in his chair and gazed at Ous as if expecting a lethal trick question. "A…dagger?" he ventured.

Ous rolled his eyes and replaced the blade in his sash. Ghulz had no idea what the weapon represented. Bolan continued on the "good Cop" line. "So the strangers left some hours after the house and Mr. Ous's family were secured?"

"Yes!"

"And you were to wait?"

"Yes! I was to receive a phone call, that the American was dead."

Ghulz flinched as Bolan's eyes narrowed. "And?"

"After that we were to finish off…" Ghulz's voice trailed off in terror beneath Ous's unforgiving glare.

"So we gather," Bolan said. "You weren't supposed to contact anyone?"

"Only…if something went wrong."

Bolan had Ghulz's cell. He considered the timetable and what the contact number in Ghulz's phone might be worth. He took out his own phone and connected to Ghulz's while Ous watched with interest. Bolan downloaded everything in the phone's memory, but there wasn't much. The security software in Bolan's special-issue phone detected no viruses or subroutines. In fact, the entire memory of the phone issued to Ghulz was the single number he was to call in an emergency. The phone had never made or received a call, text, email or image. If it had, the data had been wiped clean by a professional. "If you called, what was the code word?"

Ghulz swallowed. "I was to ask, is the lion free?"

"And then?" Bolan probed.

"And then I would receive instructions."

It wasn't subtle, but Ghulz was obviously a cutout. "In Arabic?"

"Yes."

Bolan dialed the Farm. He owned one of the most powerful cell phones on Earth. Kurtzman and his cyberteam had designed it from the ground up, and nine times out of ten it was bouncing its signal through National Security Agency satellites.

"Bear, I need a trace on a call. I'm going to make a call to the enemy. I've linked my phone with the suspect's."

"That could take a minute," Kurtzman replied. "Keep them talking if you can."

Bolan held Ghulz's phone to his face, then nodded at Ous. "If he says a single syllable you find suspicious, cut his throat."

Ous drew the dagger and placed the blade just below Ghulz's Adam's apple. "Should he be so foolish, I will cut off his head, and send it to my Christian cousins in Tajikistan, whereupon they shall toss it to their dogs. When they have finished savaging it, the eyes of Ustad Ghulz shall be filled with pig's blood and sewn shut, his mouth stuffed with the pig's genitals and sealed. Then shall his head be wrapped in the pig's offal and encased in its carcass to be buried without a marker, and, clad in such raiment, shall Ustad Ghulz go to explain his sins to He who made him."

Lightning stopped just short of flashing from Ous's eyes and smiting Ghulz where he sat. "This I swear."

Ghulz looked like he might throw up.

Bolan pressed Send. The phone rang three times and the line clicked on.

Ghulz spoke a sentence in Arabic. Bolan raised an eyebrow at Ous and the warrior shrugged. A voice spoke back. Ous mouthed words in translation. "Ustad Ghulz has failed."

Ghulz whimpered something back. "He tells his co-conspirator that the United States Marines came."

The voice on the phone spoke again.

Ous's eyes flew wide as he translated. "Ustad Ghulz is a liar. A lion and an eagle came."

The symbolism was pretty heavy-handed.

The line clicked dead.

"What'd you get, Bear?"

Kurtzman grunted unhappily. "Not enough time."

Bolan clicked off Ghulz's phone. "Bear, I got a feeling that the moment I turned on Ghulz's phone and pressed Send, I got GPSed.

"Striker! Get out of there!"

"Hold that thought." Bolan dialed another number.

Keller answered on the first ring. "Yo!"

"How soon can you and the Marines get back here?"

"Half an hour, why? Did you get anything out of Ghulz?"

"Not much, but I think we're about to get something courtesy of Ghulz."

"You're going to get hit?"

Something the size of a 155 mm howitzer round hit the house. Ghulz screamed as dust sifted down from the floor above. The second impact blew the cellar door inward, and heat and smoke roared down the stairs in a wave. Ous slashed Ghulz's bonds and ran to the other end of the cellar.

"Come!" He overturned two barrels to reveal a hatch. He pulled it open and dropped down. Between the Soviet invasion and the war on terror, Afghanistan had become a veritable termite's nest of tunnels.

Bolan shoved the shrieking Ghulz into the dark as the power cut out. The world plunged into darkness that relit Halloween orange and hell red as the third shell impacted. Bolan tossed Ghulz's phone back behind him as he dropped down and gave the cowering Ghulz a shove to motivate him onward. The soldier pulled out his tactical light. The tunnel was just big enough to move at an uncomfortable crouch. Ghulz crawled, sobbing, on hands and knees. Ous scrambled ahead. Heat seared the back of Bolan's neck, and a second later the tunnel hatch filled with rubble as the floor of the house above failed. Bolan's internal compass told him they were heading northwest in a line that was taking them to Ous's stable. His sense of direction bore out as the tunnel dead-ended with a hatch leading above.

Ghulz whimpered and Ous cuffed him to silence. Bolan and Ous crouched and listened for long moments. The shelling had stopped. Ous's tone was dangerously conversational. "Do you know? I was not aware of an artillery emplacement in the hills above my home."

"It wasn't artillery." The explosion pulse and Bolan's sense of smell told him what happened. "They're using thermobaric weapons."

Ous gave Bolan a look.

"Fuel-air explosive," Bolan explained. "I smelled the stench of the fuel over the burnt high explosive. I'd bet they're hitting us with Russian-made Shmel or Shmel-M shoulder-fired recoilless grenade launchers."

"Truly you are a fountain of knowledge. What else does this mean?"

"It means three hundred meters is the effective range and seventeen is the maximum. They're aiming at a large house and they're up in the hills firing down, so it's plunging fire. I'm guessing if they have training and want hits they're at five hundred meters or less."

"What else?"

"We need bigger guns." Bolan glanced meaningfully at his silenced submachine gun.

"God, through his servant Omar, Provides."

Ous reached into a crèche in the side of the tunnel and pulled out a crate, from which he withdrew an SVU-AS sniper rifle. He handed it to Bolan and took out a second weapon for himself along with two bandoliers of magazines for the both of them.

Bolan inspected the weapon. It was distinctly odd as sniper weapons went. It was basically the old Russian Dragunov back-flipped into a bullpup configuration, and it had the charming and somewhat mind-boggling ability for a .30-caliber sniper rifle to fire on full-auto. In the glare of the tactical light between Bolan's teeth it was clear the rifle was both well used and lovingly oiled and preserved. "You got any grenades?"

"I have two. How many would please you?"

"One'll do just fine," Bolan said.

Ous handed him a Russian RGO fragmentation grenade. "Thanks."

Ous put his shoulder against the hatch above him and shoved hard. Dirt, dung and straw cascaded down. The spooked horses nickered and shifted in their stalls at the new intrusion. Ous jumped up into the stable and pulled Ghulz up by his hair. Bolan heaved himself up and moved to the wall facing the house. He peered out a knothole at the burning pile of rubble.

"It's gone."

"So I gather." Ous slapped Ghulz to the ground. "Stay still, and I shall not kill you immediately."

Bolan glanced around through the gloom. The smell directed him to the tarp-covered pile of something in the corner. He had a reasonable suspicion it was Ous's mother-in-law, the servants and Ous's hounds. Ous glanced to where Bolan was looking, snuffed the air and then looked once more upon Ghulz. "I restrain myself."

Ghulz cringed.

Bolan watched the house burn. The phone signal would tell the enemy that he and Ous were buried in the rubble. Regardless, the enemy didn't seem to know about the tunnel.

"How shall we proceed?" Ous asked.

"They're waiting to see if anything moves. If nothing does, they're most likely going to extract, though there's a chance they may come down here and run a quick recon on the rubble before they do."

Ous squinted out a crack between the boards of the stable wall. "Can you ride a horse?"

"Yeah."

"I suggest a quick ride through the orchard and then beneath the aqueduct. I know the terrain. We can flank them within thirty minutes."

It wasn't a bad idea. The stable was a house of straw and a very big bad wolf could huff, puff and thermobarically blow the structure and person and beast within it away the moment they were divulged. They could spread to give the gunners up-range too many targets. It would most likely force an extraction on their part, but the Marine choppers were inbound. It would only—

"Ghulz!" Bolan roared.

Ustad Ghulz ran screaming from the stable.

The gate hadn't been barred. Ous raised his rifle to shoot the coward. Bolan seized Ous by the shoulder, spun him around and shoved him toward the hatch.

"Forget him! Down!" Bolan heard the rush of the rocket. Ous vaulted back down into the tunnel, and the Executioner followed a second later, slamming the hatch shut. The world blew up as the fuel-air weapon hit the stable. It stopped short of collapsing the tunnel. Bolan waited a moment as dust and dirt filtered down on him, then threw open the blackened and warped trapdoor. He found himself in a crater. Rather than burning like the house, the stable had been scattered to the four winds. The horses had been blown into chunks of smoldering meat and a smoking human leg a dozen yards away implied Ghulz had met a similar fate. The blast wave had gone on to denude the trees in the orchard of every single leaf and fruit.

Ous popped his head up and scowled around his premises. "The men left behind at the house were considered expendable."

"Yeah."

"The men on the hillside were left to watch, with the option of attacking us or killing their own men if my assassination attempt upon you failed."

"Yeah."

Ous gave Bolan a pained look. "I see, but then why did they not attack the Marines when they were at my home?"

"Because there were three helicopter loads of them and it would have accomplished nothing."

"I see. They were left to deal with NCIS agents, malingerers, or perhaps even you and me."

"Right."

"The men on the hill are considered expendable, as well?"

"Yeah—" Bolan frowned "—but I haven't made up my mind whether they know it or not."

Ous stroked his beard. "Our enemy plays a deep game. How shall we proceed?"

Bolan knew his next suggestion would most likely be in vain. "We could wait for backup?"

"They have terrorized my wife, beaten my son, abused my daughter, killed my mother-in-law, shot my hounds, burned down my house, slaughtered my horses and now the cherry crop is ruined." Ous's tone was eerily conversational as he made his list. "It is said that the man who forgives shall find his place in Paradise assured. However, I find I wish to see these men's souls in hell before I worry about my own."

"It's not unreasonable," Bolan admitted.

"No."

"You're going up that hill?" the soldier asked.

"I am."

"Do you want some company?"

"Few things would please me more," Ous said.

"Let's go." Bolan crawled to the edge of the crater and pulled down his night-vision goggles to peer through the smoke. The problem for the bad guys was that recoilless weapons belched fire from both ends. Beyond the burning house, gray smoke rose up in the hills, marking their firing position. "I make it four hundred meters from the house." Bolan tried to scan the area, but the fit between his night-vision goggles and the Russian telescopic sight wasn't ideal. The good news was that he had fired a Shmel rocket once or twice himself. They weighed nearly twenty-six pounds and most of that weight was the rocket. A mobile force wouldn't be carrying many reloads, and they'd already fired four times. The bad news was that out in the open one thermobaric detonation would be all it took to paint Bolan and Ous into swathes of shattered bones and bubbling goo across the scorched earth.

"Cover me." Bolan rose and sprinted across the killing ground. He kept the smoke of the burning house between him and the hills. The enemy opened up, but it was almost a relief to have rifles firing at him in the distance rather than rockets. Bolan made it approximately eight shooters. Ous returned fire as the Executioner ran. A thermobaric blast had knocked Ous's Landcruiser onto its side and Bolan skidded behind it. He slapped his rifle over the scorched left tire and roared behind him. "Go!"

Ous ran. The chattering of the enemy AKs were strobing orange blossoms in night. Bolan picked flowers. The short, SVU-AS rifle slammed into his shoulder, and a rifle in the hills fell silent. He took two more, and suddenly all the weapons fell silent as the enemy realized they were outranged. Ous reached his overturned truck, his breath ragged.

It was another hundred yards past the house to the start of the rugged hills and rock creeping that was more the veteran's speed. "Go."

Ous groaned but broke cover and ran. Bolan knew every step Ous took also brought him in range of the enemy rifles, but the soldier was a trained sniper and the better sprinter. He had to get Ous into the hills first. One fool did the Executioner the favor of opening fire from too long a range, and Bolan's bullet put into him.

Ous reached the rocks alive. The effort left him bent over double, but he waved Bolan forward. The big American kept the house between himself and the enemy as long as he could, then sprinted for the rocks. No fire reached out for him during his seconds' long sprint across the open ground. He crouched behind an outcropping. Ous was still gasping. Bolan considered the situation. He wasn't looking forward to climbing this hill. "They're waiting to ambush us as we come up."

"Yes," Ous agreed. "However, look to your right."

Bolan looked. To a practiced eye the land to his right formed a small alluvial fan. He smiled in the dark at the rocks that guarded its mouth. "A channel."

"A chute," Ous acknowledged. "When it rains, the water comes down the chute in a torrent. The chute goes nearly to the top of the hill. When the Soviets came to my village, we fighters scattered up into the hills. We would slither down the chute on our bellies at night to come down to the valley floor unseen. We shall now creep up it to come upon our enemies."

"Lead the way."

Ous disappeared into a crevice. Bolan slung his rifle and followed. The chute was like a narrow waterslide of stone. Aeons of rainwater had carved a serpentine course down the hillside. The sides and floor of the chute were bone-dry at the moment and made for an easy ascent. Hands and boot soles made almost no noise against the slick rock and Ous set an easy pace up the hill. They stopped at the sound of whispering voices. They were about halfway up the hill, and the rolling land gave way to "shattered castle" rock formations. It made the exact location of the enemy difficult. The problem of the valley floor repeated itself on a smaller scale. To reach the rocks they had to clear twenty-five yards of dead space. Once they reached the rocks they were going to be outnumbered and at fistfight distances. Bolan wanted an advantage.

"What do you propose?" Ous whispered.

Bolan took out his grenade and pulled the pin. He

nodded at Ous to do the same. The man scowled but did so. "You intend to fire for effect?"

"Not exactly."

"We have only two grenades," Ous reminded him. "Perhaps it would be wise to use them defensively."

"Let's see how smart these guys really are." Bolan took out his cell phone.

"What do you plan to do?" Ous queried dryly, "set it on vibrate and hurl it at them?"

Bolan's plan was a playground trick, but sometimes people forgot things in the heat of battle, and while he knew his opponents were stone-cold killers, he was hoping they were not operators. The soldier hit Ghulz's emergency preset number. Several seconds later Bolan was rewarded by the sound of Pakistani Qawali music pulsing tinnily from a cell speaker. The glow of the cell phone's display was a flare in the light amplification of Bolan's night-vision gear.

"Ah!" Ous exclaimed.

The reaction in the rocks was horror and consternation. *"Bismillah!"*

Bolan hurled his frag grenade and Ous flung his a second later. The rocks flashed yellow and pulsed smoke in tandem detonations. Horror and consternation rose to wailing and screaming. Bolan swung up his suppressed submachine gun.

"Take a prisoner if possible."

He and Ous charged. The Executioner hit the rock maze and followed the stench of spent grenade and passed the bodies of several men he'd shot. The rocket launchers needed a good bit of space for the back blast. Bolan found the dead and dying in a tiara of rock that formed cover in the front and opened into a culvert in the back. He had guessed right. A small pile of Shmel launch tubes littered the firing position. Of the four men, two were facedown unmoving. The third wheezed as he bled out on his back, and the fourth was trying to crawl away while holding his face.

Three choppers flying nap of the earth suddenly popped over the opposite ridge. A SuperCobra gunship flanked by a pair of Venoms thundered over the valley in a hostile wedge of USMC firepower.

"Cavalry's here," Bolan said.

Ous clubbed the wounded man to the dirt and sighed. "Thank, God."

Bolan gazed at the man. "You were worried?"

"Thank God they are helicopters." Ous stood at stared at the oncoming Marine aircraft and then looked at Bolan very seriously. "I never wish to fly in a plane again."

Bolan knew Ous was going to have to confront his fears in order to return to the base.

CHAPTER EIGHT

Ous survived the plane ride back to base. The lack of any parachutes in sight and a task to keep him occupied might have had something to do with it. The prisoner's shrapnel wounds were bad but not life-threatening. He had ridden a gurney in the back of the plane sutured up and morphined out of his mind. Ous had spoken to him and found that Tajik was the man's first language. He was northern Afghani from Badakhshan Province, and his name was Motahmed. In the midst of Motahmed's opiate-induced babbling the man had suddenly remembered where he was, whom he was with and what his status was, and clammed up.

Still, it was a good start.

Bolan watched as Motahmed was wheeled into the infirmary surrounded by a phalanx of MPs.

"Sir!"

The Executioner turned as a female Marine corporal ran up and handed him a folded piece of paper. "Sir, Agent Farkas asked me to give you this as soon as you got in."

The big American thanked her and read the note: Meet me in the mess tent, asap, bring Ous. It was followed by the code word Bolan had given Farkas for private communication. Agent Keller, who'd joined him, watched as Bolan folded up the note.

"What? He's still pouting because he had to stay behind on babysitting detail with the female prisoners?"

"Don't know. Speaking of the prisoners, why don't you go check on them?"

"No problem. You want to go have boy-talk, you go ahead. I'll go check on Zurisaday and the Pussycats." Keller checked the load in her pistol and wandered off toward the detention area.

Ous stared at the note. "What is going on?"

"Agent Farkas wants to have a private meeting with us, in public."

Ous followed Keller's lead and checked the load in his pistol. "Very well."

Farkas sat in the back of the mess tent, facing the entrance. He hadn't shaved and he looked distinctly unhappy. The word "haunted" came to Bolan's mind. Farkas looked relieved when Bolan and Ous entered the mess tent. It was very late or very early depending upon how you felt about matters and only a few scattered clumps of Marines sat eating or drinking coffee. Bolan and Ous grabbed some coffee and took a seat.

"Got your note," the Executioner stated. "What's up?"

Farkas looked back and forth between the two warriors. "I asked you two here because at the moment you're the only two people I trust."

Ous raised an eyebrow. So did Bolan. Ever since Ous's attempt on Bolan's life, Farkas had strenuously objected to the Afghan's continued involvement. This new outpouring of trust didn't bode anything good. "What's on your mind?"

"Listen," Farkas said, "I know there's a lot of stuff you haven't told me, that you *can't* tell me."

"You can always ask."

Farkas looked at Ous. "You went after him, because somebody had something on you, right?"

Ous stared at Farkas for long moments. "That is essentially correct." Farkas reached into his jacket and pulled out a Pesh Kabz dagger. It wasn't as nice as the one with which Ous had attacked Bolan, but the sinuous lines were unmistakable. "You found it on your bed?"

"Yeah, along with a picture of my wife."

Bolan gave Ous a hard look. He knew the man's family had been threatened, but the veteran had been holding out about the dagger. "You found the knife you tried to kill me with on your bed?"

"It was placed on my pillow—" Ous shook his head "—as I lay sleeping. With a picture of my family beneath it."

Farkas was appalled. "Well, why didn't they just kill me?"

"Because they are trying to warn you off—" Ous took out his pipe "—or, like myself, there is a task they wish you to perform."

Bolan took the agent's eye and held it. "You been tasked, Farkas?"

"No! God no!"

"You are a Westerner. They would not expect you to fully comprehend the meaning of the dagger. They are expecting you to take it as a warning or else you will be contacted again if they wish something of you."

"Who the hell are they?"

Bolan spoke very quietly. "Hashasheen."

Ous's head snapped around. His pronunciation was better. "What do you know of the Hashashiyyn?"

"They were the Nizari branch of the Ismaili Shia Muslims in medieval Persia. They were a splinter group, and as such they were persecuted. Some sources credit them with developing asymmetrical warfare, and if they didn't they took it to the next level. They used bribery, political intrigue, espionage and disinformation campaigns to keep their enemies in confusion. Throughout the Middle East and Central Asia they planted sleeper agents, and when all else failed they intimidated or assassinated the leaders of their enemies. Some people think the word assassin derives from Hashasheen. Their leader was known as the Old Man of the Mountain. Their base was high in the Kopet Mountains overlooking the Caspian Sea. It wasn't unknown for them to sell their services."

Farkas just stared. "What happened to them?"

Bolan shrugged. "They couldn't infiltrate, intimidate or assassinate the Mongol invasion. They were wiped out."

"So there's a new Old Man of the Mountain with an assassin army in Iran?"

"There was."

"What happened?"

"They couldn't intimidate or assassinate me," Bolan said. "Most got wiped out."

"Jesus…" Farkas remarked.

Ous visibly stopped himself from making the sign against the Evil Eye. He regarded Bolan long and hard. "Had any other man told me this, I would consider him insane or possessed."

"So…these guys were like, Persian ninjas?"

"In a sense. Like ninjas, mystical powers were attributed to them. They didn't do anything to dissuade anybody believing it. Espionage and intimidation were their best weapons. If you, your wife or your child wakes up with a dagger on their pillow, then you know that you and yours aren't safe anywhere. If I had to bet, somewhere on this base is a Marine who was gotten to, and told to put that knife on your bed."

"This much I agree with," Ous said. "However the dagger with which I tried to kill you was placed on my pillow, as I slept. I was in a safehouse few if any would know of, and I had taken security precautions both within and without my chamber. There is no one who could have been bribed or gotten to, to effect their egress. This was a work of great skill."

"That's troubling." Bolan nodded. "Farkas, you get anything out of Zurisaday?"

"The bitch is a goddamn cipher." Farkas scowled.

Ous puffed on his pipe. "Perhaps more of a trained sleeper agent, and an assassin."

The base general alarm and Bolan's phone rang simultaneously. "What's happening, Keller?"

Keller's voice was ragged with pain. "The bitch is loose! She slaughtered the entire holding block and just about took my head off!"

Bolan rose. "Zurisaday is loose. Farkas, stay here." His voice rose to command tones as he addressed three Marines who had risen from their seats and put hands to sidearms.

"You three! Agent Farkas may be the target of an assassination attempt. Guard him with your life!"

The Marines sounded off in a chorus. "Sir, yes, sir!"

"Ous." Bolan drew his Beretta. "With me."

Bolan and Ous stepped out into the predawn. The Afghan filled his hand with steel. "You believe she has a target? Or does she seek to escape?"

"I don't know yet, but she didn't try to escape until after we got back from your place."

"It is an interesting coincidence."

Marines were running in every direction in various states of dress and armament.

"What course of action do you suggest?" Ous asked.

"Let's wait a moment or two," Bolan suggested.

"Very well."

The two warriors' patience was rewarded as the lights

of the base went out in a rolling cascade. Some parts of Sangin were semipermanent fixtures, others, like the tents with medical or command, communication and control equipment, were equipped with emergency generators. Parts of the base rebooted into scattered emergency light. Tracts of tents and Conex containers stayed in darkness.

"She's coming," Ous observed.

Bolan took his night-vision goggles out of his hip pack and held them up to his eyes. "Yes."

Zurisaday came loping out of the gloom. Her mouth was smeared with blood and she held a Military Police collapsible baton in the open position. She caught sight of Bolan and Ous in the fading starlight. She flicked her gaze from side to side and decided that going through them was her best option. Bolan pocketed his NVGS. "Stop."

The woman came straight-on.

She wasn't afraid of the gun. Bolan was very certain the young woman wasn't afraid of anything. She intended to assassinate somebody, escape, or be killed trying, and didn't seem to have much problem with either eventuality. Bolan considered shooting her legs out from under her, but 9 mm hollowpoint rounds were known to make a mess, and femoral artery wounds bled out faster than anything other than hits to the throat.

Bolan holstered his pistol and beckoned the assassin in. Zurisaday's hair streamed behind her as she ran light-footed down the gravel path. Her lips skinned back from bloody teeth in a frozen, rictus smile. As the black of night turned to the purple of predawn, like she looked like a succubus as she came in for the kill. The soldier had beaten her once, but he'd had the element of surprise.

It seemed the assassin wanted a rematch.

"If I don't take her down, shoot her."

"As you wish," Ous stated.

Bolan strode out to meet his opponent.

He didn't relish hitting women, but when one added the descriptor sociopath-assassin, gender considerations went right out the window. Zurisaday was eerily silent and grinning as she raised her truncheon high for a wild swing at Bolan's head. He saw it for the feint it was. The strike turned into a liquid swift, softball pitch thrust straight for his solar plexus. It was a blow guaranteed to snap Bolan's xiphoid process and drive it inward, perforating the diaphragm and collapsing his lungs.

Bolan twisted his torso with the blow, and the tip of the truncheon scraped across his chest rather than punched through it. He snapped his knee into Zurisaday's stomach as she sailed past. The assassin gasped as she spun, then stumbled. Bolan hadn't collapsed her lungs, but he had driven every last ounce of air out of them, and even sociopaths needed to breathe. His strategy solidified as he continued his attack. Sociopaths generally had a movie in their head of a universe that centered around them, and they didn't like changes to the script.

Bolan's knee had been above the belt. His spear hand struck just below it and stopped just short of rupturing Zurisaday's bladder. It didn't do much for the assassin's strangled attempts at breathing, either. She wheezed like a landed fish and bent double but didn't fall. Bolan took the opportunity to drop a hammer fist over both of her kidneys. Zurisaday's claw hand toward Bolan's groin was palsied, but it was remarkable that she could still muster any offense at all. He caught her wrist and rewarded her gumption with a spear hand between the biceps and bone that crushed her medial nerve. He finished off her right arm with a knife hand into the biceps itself.

The woman didn't cry out. Her eyes flared almost in incomprehension as Bolan gave her left arm the exact same treatment. She tottered back a step with her arms hanging uselessly by her sides. She attempted a kick at Bolan's groin. He caught her ankle and worked the offered leg, spear-handling the femoral nerve and then driving his elbow into the flesh of her thigh in the mother of all charley horses. Zurisaday dropped to her knees and even more incredibly lunged her head forward like a snake striking. Her bared teeth snapped for Bolan's groin like a steel trap. He put both hands on her shoulders and tossed her into a wrestler's sprawl. Zurisaday landed facedown in the dirt. Bolan rolled across her back and gave her an elbow to both hamstrings. He flipped her over and gave her left leg a femoral spear and dealt a hammer blow to the muscle to match her right.

Bolan rose, dusted himself off and examined the woman.

He hadn't broken any of Zurisaday's bones or torn any of her tendons or ligaments, but the crushed muscles and nerves in her limbs would feel like ground meat and be about as useful for days to come. She stared up with a pure, distilled hatred that was almost palpable. If looks could have killed, bits of Bolan would have been strung around the surrounding tents like Christmas lights. The assassin was shaking, but not with pain. She hadn't killed her target or been killed in the attempt. She had been manhandled, and taken with childlike ease. The script of her movie hadn't been edited.

The film itself had snapped in the projector.

A shuddering, hissing stream of what Bolan could only suspect was sizzling invectives began spilling from Zurisaday's beautiful mouth, and it went on and on. He stood over her implacably as she spit forth her insane fury like poison.

Ous spoke quietly at Bolan's side. "I have gleaned what

is most important out of her rant. She is now repeating herself."

Zurisaday took the news like a lightning bolt.

Bolan had seen grown men and women go into fits several times in his life. Only the state of the nerves and muscles and in Zurisaday's limbs kept her reaction to Ous's words from launching into full-blown grand mal seizure. The blown pupils, rolling eyes, gnashing teeth, frothing at the mouth, whole body spasms and speaking in tongues were bad enough. Ous made the sign against the evil eye and took a prudent step back. "The woman has been possessed by evil spirits."

"For some time," Bolan agreed.

A pair of MPs ran up and skidded to a halt.

"You want us to take her back to the holding area?" the lead MP asked Bolan.

"If you would."

The second MP cleared his throat. "Uh, is she epileptic?"

"No. As far as I know, she's just pure evil."

The MPs spent several moments internalizing this. "Is she safe to transport like this?"

"She should be." Bolan considered the woman's physical breakdown and let out a tired breath. "But I'd watch out for her teeth."

CHAPTER NINE

"How did she get out?" Bolan asked.

Ous echoed the sentiment. "She had help?"

Bolan, Ous, Keller and Farkas sat around a table drinking Marine Corps coffee.

"Of a kind…" Keller rubbed her swollen jaw. Zurisaday had run over her like a freight train as she'd burst out of the holding area.

Bolan raised one eyebrow in interest. "What kind?"

Keller rolled her eyes in disgust. "The detainee offered to perform, shall we say, an act of oral outrage for one of the guards, through the bars, ostensibly in exchange for cigarettes."

Farkas sighed. "I swear this Zurisaday chick is a Marine magnet. It's like they can't resist her or something."

"Or something," Bolan was pretty sure he could see where this was going. "And?"

"And the young private was smart enough to put his sidearm in a locker, but dumb enough to think his baton would be enough to control the course of events. Needless to say, she got a hold of his baton."

Bolan grimaced. "Both of them?"

Keller shook her head ruefully. "The young military policeman's 'man baton' is still attached to him, barely. They say he'll regain full functionality in time."

"I thought her hands were cuffed behind her back."

"Yeah, well, somehow she managed to limbo her arms

underneath her to the front, all the while holding our young hero helpless in her 'jaws of death' grip."

"Talented girl," Bolan observed.

"Yeah, well, from there she also got hold of his keys, went into the cells of her fellow detainees and killed each one of them."

"She beat them to death?"

"Oh no, worse than that. They were flat-out executions. Upon initial examination it appears each woman was kicked in the stomach to bend her over and then the butt of the baton was driven into the base of her neck in a single blow. A blow with a great deal of both force and precision."

Bolan knew the technique. Someone had given the young woman a comprehensive lesson on kill shots. "Second cervical vertebrae."

"Your classic blunt-trauma neck kill. Fracture the vertebrae and sever the spinal cord, and your talented girl did it four times in less than five minutes. That's got to be some kind of record, particularly under prison break conditions." Keller gave Bolan an appraising look. "Quite frankly I'm surprised she didn't hand you your gonads this morning."

Bolan mentally reviewed his dawn battle with the assassin. "She tried."

"Well, she's back in holding under double guard." She gave Bolan another look. "The doctor got done with her about an hour ago. Says he's never seen such a spectacular array of deep tissue hematomas in his life. He says the patterns and placement of her contusions beggar his medical experience."

"Figured you wanted her back, maybe talking, and with no hope of busting out for a day or two."

"You say she started talking after the beat-down you gave her?"

"Other than her expressing unkind thoughts, I couldn't get anything out of it."

Keller glanced at Ous. "You?"

The Afghani smiled at Bolan. "She hoped that your mother might recognize you in a meat pie."

Bolan smiled. "Nice."

Keller snorted. "What else?"

"After that her words became increasingly uncultural. However, she spoke her insults in Arabic, and I can tell you from personal experience that both by the flavor of her words and her accent it is very likely she is Syrian by birth."

Keller nodded. "Well, that jibes with previous intel at least."

"There were some aspects of her rant you may find of interest," Ous stated.

"Such as?"

"Some of it was most unladylike, to be spoken by a lady—" Ous cleared his throat and nodded deferentially "—or in a lady's presence."

"Mr. Ous, are you aware of the fact I was at one time a United States naval officer?"

Ous looked to Bolan, who shrugged. "Go ahead, give her a thrill."

"Well…of interest, was that she said, 'after the council' was done with our friend, she was going to make *sarma* with the skin of his phallus and feed it to him."

Keller's nose wrinkled. "What's *sarma*?"

Bolan grinned. "Imagine an egg roll stuffed with—"

"Eew!"

The big American changed the subject. "He's right, the council part is interesting."

Farkas spoke up for the first time. He'd been very quiet since the discussion in the mess tent. "Hey, that coincides with your wiping out the modern Old Man of the Mountain and his minions in Iran."

Keller turned a droll look on Farkas. "You been holding out on me, partner?"

Bolan sat back and let Farkas tell the story of the dagger on his pillow and summed up the story of the Assassins of Alamut he'd been told. He was a trained agent and there was very little that needed correction.

Keller reserved comment until Farkas was finished. "Jesus H. Christ. Anything else I should know?"

"That's the skinny as it stands," Bolan said. "And at least now everyone in this room trusts one another."

"F'ing marvelous," Keller muttered.

Ous blinked at Keller and spoke with great seriousness. "Trust earned, indeed, is a marvelous thing. May I say, Agent Keller, that I trust you implicitly."

Ous's earnestness was just about bulletproof. Keller relented. "Yeah, well, I trust you, too."

Ous beamed.

Keller turned to Farkas. "What about you?"

Farkas shrank with shame. "Man, c'mon Kat. They put a dagger and a picture of my kids on my pillow. How many people had access? They're getting to people. I'm sorry, my first thought was maybe they'd gotten to you, too."

"Don't worry about it."

Farkas seemed to be slowly coming back to life. "So what do you think a council could mean?"

Ous blew blue smoke toward the tent ceiling. "It means there is no Old Man of the Mountain."

Farkas blinked. "Okay...and?"

Bolan gave Farkas credit for having had a hard night and held his peace.

"It means if we're dealing with a new, or splinter group

of the Assassins, they are not a cult dedicated to a charismatic leader," Ous explained.

Bolan nodded. "Or we have a council of charismatic leaders, each representing different countries, sects or areas of operation. We know they can penetrate the United States Marine Corps, and if they can do that…?" Bolan left the question in the air.

Keller didn't leave anything anywhere. Her feelings on the matter were plain. "F me."

Bolan watched as Farkas did some math. The agent stabbed a finger on the map of Afghanistan in the middle of the table. "Okay, so the Assassins of old were all about protecting the sect, playing one side against the other. So, what are these new Assassins trying to defend?"

Farkas was a good man, but his world had been seriously rattled, and Bolan cut him some more slack. "You think they're on the defensive?"

Farkas suddenly got the major message to his melon. "No, no they're not. They're playing offense."

Bolan nodded over his coffee. "There's hope."

Ous took a long tug on his pipe. He blew three smoke rings and then sent a pursed-lip stream of smoke that bull's-eyed all three like a lance. "They infiltrate us, fearing not that we can infiltrate them."

A slow smile spread across Bolan's face. "It's hubris."

"God frowns on it."

"Okay," Keller said. "What in the Blue Hell are you talking about?"

Bolan looked at Ous. Both warriors knew they'd had a meeting of the minds.

The soldier poured himself more coffee. "The Assassins trained their sleeper agents and killers from childhood, then put them in place to confound their enemies when the balloon went up on any particular front."

Keller's smile was beautiful to behold. "And these new 'council' assholes haven't had time to train anybody."

Farkas glanced around the table. "So?"

Keller dropped her elbows to the table and her face into her hands.

Farkas looked around the table in vague panic. "What?"

"Other than an inner corps of hardcore fanatics, they haven't had the time to custom-build an army of assassins. So since they're buying off the rack…"

Farkas blinked twice as the ramifications hit home. "Oh shit."

Bolan nodded. "Oh yeah."

"So what do we do?"

Keller and Ous both nodded at Bolan, who nodded at Farkas. "We switch sides."

Sangin

GHOLAM DAEI WATCHED his guest with interest. The man was stripped to the waist and was moving around Daei's personal exercise cellar. Unlike Gholam Daei's ogrelike proportions, the guest was short and as lean as a whip. The guest ran a Khyber knife through a series of exercises of the like Daei had never seen. The Khyber knife was famed throughout Central Asia, but it was particularly known as the traditional blade of an Afghan warrior. It pretty much looked like a chef's knife on steroids. Running fifty-six centimeters, this particular example was approaching swordlike proportions. Daei considered his guest's weapon somewhat exaggerated for what was supposed to be an all-around working and fighting knife, but Daei had acquired what had been asked for without question.

There was nothing exaggerated about the way the dull

gray blade hissed through the air in liquid-quick patterns of thrusts, cuts and blocks.

The guest suddenly came to an abrupt halt and sheathed the blade. Daei nodded ingratiatingly and spoke in English. "It will serve?"

The man nodded curtly and replied in Arabic. "I am becoming used to its balance. It will serve elegantly."

"I am pleased."

The guest nodded once more. "What is the status of Motahmed?"

"My informants tell me he died of his wounds in Marine Corps custody. His body is being returned to his family."

The guest stood steaming in the cool of the cellar for long moments, frowning. "Do you believe this to be the case?"

"I have no reason not to believe it. The slaughter at Ous's home and the hillside above was great. I am told the Marine medics engaged in Herculean efforts to keep him alive, and even if it is untrue, there is little he can reveal."

"Yes, it was costly, and to little effect."

Daei bristled inwardly but kept it off his face. "War has its fortunes."

The guest grunted at the wisdom of the statement. "Do we know where the family of Omar Ous is currently?"

"Currently only God and the Americans know. Neither has seen fit to reveal their location to myself or my agents."

"Then they are most likely in protective custody, and most likely no longer in Afghanistan."

Daei sighed. "Most likely."

"This American and his continued interference concern me."

There was no need to ask which American. He was a source of growing concern to Daei, as well. "We still have several Marines on Sangin Base who shiver beneath our shadow. However they are extremely valuable sources of intelligence. The loss of Corporal Convertino was tragic. We had great plans for him, and I am loath to use those remaining assets in Sangin Base in another assassination attempt against the American."

"That is understandable. However, tell me, what is the status of the NCIS agent asset, Farkas?"

Daei shook his head in very dark amusement. "Agent Farkas appears to feel that our shadow can no longer reach him, or his family, and I blame the American. It is known Farkas met with the American and Ous just as Zurisaday attempted her escape. And, speaking of the American, he defeated her in open combat, hand to hand. I believe Farkas broke silence and told of his visitation."

"Interesting. And what is the status of Farkas's family?"

"I must admit our resources in the United States are extremely limited at the moment, and almost entirely relegated to intelligence gathering. I am informed that his family continues to abide at their residence in Virginia. It is also known to me that they are under the protection of federal agents. I fear I cannot reach out across the hemisphere and touch them without grave risk of exposure. I must admit I have thought of you concerning this."

"I have far less to fear in this situation, but nonetheless, an operation within the United States is always a serious undertaking."

Daei shrugged. "I could arrange a suicide attack."

"That would defeat our purpose. Let me consider if action should be taken against the Farkas family and then when and what that action might be."

Daei bowed. "I have been instructed to obey your orders and see to your every need."

The guest grunted at the wisdom of the statement.

Daei failed to mention he also had orders to kill his

guest if and when he should become a liability. "What do you recommend?"

"Another attack at the Marine base would be foolish. They are at a high state of alert. I believe it would be wise for me to engineer an incident, one that will draw the American and Ous out of Sangin Base and into our hands. Upon consideration, it will be at that juncture that I will bring Agent Farkas back into play."

"I am intrigued. How may I be of assistance?"

"I will require you to recruit more men," the guest said, "and unlike others, despite their skills or ferocity, they must be utterly willing to die."

Sangin Base, Secure Communications Area

"UP TO SPEC?" Kurtzman asked.

Bolan looked at the paraphernalia he'd asked for. "Yeah."

Seventy-two hours of rest had done the team a world of good. It had given the enemy three days to consider the situation, as well, but Bolan was hoping they had spent it considering the ass-kickings they had taken and decided they needed more men. Mothamed had caved under pressure. Bolan was preparing to sign up for Team Jihad.

He was going undercover in Central Asia to try to get hired and penetrate a revitalized Islamic death cult, and he didn't speak Arabic, much less any of the local ethnic languages or dialects. Normally that would have been strike one, strike two and strike three right there. But Bolan had a couple of advantages. One was that Omar Ous was going to run interference for him, and two he had the technological wizardry of Aaron Kurtzman and Akira Tokaido, and Stony Man Farm's assets, including John "Cowboy" Kissinger, at his disposal.

Kurtzman watched on the laptop camera as Bolan picked up an old-fashioned, bulky, hooked-over-the-ear hearing aid with Cyrillic writing imprinted on it. "Okay, that is your lifeline. We have two satellites slaved to it and linguists who speak Arabic, Pashto, Dari-Persian and Tajik. We've locked them in a basement room of the Pentagon and they will be listening on six-hour shifts. They will be able to hear anything you hear within conversational distances and translate via satellite in real time. The rig matches an older model of Russian manufactured hearing aids that an Afghani might be able to get his hands on."

Bolan tried fitting the rig into and over his ear.

"The kicker are the batteries," Kurtzman continued. "You're going to burn through them fast. We've given you a set of spares, but turn the rig off whenever you have the opportunity."

"Got it."

"Now Afghanistan is being flooded with cheap Chinese cell phones these days. We chose an older candy-bar model to give ourselves more space to work with inside."

Bolan picked up the battered cell phone.

"It won't help you under cover so much, but the phone is satellite and can be used just like the fake hearing aid for translation. It has deep erase so any data you kill is dead, but don't worry about that because we'll be recording everything."

"Right."

"Again, if you get called or texted in foreign languages by whoever hires you, remember the hearing aid and the phone are slaved. We can translate any time of day right into your hearing aid, but there may be a slight lag, so be careful."

"Always."

"Ous will have a similar phone but different model. Oh, the antenna?"

Bolan glanced at the old-fashioned stub of black plastic antenna barrel. "What caliber?"

"Cowboy stayed Chinese. It's PRC issue 5.8 mm subsonic. Aim over your thumb-knuckle and press the Chinese logo medallion, hard."

"Nice."

"The camera function will appear to be broken. Memorize the second number I sent you to enable it. Anyone who tries to access the photos will have to know that number to view them. We want as many photo captures as possible, but be careful of who you try to capture. When you do, send and then erase as quickly as possible. We can send the photos back later if you need to show them to someone on the ground."

"Got it."

Bolan checked his weapons. The Russian bullpup sniper rifle Ous had given him was a little too fancy for his undercover role, but Bolan still wanted the power of precision shooting. Kissinger had sent him a Dragunov sniper rifle that was so battered it looked as though it was on its last legs. On the inside the action was as slick as glass and hand-tuned and accurized by the master himself. The Stechkin machine pistol next to it looked like it had seen equally hard use externally but it was likewise racing-tuned on the inside, and loaded with Russian high-impulse rounds. The fourteen-inch Khyber knife wasn't fancy, but Calvin James, the Farm's knife-fighter in residence, had put his signature shaving sharp edge on the high-carbon steel. He had done the same for the Dragunov's bayonet. The last weapon was a tiny Russian PSM pistol. To this day they were still called "suicide specials" in Russia.

"You really think you're going to get away with this?" Kurtzman asked.

To Bolan's knowledge something like this had never been tried in Central Asia. "The whole thing is going to hinge on Ous."

"You trust him?"

"Implicitly," Bolan replied.

"Well, then, the good news is your CIA groomer and her kit are in the capital. She should hit Sangin in about two hours." Kurtzman smiled knowingly, "Then the real fun begins."

"Yeah…" This was a part of the mission Bolan wasn't particularly looking forward to.

The computer wizard's smile became insufferable. "We all want pictures."

CHAPTER TEN

Bolan and Ous stepped into the meeting room.

Keller whistled. "Christ on a crutch..."

Farkas gaped in agreement. "If I didn't know you, I'd shoot you."

Ous's eyes narrowed at Farkas, who backpedaled.

"Except I'd be too scared." He looked to Bolan for a lifeline. "You, I don't even recognize."

Sunless tanning solution had darkened Bolan's face and hands a few degrees short of Ous's weathered complexion. His mustache and black beard were made of human hair and of the highest quality that the CIA provided for its covert ops, and it fell to his collarbone. The adhesive that held the false beard to his face was guaranteed for a week, and his own beard would grow right through it, though Bolan knew through personal experience that by day three the beard-itch would become almost unbearable. Hair extensions had brought his dark locks down to his shoulders to match the beard, and the CIA groomer had accentuated his eyebrows into some nebulous place between a hillbilly Spock or Satan on a bad-eyebrow day.

A series of rather painful, shaped-silicon injections had seamed the lumped lines of scar tissue across the left side of his face, throat and head. Further pigment injections over the silicon had turned them into the dulled pinks and shiny grays of the scar tissue that would explain why he couldn't talk and needed a hearing aid. It was an outstanding grooming. Bolan wore the full regalia of an Afghani tribal guerrilla and except for the arctic-blue eyes burning out of his weathered, bushy and brutally scarred countenance even Bolan's worst enemies wouldn't have recognized him—if they still lived.

Ous had performed only three changes, but they were spectacular. He had combed out and stiffened his beard and dyed it a bright orange-red with henna. It was said the Prophet Mohammed and his Caliphs had dyed their beards, and some of the ultraorthodox, particularly pockets of them in Central Asia, followed the custom. Ous had shaved his head and swapped out his omnipresent, rolled pakol for a woolly, Fezlike Karakul hat. It was quite possible Ous's mother might not have recognized him, and between them, Bolan and Ous looked mad, bad and dangerous to know. They looked like the last two men a person would ever want to meet in a ravine in Afghanistan.

Bolan's cover was simple. His name was Makeen. He was deaf in one ear and could barely hear out the other. The same U.S. bomb strike that had robbed him of most of his hearing had also torn his vocal cords and left him unable to speak. It had also killed most of his family. Ous would stress that all of these things had made him an even more dangerous sniper than he'd been before, and it was Ous who knew how to point him in the right direction.

Bolan spread his arms and did a turn. "And?"

"Super hot," Keller proclaimed. "Bind my feet, put me back in the burka and take me to your tent."

"Chinese bound women's feet," Bolan corrected.

"So?" Keller flipped her hair. "Bind my feet and take me to your tent anyway."

Ous grunted bemusedly.

Keller pointed at their route on the map. "From what we got out of Motahmed, there's some spooky recruiting going on here in the border region with Pakistan. Ous learned Motahmed was from Badakhshan, so that fits."

"And that part of the border—" Farkas shook his head "—is funhouse central."

Farkas wasn't far off in his assessment. Pakistan basically had four administrative units. Four were provinces, one was the Federal Capital Territory, and then there was that unique piece of border real estate beneath Keller's finger. It was generally known by the acronym FATA, for the Federally Administered Tribal Areas. The "Federally Administered" part of the designation could be charitably described as "hopeful." The "Tribal" part was spot on. FATA was the most impoverished part of Pakistan. The overwhelming majority of the people were rural and pastoral. The main cities could barely claim the title. Most major transactions outside them were brokered in goats, guns or opium. The Taliban presence there was powerful and well entrenched. FATA really was funhouse central, and the trifecta of God, AK-47s and tribal custom decided just about everything. There appeared to be a new player in the game who was playing the region's proclivities for all they were worth.

It was Bolan and Ous's next destination.

Ous combed his fingers through his newly orange beard. "Tell me about our insertion."

Bolan didn't figure insertion into the area would be problem. "I want to hear about extraction."

Badakshan/FATA border

BOLAN AND OUS fell out of the cabbage truck and landed among a herd of goats. They dusted themselves off as a flatbed full of disreputable individuals cascaded onto the dirt road behind them. Goats baaed and their bells tinkled.

One section of Central Asia pretty much looked like another. This section was distinguished by the fact that just about every man over the age of twelve was carrying a rifle and there was nary a woman to be seen; not even in full black regalia and accompanied by male family members. Bolan and Ous walked down the single dirt lane of the village.

The village looked like hell, Bolan thought.

The side of just about every building, including the tiny mosque, was scarred by bullet strikes and the black flash burns of recent high-explosives that the rains hadn't yet washed away. Despite the forbidding aspect of the village and its inhabitants, the improbably large number of trucks, motorcycles and people wielding cell phones spoke of the wealth the village derived from the smuggling trade.

Other than the battered mosque, the teahouse was the hotbed of civic activity. Bolan and Ous went inside. Most of the tables were taken and they took a seat on a rug in the corner. The teahouse sported a satellite dish and the Al Jazeera news network played on a flat-screen television. Interestingly enough FOX news played on another. Despite the fact that it was broadcast in English, the blonde news anchor seemed to be drawing the majority of patrons' attention and speculation. Bolan and Ous ordered tea and dumplings to break their fast. The tea was heavy with cardamom, the dumplings swam in yogurt and dill, and the bread was still hot from the oven. It was the best breakfast Bolan had eaten in days.

"What do you think?" he murmured through a mouthful of bread sopped in the dumpling sauce.

Ous spoke into his teacup. "We are already attracting a great deal of attention."

The looks they were attracting were just short of hostile. The Pashtun people were regarded as one of the most hospitable cultures on Earth. It was ingrained in their culture through Pashtunwali, or "the way of the Pashtuns." A Pashtun was required to show hospitality and profound respect to any visitor or guest, regardless of their tribe, race, religion or creed, and to do so with no hope of reward. Under a flag of truce this hospitality was shown even to sworn enemies. They were also required to give sanctuary to all who sincerely applied for it and to give them protection from their enemies, even if the applicant was a sworn enemy himself. It was one of the main reasons why it was so difficult to catch al Qaeda and Taliban operatives.

Once an al Qaeda or Taliban operative or group had been shown hospitality or asked for sanctuary, no Pashtun would give them up for any reason, and they would fight to the death to protect them. Pashtunwali was also the reason that it was almost impossible to infiltrate Pashtun Taliban organizations. The code took precedent over everything, even religion. Anyone who broke Pashtunwali would be considered not Pashtun, not human, and would be killed or cast out. As far as Bolan knew, neither the British colonials, the Soviet invaders, nor U.S. and coalition forces had ever successfully conducted an undercover operation among Pashtun guerrilla fighters.

Bolan suspected he and Ous were most likely the first to try it in some time; and at the moment the two warriors were neither guests, enemies under a flag of truce nor individuals seeking sanctuary.

They were strangers.

They did have one card to play. The coming of the Taliban had rocked traditional Pashtun culture. It had initially started with the Soviet invasion but particularly after the toppling of the Taliban and the guerrilla war that ensued, the concept of foreign fighters had seeped into Afghan warfare. So had the concept of shuffling guerrilla fighters from one area to another. Bolan and Ous were depending on this unusual break from millennia of tribal custom. Ous looked like a mad mullah and Bolan simply looked mad. For good or ill they were bound to attract attention in all the right circles, or the wrong ones, depending on one's point of view.

Attention wasn't long in coming.

A lanky man with severe chicken pox scars and whose nose had been broken so badly it sat on his face like a flattened squid approached. Bolan had taken note of him ordering the help around, and Bolan made him out to be the proprietor. The big American scratched his ear to tell his translators to look sharp. Pock-face took in Ous's hennaed beard, shaved head and woolly hat. "Peace, imam. My name is Saboor. As long as it pleases God, I am the owner of this establishment."

"Peace be upon you, Saboor. I thank you for your praise and the pleasure of this house. However, I am no imam. I am but a simple mullah, little more than one who only barely managed to memorize the Holy Koran."

The man took in Bolan's shaggy appearance and the road map of battle damage the CIA groomer had drawn upon his head and neck. "And your companion?"

"My only disciple."

"Forgive my impertinence, mullah, but you seem to have journeyed far. May I ask what province you are from?"

"Since I let go the plow and took up the Holy Koran, I have known the dust of thirty-four provinces beneath my shoes. My only home now is the Province of God." Ous smiled in a kindly fashion. "However, since you ask, long ago, long before you were born, I was born out of the dust of Farah."

Saboor contemplated this. Afghanistan had thirty-four provinces. The province of Farah was on the western edge of Afghanistan. It was about as far away as you could get from the FATA region without wandering into Iran. However both Afghanistan and Pakistan had long and storied traditions of mendicant monks and mullahs who wandered far and wide following wherever the whisper of God led them.

"And your companion?"

Ous sighed sadly and gestured at Bolan's brutally scarred visage. "To be very honest, brother, I do not know. He cannot speak, he can barely hear and he is illiterate."

"May I ask what brings you to our poor village?"

"The call of God."

"Is it permitted for me to ask what God calls for?"

"Martyrdom."

Saboor was taken aback. "Martyrdom?"

"In jihad, against the infidel invaders."

Saboor gazed upon Ous long and hard, and finally nodded. "I might know of a man whom you might meet."

Ous gave Saboor the mad mullah smile. "Every man I meet has been put upon my path by God."

Saboor's eyes widened. Bolan kept the smile off of his face. Ous had a career in the theater if he was still alive after this. "Would you meet with this man?"

"I would," Ous replied.

"Do you possess a cell phone?"

"I do."

"Would you give it to me?" Saboor asked.

"I am sworn to give whatever I have to any believer who asks."

Saboor bowed at the show of piety. "And your companion?"

"You may have all that he possesses except his rifle. I fear if you wish to relieve him of that you must do so at your peril."

Saboor nodded. "Would you take a journey with me?"

"I would, brother." Ous took his cell phone and nodded at Bolan, who took his phone out of his vest and held it out.

Saboor looked at Ous askance. "You say your friend cannot speak, and can barely hear?"

"Sadly, it is true."

"And he knows not the written word?" Saboor queried.

"Sadly, this also is true."

"Then pray why does he own a cell phone?"

"He took it from a Russian who gave us great offense, and it pleases him to take pictures," Ous said.

Saboor took the phone and gave Bolan's picture file a cursory once-over. Kurtzman had filled the phone's picture file with stills of dozens of mosques from over a dozen Afghani provinces. Saboor grunted. "Then I bid you take your fill, take your ease and accept the hospitality of my poor establishment. The journey is not long but it will not be comfortable."

Bolan made a polite gesture at his empty plate for more dumplings. He was going to take his ease and his fill while the easing and the filling were good. His instincts told him things were about to get distinctly uncomfortable for the foreseeable future.

CHAPTER ELEVEN

Federally Administered Tribal Area

"All...righty then." The woman translating for Bolan back at the Pentagon sounded very unhappy. "Do you see two men talking?" Bolan did indeed. Most of the men in the truck were dozing or smoking as the ancient, Soviet-era two-and-a-half-ton bounced over the brutal single-lane, dirt-and-rock road. Everyone was armed and phoneless. The congregation looked suspiciously like a squad.

Two dark, young, barely bearded men who looked like brothers were squatting behind the cab. They were talking in low voices and passing a thermos of tea between them. Bolan didn't understand a word of what they were saying, and Ous was puffing on his pipe unconcernedly. The soldier casually scratched his head above the hearing aid and gave it two taps in acknowledgment that he had eyes on the suspects in question. "Okay, well," the translator continued, "you caught a break. I have a decent grasp of Nuristani. It's usually classified in the Dardic languages branch of the Indo-Aryan language family. Its relation to—"

Bolan rapidly scratched his ear, which was the agreed-upon sign to get to the point. The translators he was working with were some of the top in the field of Central Asian languages. However they were professors and scholars who had been abruptly pulled out of academia for this mission with a heady mixture of carrots and sticks, rather than Pentagon or CIA agents.

The translator cleared her throat. "Okay, pertinent point. Nuristani is only spoken by tribal peoples in extremely isolated mountain regions in the Hindu Kush, it's no wonder that Ous doesn't know what's being said. In fact they are counting on the fact that you don't. What they're saying is, 'The silent one cannot be trusted.'"

Bolan glanced at the two men. They noticed him looking at them and smiled and nodded at him. The translator continued. "Some of the words I don't get but my impression is that they are planning to do you a serious mischief once you get to your destination."

The Executioner slowly lowered his head, let his eyes widen beneath his brows and leered at the two men as his finger curled around the trigger of his rifle. He lowered the muzzle in their direction.

One brother strangled on his tea. The other almost swallowed his cigarette. Since Bolan had the translators and the satellite link, the soldier and Ous had an agreement that if the Executioner took unilateral action, Ous would back his play without hesitation. Ous glanced at the two men, gave them an equally horrible smile, and spoke in Pashto. Bolan's translator translated in real time.

"You give my friend offense?"

The brothers began wringing their hands in caught-red-handed horror and spoke back in Pashto. "Mullah! Who is this man who does not speak? We do not know him! No one knows him! You vouch for him, but no one knows him!" A number of the men crowded in the trunk grumbled in agreement.

Ous went with the script. "He is touched by God."

That was met with incredulous silence.

"He is God's instrument, and does his will."

Saboor gave Ous a very long hard look. Every man in the truck was a volunteer who was willing to martyr himself against the Western invaders, but this was pushing it. "Forgive me, mullah. I mean no offense, but what do you mean by this?"

"I mean that when the infidel invaders took his ears and his tongue, he took up the rifle in God's name, and since that day his every bullet has taken an invader or one of those who aid him. He does not miss."

A dozen eyes fell on Bolan in open speculation. Since time immemorial, Afghan tribal warriors had garnered a fearsome reputation for marksmanship. Afghan mujahideen warriors had wreaked havoc on Soviet infantry, often armed with old, WW II vintage rifles. It was true that with the coming of the Taliban and the widespread availability of automatic weapons standards had slipped, but it was still a heady proclamation to make in present company.

Bolan just kept smiling insanely.

The truck ground to a halt. Saboor nodded. "If God wills, we shall see."

The men piled out of the truck. They were in a camp rather than a village. The camp lay in a narrow arroyo with camouflage netting stretched above and native felt tents beneath. The men broke up into little cliques of associates and moved into the shade of the netting. The few loners sat by themselves looking nervous. Bolan and Ous were still drawing stares. Saboor disappeared into a U.S. military tent.

Bolan and Ous took a seat on a small carpet beneath the netting and leaned against the canyon wall. The Executioner murmured into his fake beard. "Touched by God?"

"Yes. I believe I can say with a straight face that God must favor you."

"I never miss?"

"I have never known you to do so," Ous countered.

"That's a mighty big check you've written on my account," Bolan stated.

"And I fear you will have to cash it."

Saboor walked out of the tent with two men. One was the most physically intimidating specimen Bolan had seen in a long while. If he'd had smoke for legs, he could have passed for a genie come out of the bottle—a genie that specialized in breaking legs and smashing skulls rather than granting wishes. Despite being a physical giant the man carried himself like an athlete. The second man was his polar opposite, small and wiry with Asiatic eyes and a short, wispy Fu Manchu-style mustache and beard.

Bolan and Ous rose as the three men walked straight toward them. The soldier gave his ear a short scratch to let his translators know an important conversation was imminent, and they got to work as the giant spoke.

He nodded politely to Ous. "Peace be upon you, mullah."

"And upon you be peace, brother."

The giant stroked his beard. "I must say, one finds fighting mullahs quite rare in these modern times."

"It was once said that in times of peace a mullah carries the Holy Koran in his hand and preaches in the madrassa. In times of war he must carry the Holy Koran in his heart and fill his hand with a sword."

"I must say, learned one, I find your attitude quite refreshing. The old ways are always the best ways."

"You are wise," Ous agreed.

The smaller man stared at Bolan. Despite his diminutive stature, the power of the little man's hooded, almost hawklike eyes was like a left to the jaw. Bolan gave him the arctic-blue stare back. Neither man flinched. The giant noted the ocular exchange with interest. "Mullah, may I inquire of your friend?"

"I chose the path of jihad, and I met him upon the road. He was a beggar, his body broken from his wounds, and his heart broken from the loss of his family at the hands of the Christian crusaders and their bombs. I took him as a companion upon the path."

"God loves the merciful." The giant nodded sagely. "However Saboor tells me he is touched by God?"

"The crusaders took much from him. He cannot speak, and barely can he hear, and yet. God in his mercy preserved his eyes and bent them to his purpose."

The giant met Bolan's burning cobalt gaze. "And what purpose is this?"

"To gaze upon the infidel invaders through the sights of a rifle."

"He is a marksman?"

"I have never seen him miss, either in battle or in practice," Ous replied.

The giant stared at Bolan with renewed interest. "Truly?"

"I swear by God that this be true."

The giant leaned in slightly and spoke loudly and slowly. "Peace be upon you."

Bolan raised his right hand and touched his forehead in reply. The giant touched his own forehead back. The little man spoke. "I would like a demonstration."

Both Ous and the giant frowned at this rather drastic breach of hospitality protocol. The giant spread his hands. "Let them take refreshment first."

The little man nodded and turned away. The giant gestured toward the carpet. "Will you wait a little while here?"

"Of course." Ous patted Bolan on the shoulder and they

both sat again. Bolan watched the giant walk back to the tent. "What do you make of him?"

"I think he is very dangerous, and he speaks Dari with an accent I do not recognize."

"And the little guy?"

"He is Hazara." Ous grunted and shook his head. "And perhaps more dangerous still."

The Hazara people were the third largest ethnic group in Afghanistan and generally believed to be descended from Genghis Khan and the Mongol horde he had left behind garrisoning Afghanistan. Many had Asiatic features, and they were mostly Shia rather than Sunni Muslims. The combination made the Hazara people the number-one minority target in Afghanistan for ruthless discrimination. When Kabul fell to the Taliban in the midnineties, the Hazara had thrown in with the Northern Alliance, but they were too far away from their new allies. The central highlands of Hazarajat had fallen to the Taliban and the Hazara people had been brutally suppressed in a widespread series of massacres. The Taliban had gone so far as to declare the Hazara non-Muslim. Only the intervention of Coalition forces had prevented the full-scale ethnic cleansing of the Hazara people from Afghanistan. Bolan's frown matched Ous's.

It was very odd to find a Hazara in a terrorist camp.

Bolan gave his earpiece the tap that told his translators he was speaking directly to them. "Any of you speak Hazara?"

The translator nearly went into a panic. "Hazaragi? Oh my God, I mean, it is a dialect of the Persian language, but with a ton of Turkic and Mongolian loan words and idioms. To find a fluent speaker in the D.C. area would be—"

"Find one."

"Right, on it."

A young man approached and set down a battered tray. He uncovered a pot containing roasted rice with several fried eggs on top and a pile of small, round flat breads to serve as the eating utensils. He nodded respectfully at Ous and poured the tea. He looked at Bolan in a wide-eyed mixture of awe and fear and backed away.

Word of Bolan's mojo was spreading.

Bolan and Ous shoveled down eggs and rice. The eggs had been sprinkled with powdered sumac, and the balance of salty and tart was delightfully subtle. Ous leaned back and patted his stomach contentedly. Bolan refilled their teacups. Ous spoke low as he relit his pipe. "I fear your time of trial approaches."

The giant, the little man and Saboor emerged from the tent once more. Ous cleaned his pipe with a penknife unconcernedly. A small mob began to gather.

The giant approached. "You are refreshed?"

"The Pashtun reputation for hospitality is most generously deserved, my friend, and I thank you."

This was met with pleased nods and murmurs of agreement from the assembled tribesmen. The giant got down to it.

"Syed has asked for a demonstration of your friend's skill, and I must admit that I myself, and our brother mujahideen gathered here are eager to see, as well."

This was met with more murmurs of assent. Ous turned to Bolan and pantomimed aiming a rifle. The soldier nodded once.

"Let it be done," Ous said to the giant.

Bolan took up his rifle and rose. He walked out from beneath the netting and looked for a target. He found one in the hills to the east, and pointed at a young man herding goats approximately seven hundred yards away.

"Who is that young man?" Ous asked.

"Yesuh, a boy from the nearest village. He often acts as lookout and servant for the camp," Saboor answered.

Bolan tapped his hat.

"Tell Yesuh to take off his hat and hold it out."

The murmurs of interest turned to shocked whispers. A number of men broke out binoculars. The giant took out his cell phone and punched a preset number. "Yesuh, take off your hat and hold it out."

Up on the hill Yesuh stared for a moment incredulously and took off his hat. Bolan shouldered his rifle. Yesuh suddenly understood what was about to happen. The young man shook like a leaf in Bolan's scope. The pakol cap presented an approximate head-size target. It wasn't an ideal shooting situation, but Bolan had surmounted worse.

He had one supreme advantage—the weapon he carried had been hand-tuned by one of the world's greatest gunsmiths. The rifle appeared to be sporting an antique Soviet era 4x PSO-1 telescopic sight. It was anything but. The sight was really a camouflaged 2x10 with a built-in laser rangefinder.

Bolan's hand brushed the hidden laser range finding button. The range was 647 meters. There was no wind to speak of as the sun climbed to its zenith.

Yesuh shook like a leaf.

Bolan gave his elevation turret a click. Given the range and the rifle, Bolan put the crosshairs of his scope on Yesuh's fist and his next lowest stadia squarely in the middle of the cap. The rifleman's mantra rolled through Bolan's mind. Don't pull the trigger, squeeze…

Everyone's eyes flicked with increasing agitation between Yesuh on the hill and Bolan. The soldier took a breath and let out half of it. His lips moved as he exhaled. Anyone who spoke Arabic would recognize the words he silently mouthed.

Inshallah.

If God wills it.

The crowd murmured the blessing in response.

Bolan slowly took up slack on the trigger.

The trigger broke beneath Bolan's finger and the gun bucked against his shoulder. The pakol flapped and curled around Yesuh's hand as the bullet passed through it. To the youth's credit he held on to the hat.

The assembled tribesmen roared. The cap fell limp once more and Bolan slowly put four more rounds through it. Yesuh went from shaking in fear to trembling with near ecstasy at his role in this amazing event. Bolan lowered his rifle and looked at Ous. He tapped his hat and pantomimed a throwing gesture.

Ous's eyes narrowed, but a smile crossed his face as he addressed the giant. "Tell young Yesuh to toss his hat into the air as high as he can."

Yesuh wasn't the only one going into ecstasy. The muj began chanting and shouting and waving their own caps with excitement. Bolan had a last trick to play. He pushed his rifle's selector to the full-auto option the Cowboy had added with a "clack!" The dusty firing range suddenly became very quiet.

Yesuh hurled his pakol skyward.

Bolan shouldered his rifle like he was shooting skeet. He kept both eyes open and he mated his optic with his bare eye as the cap reached the top of its flight. He dropped his aim two stadia and squeezed the trigger. The Dragunov rifle went rock 'n' roll at ten rounds a second. The five rounds left in the magazine left the barrel in half that.

The pakol jerked in midair as if snatched at by an invisible hand. The cap went horizontal and lazily spun back to Yesuh. The youth caught his cap and ran in circles waving it like a maniac.

Hats flew skyward behind the firing line and men crowded around to pound Bolan's shoulders. Ous and the giant seemed well pleased. The little Hazara, Syed, looked upon Bolan with eyes devoid of emotion.

CHAPTER TWELVE

The squad was coming together. It was a suicide squad, bent on holy martyrdom, but it was coming together. Ous, in mad mullah mode, had become their patriarch. Bolan was flat-out the squad's holy sword Excalibur. The scarred stranger couldn't speak, he could barely hear and he was illiterate, and yet God himself guided the arctic-eyed maniac's hand when he pulled a trigger. He was the perfect weapon. Bolan was treated with awe, reverence, and by all and sundry as if he suffered from severe mental retardation. The squad spoke openly around him as if he were a potted plant.

All the while Bolan listened, and so did the Pentagon.

Bolan took the squad's weapons and cleaned, oiled and tuned them like an idiot savant gunsmith. Ous led the squad in prayer with the power of a born leader of men and the knowledge of one who had memorized the Holy Koran.

The giant had disappeared, leaving Saboor in charge. Saboor was necessarily vague about the exact nature of the mission. Syed was the team's taskmaster, and he scared everybody. This day he was lecturing on satchel charges, and doing so with a riding crop in his hand. The younger of the two brothers, Sohail, already had a red welt across his cheek. His crime had been speaking without being spoken to during the lecture, but Bolan was fairly certain it had much more to do with Sohail and his brother Shahid's evident hero worship of Bolan and Ous. After the beating, a thermos of tea was passed around and the tent walls pulled down to darken the interior. Syed put on a crudely filmed VHS tape about the joys of Russian Federation PVV-5A Plastic Explosive and how to make IEDs from the unexploded Russian ordnance littering Afghanistan. It was a subject Bolan was all too familiar with, so he sat like a stone Buddha staring at nothing in particular and listening to the whispers around the darkened tent.

Syed wasn't popular.

The men were muttering. Sohail clutched his livid cheek, while Shahid patted him on the shoulder and assured him the little Hazara dog turd's death was assured. The instructional tape ended. The lights came up and the squad shuffled out, heading toward the cook tent for the late-afternoon meal that served as supper. The camp was cold and lightless after dark.

Shahid tumbled to the dust as Syed tripped him as he came out of the tent.

"You liken me to dog turd?"

The little Hazara's riding crop fell across the young man's neck and shoulders like rain. "My death is assured?" Shahid screamed and thrashed as the whip was applied with a trained torturer's precision.

"Let me explain something to you. It is you and your brother who are dogs, pariah animals, eaters of shit, unclean in the eyes of God and his Prophet." Wherever Shahid tried to cover up, the crop lashed into what was newly exposed. Shahid writhed in the dust.

A dozen heavily armed men watched and did nothing. It was a tribute to the terror in which the Hazara was held. "You are a dog and I am your master," Syed continued. "But you are correct in one thing, and that is my death is assured, and I shall die as a holy martyr. The manner in which you will die has yet to be determined, and that determination will be mine."

Syed went to work with the whip in earnest.

Ous looked at Bolan, who thought the beating was going on a little too long. It was time to up the ante a little.

Bolan silently stepped forward and caught Syed's wrist. It felt like the neck of a bowling pin. His hand vised down implacably and stopped Syed's stroke. Despite being right-handed, Syed's Khyber knife flashed from its sheath in less than a heartbeat and drove for Bolan's belly. The soldier's blade was already in his right hand and the blades sparked and grated against each other. Bolan was surprised to feel Syed's wrist relax in his hand and even though the Executioner was giving Syed the bone-crusher, the little man didn't drop his lash. For a nanosecond part of Bolan vainly wished he had led with his machine pistol instead.

They were in a Federally Administered Tribal Area standoff.

It was Syed's eyes that surprised Bolan most. They had flared in surprise. Not so much in surprise that Bolan had dared to interfere with the beating, but the Executioner's read on the man told him Syed was shocked that Bolan had been able to walk up to him and grab his wrist undetected, and remain so in a non-disemboweled state.

Syed turned a very cool look on Ous. "Tell your disciple to let go of my wrist or I will cut off his hands and feet."

Ous looked at Bolan and made a show of opening his right hand. Bolan released Syed's wrist. At the same time he gambled and sheathed his blade without being told. Syed sheathed his own and stalked away.

Saboor shook his head unhappily and muttered to Ous, "You should make your disciple understand that he has made a deadly enemy."

Bolan watched the Hazara go back in the command tent.

Syed had been his deadly enemy the second Bolan had stepped down out of the truck.

BEING THE LARGEST and strongest man in camp had its disadvantages. So was being perceived as a low-grade, albeit dangerous, moron. Since he was dumb as a mule, the camp assumed he was equally as strong as one and he had been volunteered into the job of squad heavy-equipment humper. Bolan trudged stoically under the weight of his own equipment as well as a Carl Gustav recoilless rifle and a 4-round pack of practice ammo. The weapon had clearly been acquired by less than noble means from Coalition forces. The squad had left at dawn for a forced march. It was long into the afternoon, and Bolan figured they had done twenty miles. The squad staggered back under the netting and flopped onto any available carpet.

Yesuh had the midday meal going. By the smell emanating from the huge copper stewpot, it was wheat gruel mixed with bits of the previous day's barbecued goat and raisins. Yesuh was busy with an old-fashioned potato peeler shaving carrot slices across the top. Bolan felt his salivary glands activating. He put his hunger aside and turned his eye on the newcomers.

Two foreign fighters had arrived in camp the day before. Kashgar was reportedly a Chinese Tajik who hated Westerners only slightly more than he hated the People's Republic of China. He was even more Asiatic in appearance than Syed, but whereas the Hazara was built like a whippet, Kashgar was nearly Bolan's height but as lanky as a scarecrow. The other new was a Turkmen named Guwanc who bore a startling resemblance to a young President George Bush.

Both men stank like hired killers rather than jihadist martyrs in the making. They stank like security. They hardly mixed with the men and spent most of their time huddled with Syed. One or both were always near Bolan, who had a bad feeling that someone wanted to cull him from the herd. He shrugged off the launch tube and the pack of projectiles. Ous gasped as he folded himself cross-legged on the carpet. He lit his pipe and began smoking as if it were mother's milk. The tobacco seemed to steady him.

"I do not like these two new men," he commented.

Bolan grunted in assent.

"I believe they either intend to kill you so that they can bend me to their will," Ous expounded, "or, kill me so that they can use and abuse you as al-Qaeda loves to use idiot children in their nefarious schemes."

It wasn't a bad assessment.

"Yeah," Bolan agreed. "Who are you betting on?"

"I am betting on you. I think Syed has no love for you, and the combination of your skill and your handicap makes you a dangerous wild card."

Ous was full of truisms.

"That's the way I see it, too."

"I told you this was a very dangerous plan," Ous said.

"And yet you volunteered."

"I volunteered to kill the enemies of my people approximately twenty-six years ago. I will tell you this is not the most suicidal mission I have volunteered for. However it is close." Ous took a pull on his pipe and sniffed the smells coming from the cook fire. "And so far the food has been fantastic."

Ous sat up happily. "Ah!"

Yesuh came over with a large communal bowl of goat and gruel with a small tub of yogurt on the side. He placed it on the carpet, giving Ous a bow of reverence. He touched the cap Bolan had given him and bowed in hero worship.

Bolan kept the frown off his face. It was the kind of behavior that could earn Yesuh a whipping from Syed, and Bolan himself couldn't predict what would happen if he intervened in a matter of camp discipline a second time. He gave Yesuh the idiot savant nod and began shoveling food into his face.

Bolan sighed as he realized he wasn't going to get to finish his lunch.

Syed approached and addressed Ous. "Your disciple is the most accurate man in camp."

Ous nodded over his yogurt bowl. "I believe this to be so."

"When the time comes, two targets will require destruction with the rocket launcher," Syed said.

"I have never seen him fire a rocket," Ous replied honestly.

"God loves him," Syed countered.

"I believe this to be so, also," Ous replied with equal honesty.

"There are some rusting Soviet tanks just over the western hills. I wish him to practice. If he can strike them from a respectable range, his place in heaven will be assured."

Ous spoke to Bolan like an infant and made hand gestures approximating a tank and then pointed at the recoilless weapon and the practice rounds. Bolan took a moment to appear to ponder this and nodded.

Syed nodded in turn. "Tell him to go with Kashgar and Guwanc. Tell him to go now. It is a long walk to the safe place of practice. He need not carry his rifle and pistol."

Bolan rose and laid aside his rifle and machine pistol. He shouldered the recoilless rocket launcher and its impotent pack of practice rounds. He took note of Kashgar's silenced assault rifle and knew it boded nothing good for him.

"Yesuh!" Syed called. "Show them the Russian grave-yard, and perhaps you will learn something!"

Bolan didn't care for Syed's smile at all.

Yesuh was oblivious as he pulled on his hat and happily ran to join the artillery practice party. The young man's happiness was short-lived as they walked away from camp and down into the maze of ravines. Despite Yesuh being sent along as a guide, Guwanc took the lead and seemed to know exactly where he was going. Kashgar drifted back to bring up the rear. That didn't stop the two men from throwing comments back and forth and laughing. Bolan was pretty sure they were speaking Tajik.

Bolan's translator spoke up. "Okay, it's a little bit garbled on my end but they're speaking Tajik, and mostly complaining about things like the food and the company they're keeping."

Guwanc looked back and caught Bolan staring at him. He gave Bolan a smile and Yesuh a leer. The youth drifted back to walk beside Bolan. The young man was very aware that something was wrong as they went deeper into the maze. Guwanc looked back and said something to Kashgar, who said something back. Both men laughed.

Yesuh shivered.

The soldier noted they had just switched languages.

Bolan's translator started to panic. "Oh my God! I think they're speaking Chinese!" The Executioner was aware of that, and pretty sure they were speaking Mandarin. He walked on in apparent oblivious bliss.

"We're patching in a Chinese language guy! Hold on!"

Guwanc and Kashgar kept up a steady chatter broken by frequent bursts of unpleasant laughter.

Yesuh cringed closer to Bolan.

A new voice came through the earpiece. It was a female Chinese language expert and she sounded as though she had just been woken up. She spoke with a mild Chinese accent. "Hello, can you hear me?"

Bolan scratched his ear in the affirmative.

"Okay, well, it's nothing good. They're frequently referring to you as 'the retard.' Um…stuff about your parent's sexual proclivities, it sounds like they are taking you to a… vehicle graveyard?" The translator grew quiet. "Okay, basically, they're going to shoot you through the knees and then carve on you to see if they can make you talk, and if you really can't, they're going to have fun with you anyway."

Bolan contemplated the PSM assassination pistol tucked into his sheepskin vest and the Khyber knife thrust through his sash. He was pretty sure he could get the pistol out and kill one. Probably the same story with the knife. Guwanc gave Yesuh another leer and said something choice. Kashgar returned the sentiment in kind.

"Now they are talking about someone named 'Yesuh.' They're saying…" The translator trailed off for a personally disturbed moment. "The way they're talking, it sounds like he's a young man, and they're speculating on whether he is a virgin or not and, the…kinds of fun, they're going to have with him in the vehicle graveyard, as well."

Bolan dropped to one knee, put the crosshairs of the Gustav's optical sight on Guwanc's upper back and fired.

What Guwanc and Kashgar didn't know was that when Bolan had stepped behind a boulder during the morning march to relieve himself, he had loaded one of the training rounds into the rocket launcher. The training round was designed to have the same ballistics as the standard High Explosive Anti-Tank round. Thunder echoed in the ravine as Guwanc took an inert seven-pound shell between the shoulder blades at slightly more than eight hundred feet per second.

In all his years of battle Bolan had never seen a God-swat quite like it.

Guwanc flew through the air and partially flew apart at the same time. Behind Bolan, Kashgar screamed as the rocket launcher vented him with the back blast. Yesuh gaped in shock. Kashgar kept screaming as he staggered back, clawing at his head. Bolan pulled his knife. He had to give Kashgar credit. The man was tough. He'd dropped his rifle, but despite having half his face boiled off, he drew his knife. Bolan set down the smoking rocket launcher. Kashgar screamed some Chinese invective at Bolan and lunged. The soldier took off Kashgar's hand at the wrist for his trouble. The blade hissed across Kashgar's throat before he could register the loss of his hand. Kashgar gave up his cares and fell dead to the dust.

Bolan glanced at Yesuh.

Yesuh opened his mouth and then closed it again. It was evident he wanted to run but he was too scared to move. Bolan wiped off his blade on Kashgar's sash and sheathed it. He picked up the man's rifle, took his bandolier of magazines and gave them to Yesuh. The youth stared at the gift in awe. Bolan went through Kashgar's and Guwanc's clothes but found nothing useful. He laid the rocket launcher back across his shoulder and pointed down the path with a shrug. Yesuh gaped in shock and nodded back.

"Yes, Mighty One!"

Yesuh lead Bolan to the practice range.

CHAPTER THIRTEEN

It was a fascinating story. Syed stopped short of turning to stone while he listened to it. The camp stood around in complete silence while Saboor asked Yesuh to tell the tale a third time. It was a simple story and Yesuh didn't have much problem sticking to it, plus it had the benefit of being the God's truth as far as Yesuh saw it. Kashgar and Guwanc had repeatedly laughed at the Mighty One. The Mighty One, hard of hearing that he was, had had enough and slain them. Then Yesuh, at the Mighty One's request, had led him to the valley of slain Russian tanks. Whereupon the Mighty One had put three practice rounds into the rusting hulk of a Soviet invasion-era armored personnel carrier at a range of 700 meters. Then they had taken a light lunch Yesuh had packed and returned. Bolan kept the smile off his face as Yesuh proclaimed that the Mighty One had given him Kashgar's rifle, and, that since the Mighty One had slain Kashgar, the rifle was the Mighty One's to do with as he saw fit, and Yesuh intended to keep it.

Bolan stood impassively during the interrogation.

Sohail and Shahid ran back into camp breathlessly. According to Shahid, Kashgar had been burned and slaughtered. The state of Guwanc's corpse beggared description. Once again Pashtunwali was on Bolan's side. Perhaps the greatest pillar of "The Way of the Pahstuns" was *Badal*. Its literal translation was "Justice," but all too often it was equated with revenge. Even a mere taunt generally required the shedding of blood. Central Asia was a rough place, and the best that the mentally or physically handicapped could hope for was benign neglect. Usually their lot was horrific abuse. However, Bolan wasn't a drooling idiot. He was the Mighty One, and if the Mighty One was indeed an idiot, then he was an idiot savant when it came to violence.

Kashgar and Gawanc had been foolish enough to taunt the Mighty One. If the Mighty One had slain them in almost biblical fashion, well?

Badal.

All was well with the world.

They were foreign fighters, and no one liked them anyway.

Saboor stared at Bolan as if he had just dropped in from the planet Mars. Syed eyed Bolan with reptilian cold. Yesuh looked up to Bolan like God on High. Everyone else stared in semireligious awe. The Mighty One's mojo was going through the roof.

Ous shrugged. "Forgive me, brothers, but is this matter finished?"

Saboor opened his mouth and closed it. He turned to Syed, who spun on his heel and walked away. Bolan measured his nemesis. Syed was backing down just a little too much for the soldier's taste. The translator spoke in his ear. "I have a priority signal coming through from Control."

Bolan scratched his ear to signal in the affirmative. Agent Keller spoke in his ear. "Okay, Cooper. I've got bad news. Zurisaday escaped custody this morning. Without a trace. Not even a blip on the surveillance camera. One second she's sitting cross-legged in a corner of her cell staring like the psycho she is, and the next she's just gone. Don't ask me how. The Pentagon is sending a counterintelligence and containment agent, whatever the hell that is, but currently no one has a clue."

Bolan didn't know exactly how Zurisaday had escaped from a U.S. military base, but he did have a clue. The assassin-seductress had escaped the same way a dagger had been placed on Ous's and Farkas's pillows while they slept. "Watch your ass," Keller concluded.

It wasn't bad advice.

BOLAN RESTRAINED HIMSELF from scratching, and contemplated the wind. It whipped and plucked at the camouflage netting and the tents. Everyone knew a sandstorm was coming. He kept his fingers away from his beard through sheer force of will. The itch was turning into a little ripple of hell across his features. His genuine beard was coming in. His own hair pushed through the adhesive and fought for space with the fake beard like the slow-motion violence of trees fighting for sunlight in the forest. The battle for Bolan's face itched like a thousand mosquito bites longing to be scratched. He knew once he started scratching, his camouflage would be a highly suspicious and bloody patchwork within hours. Bolan drank tea and endured.

The good news was that he now had four live, antitank rounds for the recoilless rocket launcher at his disposal. Bolan watched longingly as Ous gave his own hennaed beard a good, long scratching. Ous leaned back and lit his pipe.

"So, brother. Agent Keller reports Zurisaday has escaped?"

Bolan smiled. Ous had taken to calling him "brother." It wasn't a bad sobriquet for the situation. They were brothers in arms, and brothers on a suicide mission to infiltrate a suicide mission. "Seems so."

"I find this profoundly disturbing."

Bolan had to admit it wasn't good news.

"Do you believe she will come here?" Ous asked.

It was an interesting thought. The hearing aid Bolan wore allowed both Keller's team and the Farm to track his whereabouts. Gunships and marines were waiting for him hot on the pad 24/7. Bolan would give a lot to listen in on a conversation between the giant and Zurisaday. On the other hand the giant wasn't here and if and when Zurisaday showed up, Bolan didn't think his role camouflage would fool the female assassin for long.

"Bismillah!" Ous exclaimed. "Who do you think that woman is?"

A woman in full burka walked out of the shadows of the ravine accompanied by two strange men who walked in as though they owned the place. The sight of a woman in a Taliban suicide-mission camp had all eyes front and forward. The woman ignored the looks and stares. Her bodyguards glared bloody murder at anyone foolish enough to let them see their roving eyes. Bolan pulled his pakol low across his brow and nestled deeper into the shadows of the boulders that demarcated his and Ous's personal space. Ous was right. A burka hid a woman from head to toe, but the discerning eye could see all. Bolan had seen that carriage, that ankle, and that body swaying beneath the folds of a burka before.

A seductress and assassin known by the name Zurisaday was in camp.

She had arrived in the FATA from her escape from the holding cell at Sangin Base in less than forty-eight hours. That implied all sorts of things. One of which almost had to be an airdrop, and that implied a whole other set of hostile well-organized and structured variables. The situation was getting worse by the second. Ous frowned around the stem of his pipe. "God help us, but do you think that young woman could be—"

"Yeah, it's her." Bolan tapped his earpiece for attention. "Message for Control, Zurisaday is in camp. I—"

Keller's voice came back immediately. "No way!"

"Way."

"I'm arranging immediate extraction! Gunships are inbound! You're—"

"You're going to get me, Ous and Yesuh killed."

"Striker, she'll make you."

"That's possible."

Keller's angry silence ensued. "You're forcing me into a very bad place."

"You're going to force me to kill everyone in this camp. Some are excellent intelligence resources. Belay that order."

"Holding, Striker, but damn it."

"Copy that," Bolan agreed. "We're just going wait and see what dawn brings."

"Yeah, well, come dawn me and the gunships are still ETA forty-five minutes to your position. If and when the shit comes down, you'll be temporarily on your own, Striker."

It wasn't exactly the first time Bolan had been in this position, but he had to admit it was a slightly more heinous version than usual. "Copy that."

"You're awfully damn calm."

Bolan sighed. "I'm crying on the inside."

"Oh, F you."

"You know? I like the way you don't swear."

"Jack hole."

Bolan smiled. "That's the spirit, soldier."

"I'm NCIS. I'm a sailor, bum-wipe."

"I stand corrected."

"Do you always talk across secure channels like this?" Keller asked.

"What's the point of a secure channel if you can't?"

"Speaking of secure channels, how are your batteries?"

"I'm down to the last pair, and since they took my phone I can't recharge," Bolan replied.

"I don't know how I can get you more but I'll see what I can do. Sneaking someone into camp is going to be next to impossible. We'll have to do some kind of airdrop."

Bolan listened as the wind whistled and moaned through the canyons. An airdrop was going to be problematic. The storm was almost upon him, in more ways than one.

BOLAN STOOD SENTRY. He stared out into the howling sandstorm through the slit in the shemagh tied around his head, and he hunched deeper into his shawl. He stood at the mouth of a canyon but the wind roared right up it like a funnel. The sun was setting and the world was slowly turning orange. Come night it would be a pitch-black maelstrom. Ostensibly he was supposed to be watching the road. It seemed like a somewhat frivolous activity with sixty-mile-per-hour winds and visibility down to ten feet. It struck Bolan as somewhat strange that Syed would post a sentry who was mute and could barely hear a hundred yards from camp during the worst sandstorm in a decade. The camp wasn't really expecting any visitors.

Bolan was.

He adjusted his shemagh slightly and turned on his translator-transmitter with the same movement. A new voice came through the earpiece. "Good morning, Striker. Or should I say good evening. Ready on our end."

Bolan coughed three short coughs to copy that. He was aware that he had company, but he didn't break role and acknowledge it. The soldier stood sentry and waited. It was Syed's move.

He didn't have long to wait.

The Hazara walked into Bolan's field of vision but without any pretense of stealth. Bolan gave him a slight, startled motion and then resumed staring into the sandstorm. The orange tint faded from the dust and sand filling the air. The sun fell behind the mountains and the world turned pink. Syed stood about ten feet away. He spoke loud enough to be heard above the noise of the wind. He spoke in Arabic.

"I do not believe you are deaf."

Bolan stared impassively into the storm as the rapidly falling sun took the dust through its spectrum.

"Nor do I believe that you are mute. My first guess is that you are Pakistani special forces, though we have no record of you. You are going to tell me who you are and whom you work for. Should you refuse, I think we both know that I can make you."

For a brief ephemeral moment the dying rays of the sun turned the little world of the canyon a deep, bloody red. Bolan flexed his limited Japanese. "Excuse me, but are you Iga, or Koga clan ninja?"

Bolan's translator balked. "What the hell—?"

Syed's sword-size Khyber knife hissed from its sheath. Bolan shouldered the Dragunov and dropped the hammer on the false Hazara. The hammer fell with an impotent click on an empty chamber.

Syed smiled and spoke in English. "Tell me, have you known many of us?"

"I've killed members of various clans."

Syed nodded slowly. The reptilian look came into his eyes. "I believe you."

"You tampered with my rifle. I'd love to know how you managed that."

Syed smiled. "I am ninja."

"I don't suppose we could talk about this?"

"Oh, we are going to spend a very long time talking about this. I suspect you will answer my every question. May I recommend you surrender? Depending how much your government values you, there is chance that you might survive the ordeal as a bargaining chip."

"I'm afraid I'm expendable."

"And since my clan has taken money—" Syed stepped forward with his sword-size knife held in low guard in front of him "—so am I." He smiled as Bolan's hand went to his own blade. The soldier knew from firsthand experience that what most people believed about ninjas was Hollywood crap. They weren't mystical, triple backflipping kung-fu warriors. From time immemorial to the modern day, ninjas were primarily spies, saboteurs and assassins, usually in that order. They had been the first in medieval Japan to embrace gunpowder. Modern ninjas embraced the most cutting-edge technologies to accomplish their missions. Oh, they still kept the swords and black pajamas on hand and they practiced assiduously with them, mostly to terrorize people or because they also embraced low-tech answers, as well; however, the fact remained that if a ninja found himself in a stand-up fight he had screwed up or gotten caught with his pants down.

Then again, Bolan had never heard of anybody beating a ninja in a knife fight, and Syed's pants seemed firmly in place. The dead slack of the Dragunov's trigger proved who had been caught flat-footed.

Syed still smiled as he came forward.

Bolan knew he wasn't going to beat Syed blade to blade. So did Syed. The Executioner drew his Khyber knife and flung it. The huge cleaver revolved through the air for Syed's face. The blades clanged as the ninja slapped Bolan's weapon out of the air contemptuously.

"Come now, you must—" The throw gave Bolan a

moment to jump back a good three steps. He took the heartbeat's worth of breathing room to draw his bayonet and click it onto the muzzle of the Dragunov. Bolan lowered the blade-mounted rifle between them like a spear.

Syed scowled.

Bolan's translator shouted across the link. "Striker! Striker!"

He ignored his linguist and lunged. Syed read Bolan's thrust correctly as a feint. Syed brought up his blade. Bolan's torqued the long rifle around for a jaw-breaker buttstroke. His opponent saw that, as well, and leaned away from it with ease. But the buttstroke was a feint, as well. In a knife fight the primary target was the other man's weapon. At over nine pounds and more than four feet in length the Dragunov was large. To partially offset that, Mr. Dragunov had designed the weapon with a skeleton stock. Bolan's buttstroke short-arced down over Syed's blade. The cutout slid over Syed's knife, his hand and wrist and jammed halfway down his forearm.

For the second time in their brief association, Syed's eyes flew wide in shock.

Bolan twisted the rifle with every ounce of strength he had.

Syed's wrist snapped and the blade fell from his hand.

The man's round kick thudded into Bolan's thigh. He had been trying to shatter a knee, but the angle and the rifle between threw him off. Bolan turned, dropped to one knee and heaved his adversary over his shoulder by sheer muscular force. Syed went flying. The ninja's locked and broken arm prevented him from rolling out of the throw or slapping out to break his fall. He bounced with spectacular force.

Syed's broken bones splintered as Bolan brutally torqued the rifle around again to snap the barrel across

the ninja's throat. That second moment of shock gave Bolan
the heartbeat he needed to control the ninja's free hand.
The soldier put a knee and his 220 pounds on the Russian
rifle, crushing Syed's trachea. Bolan saw white as Syed's
knee bounced into his kidney. He took the pain of a second
and third blow. Syed contorted like a yoga master and tried
to hook a leg around Bolan's neck to throw him off. The
soldier shrugged off the leg and kept pressing down. Cartilage in Syed's throat crackled but stopped just short of
popping.

The light in the canyon turned purple. So did Syed.

The ninja's struggles went spasmodic. His writhings
and attacks slowed as Bolan relentlessly choked him out
with the unyielding steel of the Dragunov's barrel. Syed
was turning a nice cyanotic blue. Bolan watched the light
of life behind the man's eyes die.

Bolan let up at the last second.

Syed gave a strangled gasp. Bolan rammed his thumbs
into the enfeebled ninja's carotids. Syed's brain was already
starving for oxygen but Bolan gave him a full ten seconds
of compression to make sure the ninja was really unconscious.

Ninjas were tricky. Bolan had learned that long ago, the
hard way.

Bolan disengaged the rifle from the ninja's shattered
arm and rose. He had to use the weapon as a crutch to
lever himself up. He would be black and blue where the
ninja had hit him. His kidneys ached horribly. Bolan gave it
fifty-fifty whether he would be peeing blood in the morning. Then again, you didn't capture a ninja alive every day.
As a matter of fact it happened just about never.

Bolan considered his catch.

Tying up Syed was out. Ninjas had a habit of not staying tied up.

The soldier raised the butt of the Dragunov and knee-capped the man. Syed groaned but remained unconscious.

Night was falling fast.

"This is Striker, I'm all right. Put Control on the line."

"Already here," Keller replied. "Was waiting on you."

"You remember what I said about the bad guys buying their assassins off the rack?"

"Yeah."

Keller couldn't keep the disbelief out of her voice when he told her. "A ninja?"

"Yeah, and he's alive. You need to get someone here to pick him up, stat."

"In this storm?"

"The storm is supposed to last until dawn, and it's the only cover you're going to get."

"Right. I'm on it."

"And bring me some batteries."

"Anything else?"

Bolan swiftly checked his rifle. "A new trigger group for a Dragunov SVD."

"Oh-hh...kay."

Bolan shook his head as he reviewed what if any opportunity he'd given the ninja to tamper with his weapon. Probably when they had sent him off to rocket practice. He stared down at the wheezing, temporarily crippled ninja and wondered how the Mighty One was going to get out of this one.

CHAPTER FOURTEEN

Bolan stepped into camp as the sun rose and the storm abated. He walked in with fresh batteries and a new trigger group for his rifle. He entered camp without Syed. The entire camp was armed, awake, and awaiting who might step out of the storm. Bolan had known when he had been volunteered for guard duty something was up, and he and Ous had worked out their script if Bolan came back alive and alone. He strode straight up to Ous and narrowed his eyes to tell his partner Syed wasn't coming back. Bolan made a number of angry gestures pointing back the way he had come, pointing toward the tank graveyard and then pointing at Saboor.

Ous watched the performance and turned to Saboor with a sigh. "I believe my disciple is growing weary of your friends insulting him, much less attempting to kill him. I believe he is not convinced that you are our friend."

Bolan pointed west.

"I believe my friend thinks it would be best if he and I left this camp."

Saboor gave Bolan a very unhappy look. "I will not stop you should you wish to leave, but I will tell you, our mission is nigh. Indeed, we leave tomorrow at dawn. His skills will be utterly necessary to our success. I beg you to stay."

"If I stay, he will, but out of loyalty to me."

"I understand this. Please try to tell him that Guwanc

and Kashgar were little more than mercenaries who fought for money, and no one can read the mind of a Hazara. Those who remain in this camp are pure, and their place in heaven assured. We need the Mighty One, and we need you, learned one."

Agent Keller spoke in Bolan's ear. "If you feel good about it, I'd really like you to continue the mission. Your ninja has clammed up, like, well, like you'd expect a ninja to clam up. It's going to take time to turn him into any kind of an intelligence asset, and right now we still have no clue what Saboor, Zurisaday and your giant have in mind."

Bolan stared at Ous, who went into a very long and involved pantomime while speaking to him very loudly in Dari Persian. When Ous was finished, Bolan grunted and stalked away.

Ous turned to Saboor. "We will stay."

Saboor clapped his hands. "Excellent, by the way, can either of you drive a truck?"

BOLAN DROVE and Ous rode shotgun. The battered ZIS 151 flatbed lurched and bounced over the mountain track like a ship in heavy seas. The ZIS had once mounted thirty-six tubes for launching Soviet-era 82 mm artillery rockets. The rocket launchers and the mount had been removed, and the ZIS had been crudely converted into a fence truck for livestock. The flatbed bucked as it mounted protruding rocks and dropped as it hit dips and potholes. The road looked like it had taken a recent salvo of Soviet artillery rockets. Bolan knew from experience this was the state of most roads in Afghanistan. There was no shoulder, no guardrail, and the mountain road fell away scant inches from the vehicle's wheels. "Infrastructure" was a strange and wonderful word that had yet to make much headway in Afghanistan.

Saboor led the convoy in an equally old Volga station wagon that someone had turned into a convertible with a hacksaw. He had Zurisaday and Yesuh with him posing as his wife and son, and two goats in the back for good measure. They were about seventy-five yards ahead. If they were stopped for any reason, they were unrelated travelers and Ous would complain that the car ahead was slowing them. The rest of the suicide squad was staying half a mile back and were evenly spread out between old Toyota Tacomas in fairly decent shape. Zurisaday's two bodyguards were each in one of the trucks.

"What do you believe our objective to be?" Ous asked.

"Given that we've got a twelve-man squad, a flatbed, and a Carl Gustav recoilless rocket launcher, I would say there's a truck bomb in someone's future. The Goose is to pave the way for the bomb," Bolan reasoned. "What's bothering me is that we're across the Pakistan border in the FATA region. It's hard to imagine what our target could be unless we cross west soon. There are no Coalition forces anywhere nearby or any major cities."

"Perhaps we are going to, as Agent Keller would say, 'settle the hash' of some recalcitrant warlord?"

"Hard to imagine getting a bunch of wannabe martyrs motivated with that for an objective."

"Perhaps that is why we have not been told of our objective?"

"Would you want a palace revolt with this crew?"

"No, and indeed, twice you have brought our happy band of martyrs close to just such a thing."

Bolan nodded. "It risked the mission, but both times the alternative was my being tortured until I talked."

"Yes, the mission continues, and I will admit I prefer both you and Yesuh intact."

"Something else is going on. I just haven't figured it out yet."

Saboor's brake lights flashed ahead. The Soviet-era handheld radio unit sitting on the dash squawked. "Stop the truck."

Bolan braked with fifty yards between them.

The radio crackled. "Turn off the engine."

Bolan kept one foot on the brake, one on the gas and the engine running. Saboor stood in the driver's seat. Yesuh looked up from between the goats in the back to find himself staring down the barrel of Saboor's 9 mm pistol. Zurisaday stood in the passenger seat, burka and all, and snapped open the telescoping tube of an RPG-18 anti-tank rocket into the firing position.

Bolan's earpiece crackled. Keller's voice came across the line. "What's happening?"

"We're made."

"Oh my God. Cooper, you're over thirty kilometers on the wrong side of the Pakistan border. I don't know if I can authorize gunships or extraction. It will take time to coordinate with our Pakistani—"

"Copy that, I'll get back to you."

Saboor spoke into his handheld radio. This time he spoke in English. "Turn off the engine and throw out your weapons, or I will shoot the boy."

"Should he do that," Ous said, "he risks a blood feud with Yesuh's village."

"That won't be enough to stop him," Bolan said.

"Because he and the ninja were perfectly willing to let him be raped and tortured?"

"No, that was something guilt and shame would prevent young Yesuh from ever admitting."

Ous grimaced. "So, Saboor will shoot the boy no matter what we do?"

"Yesuh has only one chance."

"And what is that?" Ous queried.

Zurisaday gave Bolan a happy wave over her launch tube.

Bolan came to his decision. "We make him irrelevant."

Ous frowned. "And how does he—"

The soldier stomped on the gas. The ZIS lurched forward and Bolan cranked the wheel.

Zurisaday pumped her trigger and the RPG-18 belched smoke and fire.

Bolan drove off the cliff. It wasn't truly a cliff, but it was an incline that could be charitably described as precipitous. There was no way to drive down the mountain, and there was no road waiting at the bottom. The best Bolan could hope for would be a controlled crash. He had no time for Zurisaday's rocket. The fact the he and Ous were not ascending heavenward on a pillar of fire told him she had missed. A tightly contained corner in the back of his mind wondered about whether she had a reload. Bolan chose a line down the mountainside that avoided the worst of the outcropping and scrubby, twisted pines. The worst was all he could avoid.

A prayer tore out of Ous's mouth as the truck took a horrific bounce.

The wheel went greasy slick beneath Bolan's hand as the tires beneath him bit into nothing but air. The truck bounced again and went fully airborne as it flew off a ridge of protruding rock. The brown river below flew up at them with sickening speed. Bolan shoved himself across the bench seat to avoid getting impaled by the steering column. "Hold on!"

The flatbed hit the stream bumper-first. Ous lost his bracing and took a good bounce on the dashboard. Bolan partially lost his balance with the impact and Ous got the hammer and anvil treatment as he cushioned the soldier's bounce. The truck stood teetering on its nose for several groaning seconds and slowly flipped. The homemade iron fencing in the bed bent and lessened the impact. The truck had no seat belts. Bolan and Ous lay wadded upside down on the roof of the cab in about a foot of water.

"Ous!"

The Afghan gasped something unintelligible.

Bolan tried to wriggle himself upright. "We've gotta—"

Zurisaday's second rocket whooshed into the exposed back axle of the flatbed. The chassis shuddered and heat washed past the windows.

The soldier grabbed at the strap of his rifle, but it was trapped behind the seat. He pulled his Stechkin and began hauling on Ous. The man groaned. An object clattered off the bumper. The soldier watched as the Russian frag grenade landed on the large flat rock the truck had barely missed. Bolan flipped his machine pistol to full-auto, shoved his hand out the window and fired. His burst sent the oval grenade into a violent spin. Luckily, high explosive, Russian or otherwise, it wasn't detonated by impact. The soldier's second burst skipped the grenade off the rock and into the water. A geyser fountained into the air with the detonation. A second later several small fish and a turtle floated by belly-up.

"Brother!" Bolan yelled. "We have to go!"

Ous's groans turned to gasps of effort as he followed Bolan's pull. Another grenade landed behind the front tires and clattered into the engine compartment. Smoke and sparks blasted from the vents as it detonated. Bolan kicked open the driver's door and rose with his Stechkin leveled. Two bullets from Saboor's pistol whined into the bowels of the truck. The Executioner burned the rest of his magazine on full-auto toward the top of the cliff. Saboor ducked back.

Bolan grabbed Ous and dragged him out of the truck. The Afghani sagged against the driver's side wheel. Throwing him into a firemen's carry, the Executioner broke into a labored run. Water splashed around him knee-deep.

He reached shore, staggering forward, determined to put an outcropping between himself and Saboor's unrelenting fire.

Bolan unloaded Ous to the ground. "You all right?"

"Just...the wind...knocked from me," Ous spluttered. "I will be fine."

The soldier wasn't so sure. "Control, do you still have a fix on our position?"

The earpiece responded with an empty hiss. Bolan pulled the equipment from his ear. The dunking hadn't done it any good. There was still a tiny hope that even though he couldn't communicate Keller could still track him.

Ous stood and steadied himself against the rock wall. "The fire from the top of the gorge has stopped."

Bolan put his gear in his pocket. He would fiddle with it later. Right now they needed to do some distance. "They'll be organizing a hunting party."

"Do you think Saboor could convince our comrades to hunt me?" Ous smiled wanly. "Much less the Mighty One?"

"No." Bolan glanced up at the sun. It was around ten o'clock in morning. He thought about Zurisaday's two mysterious bodyguards. "They'll be bringing in ringers."

Sangin

GHOLAM DAEI WASN'T pleased. "They drove off the cliff?"

Daei could almost hear Saboor cringing. "Yes, the truck

flipped at the bottom of the gorge. Then Zurisaday put a rocket into it."

"And yet they live?"

"Yes, we dropped grenades on them and myself and the Mighty One exchanged fire."

"The Mighty One..." Daei shook his massive, shaggy head. The huge muscles of his chest, arms and shoulders flexed of their own volition. Daei yearned to show this unfortunate freak that had fallen into their midst what might truly was. "Describe him to me again."

Saboor ran the litany of the stranger, tall, dark, forbidding. Stronger than he looked, and he looked formidably strong in the first place. Horrible scarring on the side of his face and neck. Wild hair and beard like a mystic madman out of the desert. God himself guided the man's hand when he pulled the trigger. An ice-blue gaze that would put a chill in the heart in even the most dedicated martyr. What he had done to Kashgar and Guwanc had been horrific. Syed's body had never been found.

Daei frowned in thought. "Tell me about his eyes again."

"He looks at you and you cannot meet his gaze! Never have I seen such eyes! He—"

"Put Zurisaday on the line."

The woman's dulcet, alto voice spoke in Arabic. "Yes?"

"The Mighty One, did you see him?"

"Only from a distance, and we were all dressed against the storm. I regret to say at the time I had many things on my mind, and the story of a retarded rifleman in the ranks was one of the least of them."

"That is understandable. Tell me. Do you have a paper and pencil handy?"

"I always keep a pad nearby."

Daei smiled. Zurisaday was a trained assassin, and to ensure her ends she had a very diversified set of skills.

"Have Saboor describe the Mighty One to you. In detail, and sketch him."

"That will take some minutes."

"I have the time." Zurisaday had initially been trained as an espionage agent. Her skill at sketching people she had met from memory was astounding. Saboor rattled off his litany of the Mighty One's attributes a third time. Ten minutes later Zurisaday spoke.

"A formidable man. I am sending you a picture."

Daei's phone toned and he opened the picture message. A very dangerous smile passed over his face. "Now I want you to imagine his cobalt-blue eyes, removed the hair, the mustache, the beard and the scar tissue. Imagine him."

"He is the man who captured me." Zurisaday's voice was cold with certainty. "It is the man who is assisting Agent Keller's investigation."

"I am also rather convinced that the man with him is Omar Ous."

"I concur. It is perhaps the most ambitious undercover operation I have ever heard of. An insane risk. Such a thing has never been done."

"Neither has capturing a ninja. Yet I believe that our friend is alive and in unfriendly hands."

It was the first time Daei ever heard curiosity in Zurisaday's voice. "Can a ninja be broken?"

Daei looked at his scarred fist. "I have yet to meet a man who cannot, and speaking of the broken, our friends have finally overreached themselves."

A purr of satisfaction came into Zurisaday's voice. "Yes, they are friendless and alone, on foot, on the wrong side of the border."

"I am sending you a team."

CHAPTER FIFTEEN

For a rangy guy Ous felt like a heavyweight. Of course one hundred degree heat and hours spent staggering through endless canyons in Afghanistan's summer sun could put weight on a man, particularly if you were the one who had to carry him. Ous rode Bolan piggyback and drifted in and out of wheezing consciousness. The old warrior wasn't spitting up blood yet, but the soldier was pretty sure the veteran had a pulmonary contusion. One or both of his lungs had been bruised when the truck had hit the creek nose-first, and he had met the dashboard.

They had walked away from the river and not found a water source since. It was three o'clock in the afternoon. The temperature might have edged a degree or two away from one hundred degrees Fahrenheit. There was still plenty of time to die of heat prostration. Failing that, the temperature in the mountains would drop like a rock come sundown.

Bolan looked up as rotors thundered over the canyons. He stepped under a rock overhang and set Ous down. He watched from hiding as a pair of Pakistani army helicopters roared overhead. Ous's voice was a rasp. "Perhaps we should attempt to contact them."

"Why?"

"Well, the last I heard Pakistan and the United States were allies. Particularly their secular army generals."

"That's true, but there's one problem."

"What is that?"

The Pakistani army flies Pumas, Alouette IIIs and Lamas. Those are Dauphins."

Ous watched the helicopters pass out of visual over the ridgeline. "You are very well informed."

"I've worked hard to become so."

"You think they fly under false colors?"

"I do."

"And they hunt us?"

"We're in the FATA, and the Federally Administered Tribal Areas don't like the federal administration. Military helicopters tend to be bullet magnets in this corner of Pakistani airspace."

"And our friends feel comfortable flying low and slow in a search pattern."

"Someone spread the word," Bolan stated.

"So what do we do?"

"Best I can figure, we have a long hike ahead of us."

Ous sighed. He didn't seem pleased by the prospect. "Ah."

"The good news is that they aren't gunships."

"What is the bad news?" Ous asked.

"Dauphins can hold up to eleven passengers."

"Two squads," Ous calculated. "Half a platoon."

"And they could be ninjas."

"Well, if there are twenty-two ninjas, at least they are twenty-two ninjas without gunships."

Bolan smiled tiredly. "You're a good man, Ous."

"I feel like a very old man."

"I'd call you distinguished."

Ous laughed and it broke into coughing. He looked at his hand and there were a few tiny specks of blood in his sputum. He matched Bolan's weary smile. "Brother, let us walk a little farther."

The Afghan stood, then sat back down again.

Bolan drew his machine pistol as he heard the crunch of boots in the gravel of the canyon floor. "Someone's coming."

Ous pulled his pistol.

Seven men rounded a bend in the canyon. Their shoulders were hunched as men did when there were rotorcraft in the air, and their eyes scanned the skies above as they moved. They wore local garb, and each man carried a Kalashnikov of some derivation. Their beards put Bolan's CIA special to shame. They weren't ninjas. These were guys who put the "Tribal" in the phrase Federally Administered Tribal Area. Bolan and Ous weren't exactly slouches when it came to not being seen, and it took the troop of Pashtuns a moment before they became aware of the two men crouching beneath the overhang.

The Pashtuns spoke as one man. *"Bismillah!"*

They took in Bolan's horrific visage and the holy man lying in the shadow wheezing. The soldier slowly lowered his pistol and shoved it back in his sash. These men were clearly not happy about the choppers in the sky, and Bolan figured his chances of hiking out of the FATA to the Afghan border with Ous on his back were pretty much zero. He played his last card. He looked up into the sky meaningfully and then at the gray beard who appeared to be the leader. Bolan spoke one of the few words of Pashto he knew.

"Nanawatai."

The Pashtuns gaped in shock.

Bolan had just asked the tribesmen for sanctuary.

The headman gave Bolan a squint that would have done Dirty Harry proud. His men all clutched their AKs and looked to the headman warily. The headman took a long breath and pulled himself up with great dignity. The iron code of Pashtunwali had the old man by the short hairs, and they both knew it. He deliberately walked over and knelt to give Ous a consoling pat on the shoulder. The two men passed a few words. The headman stood and gave Bolan a bow. The soldier didn't need to know the language. The headman had bid them welcome.

He might well have signed his village's death warrant, as well, but Bolan figured the headman suspected that already. The old man nodded at two of his men and they solicitously put Ous into a seated two-man carry. Their efficiency told Bolan the villagers were no strangers to carrying casualties. The big American fell into step with Ous's bearers as the troop of warriors reversed course and went back the way they came. Ous spent a little time speaking with the men carrying him. The old guerrilla seemed to be ingratiating himself. The stony reserve of the tribesmen carrying him went from smiles to a few rueful laughs.

Bolan's forbidding form remained a source of furtive, wary looks.

They passed through passages among the rocks and over cliff paths that would have given a mountain goat pause. They came upon the village abruptly. About a third of the village was half carved, half squatted under a vast pocket in the rock face like a Hopi Pueblo. The rest spilled down the hillside and nestled next to a river. The other side of the canyon was terraced farmland. The village was like a little, hidden Shangri-la. Bolan gazed across the vertical acres of poppy flowers twining around river driftwood trellises.

This Shangri-la was dealing in opium rather than mystical enlightenment.

It wasn't so hidden, either. Shell craters showed this piece of real estate had been fought over, and recently. At the sight of visitors, villagers began moving in all directions. Bolan noted that the women visible in the village wore headscarves but not the full burka. They peered openly at Ous sympathetically and at Bolan in concerned speculation. The women's dress and behavior told Bolan the Taliban didn't have control of the village.

A maze of ladders and steep steps took Bolan and Ous up into the cave section of the village. The headman put them in a carpeted cube of a room and steaming bowls of heavily dilled noodle soup arrived in short order along with the ubiquitous pot of tea. The headman and his right-hand man swiftly disappeared.

Ous fired up his pipe, hacked from his bruised lungs and put the pipe away.

Bolan checked the loads in his pistol. "Bad idea, brother."

"Habit is stronger than reason," Ous agreed. "The headman's name is Bilal. He has sent someone to the next village. They have some sort of a doctor there."

"Kind of them. What will they do next?"

"You have invoked *nanawatai*. As you may have surmised, Bilal was initially displeased but he has granted it and his men have gone along with it."

"How long can we count on their hospitality?" Bolan asked.

"That is a good question. We are strangers. Though *nanawatai* has been granted, the situation must be investigated. I suspect the village elders are having a very interesting meeting about us. I have told them I am very weary and might we rest for a little while."

"You had your litter-bearers smiling," Bolan observed.

"Oh, well. I have fought beside Pashtuns before. I made all the correct gestures and pleasing observations that a visitor should."

"They don't seem to be Taliban."

"No, indeed I believe the situation here in this village is tenuous." Ous raised a questioning eyebrow. "You wish to continue the wandering imam and Mighty One act?"

"No, that one's run its course and the satellite link to my translator and Keller are shot. Do you know how to cut hair?"

"The first job I ever had was that of a barber," Ous admitted. "Though I may be a little rusty."

"Then I'd like you to ask for a razor, a comb and some scissors."

Ous spent long moments scrutinizing Bolan's role camouflage. "Do you believe that is wise?"

"I think the God's honest truth is the only way to go with these people, and I'd rather it be us pulling the big reveal rather than the bad guys ratting us out on it."

"And how will we explain your miraculous transformation? If they believe that *nanawatai* was granted under false pretenses, the consequences may well be grim."

"These people don't like the Taliban?" Bolan asked.

"I believe they despise them."

Bolan shrugged. "Well, do you think the villagers might be amused by the trick we pulled on their enemies?"

A slow smile spread across the old guerrilla fighter's face. "They just might."

THE MEETING NEARLY broke into a riot as Bolan walked in. The shawl and cap were gone. So were his Central Asia hair and beard. Ous had clipped his hair into a shaggy yet serviceable haircut. There was nothing Bolan could do about the cosmetic scar tissue lining the left side of his face and neck or his fake tan, but they were all the more startling with the mustache and beard gone. Bolan looked like a Special Forces operative who had long ago gone to the Dark Side. Shouting broke out among the village elders.

Bolan bowed to Bilal. *"Salam."*

Bilal grunted back a surly "Salam" in return as Bolan helped Ous to a cushion and took a seat.

"Well," Ous said, "what shall I tell them?"

"Everything."

"Very well…" Ous began speaking in Pashto. He spoke for about fifteen minutes. He omitted names but otherwise told the villagers of his experiences since hooking up with Bolan. The village elders and warriors listened silently. Throughout Ous's summation, the soldier received increasing looks of incredulity, disbelief and awe.

When he finished, a profound silence filled the room. Ous turned to Bolan. "They particularly liked the part about killing two Taliban with one dummy rocket."

"Tell Bilal I am willing to answer any questions he may have. Translate for us directly." The first trick in a situation like this was to maintain eye contact and talk to the other person as if they understood everything you said. A pro never looked at the translator. The translator never personally interrupted unless absolutely necessary. Ous seemed to have done this before. He took a seat halfway between Bolan and Bilal and slightly off to the side.

Bilal got straight to the point. "You have seen our fields."

There was no point in denying it. "Yes."

"The United States Military is dedicated to eradicating our fields."

"That is in Afghanistan. This is the FATA. Pakistan is a valued ally of the United States, and the U.S. Military has no presence, much less jurisdiction here."

"But," Bilal protested, "the United States Military—"

"I am not a member of the United States Military."

It was a very old page from Bolan's playbook, but like a boxer with a sweet, right-hand lead it almost never failed to wow them even in the cheap seats. Stunned amazement reigned in the headman's salon. "But you are an American?" Bilal asked.

"Yes."

"But you are not a member of the United States Military?" Bilal pressed.

"No."

"Then why are you here?"

"To prevent the Taliban from engaging in acts of terror," Bolan replied.

"You seem to spend more time killing them."

Bolan shrugged. "Can you think of a better way to stop them?"

Amused grunts ran around the room at Bolan's wisdom. Bilal looked skyward and made a helicopter motion with his hand. "There is a man, his name is Saboor. He has—"

"I know him," Bolan said. "He needs killing."

The elders nodded and stroked their beards at the wisdom of this, as well. Bilal gave Bolan a very hard look of concern. "There is a man. A terrible man. A devil. His name is Syed. He came here two weeks ago and he—"

"I broke his arms and legs and gave him to the United States Military as a gift."

The room erupted. Bilal broke translation and laid into Ous rapid-fire. Ous nodded and turned to Bolan. "I have told him that even in the camp of our enemies you were known as the Mighty One."

Bolan locked his gaze with Bilal once more. "I don't claim it, but some have said it."

"What do you wish of us?" Bilal asked.

"The hospitality of the Pashtuns is known from sea to sea. My friend was injured in battle, and you have shown him and me every kindness. I fear because of it Saboor and his devils will come. This is Pakistani soil, sovereign, and I can't bring the might of the United States Military to help. I have already endangered your village, but the danger will be less if we leave. For my friend's sake, I would ask for one night of rest, a sack of grain, dried meat, and a bottle of water and we will leave."

Bilal's ancient face wrinkled. The law of *nanawatai* was iron, Bolan had just told the old man he would relinquish it and walk out with Ous into the FATA and die. Bilal was visibly moved by Bolan's bravery. "You shame me."

"Then I crave a boon."

Bilal stroked his beard in sudden suspicion. "What is that?"

"If you have one, a rifle with a telescopic sight," Bolan said.

The request was met with grins and a great deal of knee slapping. Bilal smiled happily. "My second son, Shahzad, will slaughter a goat."

Bolan bowed in gratitude. "*Salam*, Bilal."

"After you have been feasted," Bilal continued, "we shall see about a rifle." The old man's hand creaked into a fist. "And then we shall bid this pig Saboor defiance."

OUS RESTED comfortably on cushions in Bilal's house with his fingers laced across a belly distended with roasted goat. Bolan cleaned his Stechkin and drank tea. They had been shown every comfort except one. No one had offered to let them use a phone, and Bolan had decided it might make things awkward to ask, at least until he and Ous had earned a little more trust. Bilal's son Jadeed entering the room excitedly waving a museum piece. At one point it had been a British Lee-Enfield Mark VI infantry rifle. Someone had long ago given it a Monte Carlo-style sporting stock and a dubious-looking Chinese copy of a Bushnell six-power scope. Bolan removed the magazine.

The weapon took .303 ammunition, however the magazine was loaded with gleaming new Federal Power-Shok soft-point ammunition.

"Three-oh-three!" Jadeed grinned. It might well have been his only English.

Bolan clicked the magazine back in place, racked a round and pushed on the safety. "Yeah, .303."

Jadeed handed Bolan a homemade bandolier full of homemade, 5-round charger clips for the WWII-vintage weapon. They both looked up at the sound of rotors in the distance.

Bolan knelt beside Ous. "Can you walk?"

"I need a rifle and perhaps a shoulder to lean on just a little."

Jadeed helped Ous up without being asked, and the two men spoke. Bolan went outside. Bilal and several villagers stood with rifles in hand looking to the ravine to the east. The headman held up one finger, then pointed toward the eastern hills. One chopper had deployed its passengers. Bolan held up two fingers in question. Bilal shrugged.

Bolan had a bad feeling the village was being flanked. He followed Bilal down to the hill to the creek that split the little canyon. A nice six-foot adobe wall girded the frontal arc of the village, and decades of fighting had taught them to put in a firing step for ease of shooting over it. Bilal stepped out into the opening in the wall. It had no gate. Beyond the wall were pens for the village livestock.

Bolan stepped out next to Bilal. Ous came a moment later, leaning heavily on Jadeed. "You all right?"

"Yes."

Armed villagers began lining the wall while women and boys drove livestock from the pens into the village. Bolan took a moment to peer down his scope. It seemed to be in order. There was no time to check its zero. He was just going to have to hope that its owner took shooting seriously. "There's going to be a parley?"

Ous nodded. "In this situation it is traditional."

"Ask him who's got the back door."

Ous translated. "He says the cliffs behind the village are insurmountable, and should they try to deploy men at the peak from a helicopter they will receive a very hard welcome."

Bilal held up both hands as though he was behind the spade grips of a heavy machine gun. "Dah-dah-dah-dah-dah!" he proclaimed.

Jadeed happily mimed, holding a rocket launcher over one shoulder. "Toof!"

The villagers had crew-served weapons in the crags overlooking the village and the land behind it.

A man stepped out of the gully that led away from the canyon. It wasn't Saboor. He was dressed like a soldier in Pakistani army disruptive camo and wore a dark blue beret. His uniform was devoid of rank or unit badges. He cradled an FN 2000 assault rifle. The weapon was Pakistani special forces issue. The rifle's almost organic curves made it look vaguely like a submarine or a dolphin. The 40 mm grenade launcher tube mounted below the barrel spoiled the effect.

Ous translated as the man shouted out. "I am Major Noor! I demand, in the name of God and his Prophet Mohammed, and the Pakistani State that the village give up the American commando and the Afghani traitor to the faith who have violated Pakistani sovereign law and soil!"

"Sanctuary has been granted!" Bilal shouted back. "Hospitality has been shown. If you are truly a Pakistani, you know we cannot give up these men, at least until the situation has been clarified. I implore you! Come into our village as an honored guest! Accept our hospitality, and present your case against these men."

The man stepped out of view for several moments. The villagers lining the wall muttered and nervously fondled their weapons. The soldier returned.

"The surrender of the fugitives, as well as the surrender of the village, will be unconditional and immediate!"

Ous broke translation and turned to Bolan. "There's going to be a fight."

Bolan had guessed that. He still had a very bad feeling. The enemy had at most two squads of men, yet they seemed very confident that they could take the fortified village.

Major Noor began shouting angrily. The fighters along the wall became more agitated. Ous shrugged. "It is not worth repeating except that he is threatening to level the village if Bilal and his people do not give us up."

The men along the wall went from agitated to angry.

"And now?"

"He has finished threatening. Now he has moved on to insult," Ous stated.

"Oh?"

"Yes, he is— Oh! Now, that was a good one, and it was directed at you."

"What did he say?" Bolan asked.

"Some of the flourishes do not easily translate. However, he is strongly implying that you are the sort of American infidel who has sex with his sister on his mother's grave while his retarded father watches from his wheelchair."

In a society where even the slightest taunt meant a killing and the killing result in a blood feud that might last for centuries, Pashtuns believed you might as well make your insults count. Bolan gave his adversary full marks. "Wow."

"Yes," Ous agreed. "I particularly like the part about the wheelchair. It really tied it all together. I will have to remember that one should we leave this village alive." Ous cocked his head in question. "Would you like me to impart anything in reply?"

Bolan considered a few choice ones he had heard in his travels across the Middle East and passed them onto Ous.

"Oh, they are very good!" Ous cupped his hands beside his mouth and happily shouted across the killing zone. Bilal and his men laughed out loud. Everyone on the wall whirled at the sound of an explosion at the top of the crags. The explosion was followed by the sound of crew-served weapon fire. Not the "dah-dah-dah-dah-dah!" of a heavy machine gun or the "Toof!" of a rocket launcher. It was tube noise.

Mortars.

Bilal began snarling.

Ous shook his head. "Bilal says it is impossible. No one can climb the crags behind us, much less do so unseen."

Bolan shook his head. "Ninjas are famous for getting into impossible places, and doing so unseen."

Mortar bombs began falling on the village. Men and women screamed. The enemy was using white phosphorus. They were going to burn the village to the ground. Ous pushed off the safety on his rifle. "Bilal says there is one thing our enemies cannot know."

"What's that?"

"The secret way to the top."

Bolan slung his rifle and drew his machine pistol. "Show me."

CHAPTER SIXTEEN

The shaft was nearly vertical. With a few sinuous deviations the natural chimney in the rock led straight up from behind the cliff section of village. Hand- and footholds carved into the shaft long ago presented a precarious route up through the rock. The shaft was widening as they reached top—wide enough to admit two men, but that only meant if you slipped there was nothing but air to fall back against. A man named Latif led the way with an old military flashlight lashed to his back. Ous couldn't make the climb in his condition, so Bolan was going up with Latif and two men named Ali and Arian. They spoke no English. Bolan had given them their orders through Ous. He'd kept it simple.

They were going up top to kill everyone who wasn't local.

Several strange, horizontal shafts of light crisscrossed at the top of the shaft. The villagers had taken heavy canvas and stiffened it with lime. The material was stretched over a wicker frame to artfully appear to be a boulder to a casual observer, particularly one who was airborne and looking down. The sneak attack above had perforated the camouflage in several places.

Latif looked down and gave Bolan an unhappy look. The Executioner gestured with one hand that he was willing to switch places. The guide vehemently shook his head. The tribal warrior loosened his pistol in its holster and stuck his knife between his teeth. Islam's war cry hissed from between Latif's teeth as he threw back the wicker frame. *"Allahu Ak—"*

Latif's head flew off his shoulders in the single flash of a sword. Bolan hugged the walls as the decapitated head and the dagger Latif had held in his teeth fell down the shaft. Arian screamed as Latif's head hit him in the face, and he lost his hold and fell down the shaft. Bolan was bathed in a curtain of blood as Latif's body followed, and he nearly lost his hold on the rock ladder as Jadeed's corpse collided with him in its descent down the shaft. The big American squinted up into the sunlight through the blood streaming in his eyes.

A hand grenade dropped from above.

Bolan reached out a hand and snatched the grenade out of the air. He tossed the fusing grenade back up and gritted his teeth. The munition just disappeared over the lip of the shaft and detonated. Bolan scrabbled for purchase on the blood-slick rock and went over the top, finding himself right among the mortars. They were commando mortars, 60 mm, small and light enough for a man to carry on his back. There were four two-man teams. The ninjas wore Pakistani special forces camouflage and had shemaghs wrapped around their faces. Most of them had been kneeling to load and fire down on the village, and to climb the cliff face they had abjured body armor.

Bolan's grenade-return service had wreaked havoc among them.

Four lay on the ground dead or badly wounded. Two more were on hands and knees clawing at the wounds shredding their bodies. Two still had fight in them. They abandoned their mortar and bombs and reached for steel. The range was point-blank. Bolan's machine pistol triphammered 3-round bursts into the shrouded faces. One of the wounded tried to rise, and the soldier hammered him back down without mercy.

One of the "dead" ninjas popped up like a jumping jack. The long sound suppressor tube on his pistol hindered his lightning-fast draw. The ninja was fast but couldn't take Bolan. He burned the rest of his magazine into the ninja's center body mass. As the man fell, one of his comrades rose. This one wasn't faking his wounds, yet his sword hissed from the sheath behind his back. Bolan's pistol was racked open on a smoking empty chamber. He dropped the Stechkin and drew his blade.

"Allahu Akbar!" Ali fired a dozen rounds from his AK into the ninja's back. The attacker staggered, flapping his limbs under the onslaught. Several of the bullets passing through his body whip-cracked dangerously close to Bolan's head. The perforated ninja fell on his face and lay unmoving. Ali roared in triumph. *"Allahu Akbar!"* Then shot the remaining ninjas.

"Damn right," Bolan agreed. He quickly surveyed the situation. The villagers who had been sent up to the peak had been caught by surprise. Their bodies lay in a pile off to one side. All bore shrapnel and blast wounds, and all of them had their throats cut. A Pakistani 12.7 mm air defense gun squatted on its tripod in a circle of piled rocks. Down below, the village was receiving mortar fire from Major Noor's position. There was little the villagers could do about it. The ground between the ravine and the village was strewed with dead heroes who had tried to charge the hidden mortars. Fierce tears stained Ali's face as he shook his fist in rage. Bolan couldn't quite see the mortars below, but mortars were indirect fire weapons, and their advantages worked both ways.

Bolan righted one of the ninja's pack mortars and examined it for damage. Ali didn't speak English, but he didn't need to. Bolan pointed. "Hey, Ali, pass me a mortar bomb."

Ali stopped short of clapping his hands. He gathered up the remaining six bombs. The mortar was a very simple affair. It had no bipod. You put your foot on the tube base and held the handle. A straight white line painted up the tube served as the sight, and a simple drum gave elevation. Bolan put his foot on the tube base and did a little math and applied a little Kentucky windage. "Now."

Ali dropped the bomb down the tube and jumped away.

The mortar thumped and the bomb arced over the little valley. Bolan had aimed slightly behind Noor's position. A plume of white phosphorus shot skyward and burning phosphorus arced through the air in streamers that cut off retreat down the ravine. Bolan adjusted the tube's elevation a hair and held up three fingers. "Ali, again, three more!"

Ali met his mortar team responsibilities with profound enthusiasm.

The three bombs arced straight into the target area. Some of Noor's men burst out of the ravine screaming and flailing at the fire clinging to their bodies and ran for the creek. It would do them no good. White Phosphorus burned under water. The villagers manning the wall ended their suffering in a deafening fusillade of automatic rifle fire. Smoldering bodies slowly drifted down the creek. They left behind the stench of burning metal and barbecued flesh. A secondary explosion and a pulse of smoke billowed out of the ravine. The black smoke from the hidden position told Bolan that Noor's helicopter had burned and exploded.

The Executioner walked over to the Pakistani air defense weapon and waited for the second helicopter.

The graceful Dauphin streaked along ravines as it came in flying nap of the earth. Bolan racked back the big bolt and chambered a 12.7 mm round. He lowered the heavy machine gun's muzzle and glared through the steel grid of the antiaircraft sight. He tracked the chopper as it streaked along the ridgeline. The pilot was good, but it seemed as if communication between the ninjas and their cohorts wasn't what it could be. Once the ninjas had taken their objective, the helicopter crew seemed to have assumed the village's heavy weapons had been disabled. They didn't realize the big weapon had simply changed hands, and changed hands twice.

Bolan eyed the twin rocket pods adorning the Dauphin's lower fuselage. Maximum effective range was about eight thousand meters, depending on the warhead and the platform. The helicopter was coming in low and fast and would want to stay out of small arms range. Two thousand meters would be about right, and that was the about the maximum on the weapon Bolan held. He shook his head. The village might have to take the aerial bombardment before he could get a shot at the chopper.

The pilot obliged Bolan by doing his firing pop-up at fifteen hundred.

Bolan's thumbs shoved down the paddle trigger. The big weapon rattled and roared, and tracers streamed across the valley. The helicopter was coming in nearly straight-on to deliver its rockets into the village proper. Bolan walked his tracers into the cockpit glass.

"Allahu Akbar!" Ali roared.

Bolan kept the trigger down until the weapon spit out the last, smoking empty brass shell casing. The helicopter dipped its nose and began its death spiral. It jerked and spun wildly as someone still living within tried to fight the controls left behind by the dead pilot. The rotors sheared off as the chopper stuck the wall of the canyon, and it instantly went from death spiral to dropping like a rock. The rotorless fuselage struck the valley floor and broke its back over a boulder.

The village erupted into cheers.

Bolan hooked a fresh can of ammo on the big gun and racked the bolt back on a new belt of ammo. Ali's cell phone rang. He answered it eagerly and almost instantly pressed it into the Executioner's hands.

"How's it going down there, brother?" Bolan asked.

"Well, brother, first of all," Ous replied, "Bilal wanted me to tell you that he now believes everything he has been told about the Mighty One."

"Would you please tell Bilal that the Mighty One respectfully asked if he might make a phone call to tell his people that he is all right and where they can meet him on the Afghani border?"

"Brother, you may make your call," Ous replied a moment later.

BOLAN WALKED into the conference room. It had been a two-day hike out of the FATA. Bilal had been kind enough to provide an armed escort and a pair of litter-bearers for Ous. The soldier was exhausted, but he knew Keller was eager for a face-to-face debrief.

Keller smiled as Bolan took a seat. "You know, I kind of miss the beard."

"What do you have on our Major Noor?"

"The Pakistani Military says there are no Major Noors in their special forces. There are currently two Major Noors in the regular army, both accounted for, and neither answering your description."

"Any forensic luck on the village battle?"

"We managed to insert a team. It took us a day. We asked Bilal to leave everything where it lay, but a third of the village was burned down and after their initial excitement at the victory they were in a bad mood. The bodies that weren't burned beyond recognition were stripped and mutilated. We got there seventy-two hours later, and the bodies had been thrown in a pile and left in the sun. The vultures had been feasting."

"One of the helicopters was a burned-out hulk. The villagers had stripped the other down to the frame. The Pakistan Military claims it isn't missing any choppers."

Bolan knew the answer to his next question, but he asked anyway. He was always willing to be surprised. "Have we contacted the Japanese?"

Keller sighed. "The Japanese Public Security Intelligence Agency says there are no such things as ninjas, nor have there been since the feudal Shogunate."

It was the PSIA's standard answer on that one. No surprise there. There were even rumors in certain circles that at least one ninja clan was an arms-length PSIA asset. "So, how's my ninja?"

"Inscrutable."

"They tend to be that way."

Keller smiled. "You've known many?"

"A few."

Keller just shook her head. She was starting to believe in the Mighty One, as well. Her bemusement sank into a frown. "We've got some new data on Zurisaday."

"Yeah?"

"We think we know who she is."

Bolan could tell by Keller's face he wasn't going to like the answer. "Who?"

"Your friend 'the Bear' was kind enough to contact me after you went missing. He told me that he has it on good authority her name is Na'ama Shushan."

"That's a Hebrew name," Bolan stated.

"Yes. You said it. Assassins, off the rack."

There was a group of people who could rival the ninjas when it came to infiltration, espionage, sabotage and assassination, and that group was the Israeli Mossad. Over the years Bolan and other members of Stony Man Farm had worked with the Mossad and its agents. They had some markers to call on. Kurtzman had had a hunch and called in all of them.

"She must have been a real embarrassment to the Mossad," Bolan said.

"She disappeared during a mission. Since there was no ransom or prisoner exchange deal, it was assumed she'd been killed."

"She was captured."

"The Mossad currently believes that she was captured and turned."

Bolan could see why Israeli Intelligence hadn't shared everything. Having one of their own turned by the enemy and using the skills they had taught her to kill Israeli targets was unthinkable. It seemed the unthinkable had happened. "What else did they give us?"

"The Bear let them know that we had her. They immediately wanted to send an agent. When they found out she had escaped, they canceled the trip and clammed up again. You were in-country and incommunicado when this happened. Your friend said this struck him as very odd, and I guess he did whatever he did to make them spill. They gave us the whole shebang on her. There were some flags on her psych profile, but you'd expect that on a woman who accepts the job of seducing and killing enemies of the state."

"I think she was much more excited about the seducing and killing rather than the protecting the State of Israel part." Bolan considered his encounters with her. "Frankly, after she was captured, I don't think it took much to turn her."

"Bitch probably took it as a golden opportunity," Keller muttered.

"And exactly the kind of woman whoever the new player on the scene would hire."

"That's how I see it," Keller agreed.

Bolan reflected a moment. "I think she's still in Pakistan."

"She and Saboor certainly know by now that you and Ous escaped. I'm betting they're long gone."

"They have a target in Pakistan."

"There really aren't a lot of high-priority Western targets in Pakistan."

"The target is Pakistan," Bolan told her.

"You're saying everything that's happened in Afghanistan was a feint?" Keller said.

"No, they were targets. Good enough to keep you and me from looking east. Even when we knew they were in the FATA and I was among them, we were still trying to figure out how they could launch an attack into Afghanistan."

"Okay, now you're scaring me. What kind of target?" Keller asked.

"One that would turn Pakistan from the West, one so bad that the army wouldn't be able to stop radical Islamists from taking over the country." Bolan went worst-case scenario. "Or started a nuclear exchange between Pakistan and India."

"Tell me—the Mighty One has something up his sleeve?" Keller asked hopefully.

"I have two, but they're slim."

"Do tell?"

"One is my rifle. We dressed it up to look like a workhorse," Bolan said.

"There's a tracking device on it!"

"They probably gave the rifle to someone. The scope has a laser range finder. If someone figured that out, then we have to hope that someone higher up said, "'Ooh, CIA special, gimme.'"

"Is it tracking now?"

"It's passive. The Radio Frequency Identification Tag doesn't go active until something, in this case an NSA satellite, hits it with the right frequency."

"So how come we haven't pinged your rifle already?" Keller asked.

"I figured we'd let it travel for a few days, see where it ends up."

"Good thinking. It's kinda gutsy when you've gone dark for three days and we don't know whether you're dead, drunk or in jail, but good thinking."

"The second option is my phone," Bolan suggested.

"Nice."

"They probably looked through it for pictures and numbers. If they took it apart then they found the hidden gun function, and then they most likely gave it a hard second look. If they have any kind of counterintelligence operation, they might just have booted it up the food chain."

"But they would know if it was sending off a signal."

"That's right. Again, that's why we don't fire off the RFID inside until the last second," Bolan stated.

"What's to prevent their people from discovering the RFID even it hasn't gone active?"

"The RFID is buried in the metal parts of the phone's body. We're just going to have to pray that my people's hiding skills are better than the enemies seeking."

"So when do we activate the RFIDs?" Keller asked.

"Now."

CHAPTER SEVENTEEN

Islamabad, Pakistan

A short, very pregnant woman in full burka hurried across the street accompanied by a gruesome individual wearing a turban. Bolan sat on the patio of a bread shop, munching a pastry and drinking Turkish-style coffee out of an ibrik urn. Farkas sat across from him looking nervous. The groomers had done a good job with the beard and local clothing, but it was kind of like putting perfume on a pig. He just didn't carry himself like a local. Bolan was in full regalia himself, but the scar tissue had been removed and his hair and beard were now brown. With the contact lenses, so were his eyes. The pregnant woman and her companion sat at the bus stop a few yards away from the patio.

Bolan was mildly surprised when the pregnant woman made eye contact.

He kept the smile off his face as he recognized the hazel gaze of NCIS Agent Keller flashing at him through the eye slit. Donning a burka made wearing a wire a piece of cake. The soldier whispered his admiration for Keller's third-trimester couture into his coffee. "Wow, I didn't know my boys worked that fast."

Keller weighed in through the receiver Bolan wore beneath his turban. "It's an empathy belly pregnancy simulator, jackass, and the damn thing weighs thirty pounds.

After Ous's little lecture on the joys of figure and flow recognition through the folds of a burka I figured it would be the easiest way to change my shape and stride. I borrowed it from a very sensitive young Marine embassy guard who wants to empathize with wife's joy and pain, and not even the Taliban messes with a pregnant woman."

Bolan eyed the bad-ass escorting her. His very real facial scarring made the fake battle damage Bolan had worn look like a shaving accident. The man looked as though he'd French-kissed a claymore mine and lived to tell about it. "Who's your date?"

"We are very grateful to receive Subedar Babar on loan from the Black Storks."

Subedar was a junior commissioned officer rank in most of the former British colonies in Central and South Asia. Black Storks meant the Subedar was Pakistani Special Service Group. They'd acquired the nickname when the unit had crossed into Pakistan during the Soviet invasion and fought the Russians posing as mujahideen. Bolan had worked with some of their members before. In the world of international special forces, they were considered something of a cowboy outfit. All too often Pakistani army command used them as shock troops rather than genuine spec ops warriors.

As wild and woolly as they were, they had earned a well-deserved reputation for toughness. They liked to fight, and unlike a lot of high-tech special operations groups around the world that trained often but fought little, the Black Storks had seen nearly continuous action since 1965. Any man above the rank of private had most likely been in-country multiple times, and sadly, and all too often, in-country for the Black Storks was their own backyard. Bolan wasn't surprised to see a man like Babar operating in the Federally Administered Tribal Area.

Bolan and Babar exchanged barely perceptible nods.

The United States wasn't allowed to run independent missions in Pakistan.

"How's Ous?"

"Resting angrily. He wants to be here. The doctors nearly had to use restraints," Keller said.

"Bear, what's the status on my rifle?" Bolan said.

"No movement, Striker." Kurtzman's voice came back over the receiver. "Unfortunately we don't have satellite eyes on. As you can imagine, most of the satellites we have stationed over this part of South Asia are heavily tasked at the moment."

"Can you get me a transient?" Bolan asked.

"We can get you a two-hour window in eight hours."

"What's the status on the RFID battery? Best estimate? Maybe about the same, maybe a little longer, maybe a little less."

"Bear, I say we go in now. Keller?"

"I agree."

"With a four-man team?" Kurtzman asked. The fact that they knew nothing about Subedar Babar was left unsaid.

"This is a clock-is-ticking situation. I'm willing and so is Keller. I'm calling it a go."

"All right. Keller and Babar are going to take the bus ten blocks up to the objective. We own the driver, and their equipment is on board. It will have a no fares sign on it but will stop for them. They'll get dropped off near the objective and make their approach openly from the street. You and Farkas are going to be picked up in a cab. Your equipment is inside and you'll be delivered to an alley near the back. Keller and Babar are going to make a small diversion out front. That's when you and Farkas are go in the back."

"What kind of resistance?"

"Our CIA scouts say one man openly standing guard

out front. One in back. We have no idea how many may be inside. No one has come in or out since they began observation. The guard out front switched off with someone inside, so I would assume at least four. Given the nature of the target, I would assume everyone inside is heavy."

The cab pulled up to the bakery and the driver grinned and waved. Bolan rose. "We're a go." He and Farkas slid into the back of the cab. The driver passed them two small suitcases. Bolan flipped the latches. The contents were definitely old school and acquired from Pakistani sources. He took out his weapon and held it low. The Uzi submachine gun had seen some hard use. The weapon was accompanied by a foot-long, canvas-wrapped suppressor tube, six loaded magazines and an assortment of grenades. There was a second weapon and accessories just like it in the case.

Bolan looked over at Farkas.

He really looked like he missed his government-issue weapons. Bolan loaded his pockets with two ancient M-67 fragmentation grenades that still had dust on them, a tear gas grenade with a suspicious dent and, thankfully, a shiny new flash-bang.

The Toyota cab wound through the back streets of Islamabad. The capital of Pakistan was a major world metropolis and had been built nearly from the ground up in the 1950s. The cab took them beyond the administrative district into the suburbs. Middle Eastern and South Asian housing styles didn't go in for front yards, backyards or lawns. They liked private courtyards within. That left many houses presenting a solid, often forbidding face to the sidewalk.

The cabdriver pulled over. He was Pakistani but a CIA asset. "Down the street, take a left, down the alley. Fourth door on the right. I will be waiting here if you need alternate extraction." He paused a moment as he listened to his earpiece. "Our spotter says there is currently one man still guarding the back. Definitely armed. We are five minutes from front door diversion."

"Thanks." Bolan and Farkas took their cases and began slowly walking down the street. The avenue had no street-lights, numbers or signs. In the Middle Eastern and South Asian cultures the prevailing theory in most neighborhoods was if you didn't know your destination, then you most likely weren't welcome there anyway.

Bolan palmed a frag grenade as he and Farkas turned the corner and began their approach.

Their intel was good. Four doors down a large man in a tracksuit who obviously had a weapon under his left arm stood smoking, and he seemed bored as most guards usually were. Bolan timed his pace. The guard instantly came to attention as the two strangers approached. The Executioner broke eye contact as if he were intimidated and mumbled as he closed in, *"Salam."*

The guard deigned to incline his head slightly. *"Sala—"* He raised his head at the sound of a scream out front. It was clear at the same time someone had spoken in his ear-piece to him. As the sentry raised his head, Bolan hit him with an uppercut that had the weight of the grenade in his hand behind it. The sentry's jaw broke, and his eyes rolled back in his head as he sagged against the door and fell. The screaming out front continued as Keller made noise like she was being beaten.

They didn't have much time.

The door was heavy, blue-painted wood with a massive brass lock. Security was likely very simple. No one opened the door unless the guard outside gave the call sign. Bolan broke out his picks and swiftly worked the lock. Farkas locked and loaded the Uzis and spun the suppressors over their muzzles. The old brass tumblers turned under the soldier's torsion wrenches, and the bolt slide back with a click. Bolan took a weapon and a magazine pack from Farkas and opened the door. The interior alcove was tile floor and bare walls.

He spoke into his wire. "Sentry down, we're in."

"Copy that," Keller came back.

Bolan moved down a narrow, dim hall toward the sounds of talking and professional sports. He stopped at the open entryway. It wasn't unknown to find four men in this part of the world sitting on a sofa watching cricket on television. Back in the FATA the fact that all the men had automatic weapons close at hand wouldn't have raised many eyebrows, either. The fact that they wore Western clothes and this was suburban Islamabad raised the bar of suspicion slightly. Bolan stepped into the room followed by Farkas. The jaws of the four sports fans dropped in unison. Bolan raised his finger to his lips in the universal gesture. "Who speaks English?"

The man on the far left of the couch raised a shaky hand. "I—"

The man on the far right lunged for his weapon, snarling something. The other two followed. Bolan's Uzi chuffed in three rapid bursts and three of the gunmen sagged into the couch never to rise again. The man on the left screamed and covered his head. Responding shouts echoed through the house.

Keller spoke across the wire. "Sentry down! We're in!"

"Copy that!" Bolan put his foot on the talker's chest and let him admire the smoke oozing out of the Uzi's suppressor an inch from the bridge of his nose. "How many more?"

"Four!" the man gasped. "No! Five!"

"Where?"

"Upstairs!"

"Computer! Where?"

"Up—" Bolan drove the steel strut of the Uzi's folding stock into the side of the man's neck. He went white and went fetal.

"Farkas, on my six!" Bolan swept the bottom floor. He and Farkas linked with Keller and Babar. Keller had ditched her burka and wore armor and a NCIS windbreaker. Bolan loped up the stairs. "Keller, break right!"

Bolan broke left, hearing furious activity in the room at the end of the hall. He kicked the door and the man inside screamed. The man was in front of a desktop furiously deleting files. Bolan walked his fire across the desk and put three rounds into the power strip. Computer activity instantly ceased. The technician snarled in rage and went for the pistol on the desk. He screamed in pain as Bolan put a burst through his hand and all quick-draw activity ceased, as well. "Farkas, secure him and the computer!"

Bolan moved to the other end of the hall.

Keller and Babar were in the entry position on either side of a heavy wooden door. Babar was getting ready to kick it. Keller jerked a thumb. "We got three hostiles in there."

Beyond the door a desk crashed as it was turned over. The bad guys were barricading themselves in. Babar nodded. "On three. One, two—" Bolan recognized a muffled click-clack sound beneath Babar's countdown, and he held up a hand to wait. Babar frowned. "What?"

"Squad Automatic Weapon," the soldier explained, taking out his tear gas grenade.

Babar frowned.

The Executioner pointed to the open transom above the door.

Babar beamed and took out tear gas, as well. The two men pulled pins and two cylinders looped over the transom. The effect inside was immediate. A light machine gun began chewing holes in the door at 800 rounds per minute. Everyone hugged the wall. Two grenades for a single room would very quickly turn into a lethal concentration. Long before that it would become intolerable. The weapon within died as its belt ran dry. A ragged, coughing, *"Allahu Akbar!"* tore from several throats. Bolan motioned for Keller and Babar to fall back to the bedroom door down the hall. The Executioner stayed plastered against the wall. Tear gas oozed out of the transom and fell down the door like a waterfall of fog. Behind the door, men hacked and screamed. AKs opened up and tore more holes low through the door as someone else pulled the bar. Bolan yanked the pin on his flash-bang and tossed it to the floor. The door flew open in a flurry of AK fire.

Bolan covered his eyes with his hands and stuck his thumbs in his ears.

The terrorists came through the door like Butch and Sundance in Bolivia. The flash-bang went off, the blast effect sending the CS whirling in crazy eddying gas devils. The first two men out the door staggered like drunks, blinded from the flash and their inner ears overcome from the blast wave and the decibels. Bolan let them go past firing blindly.

The third man charged out.

He'd reloaded his SAW and he came out blazing, hosing down the hallway as well as his sensory compromised compatriots. Bolan stuck out a leg, and the terrorist went flying, swan-diving to the tiles. Bolan was on him instantly. He rolled the gasping, wheezing, stunned terrorist over and put a knee in his chest. Despite the tear gas stinging his eyes and beginning to burn his lungs, Bolan smiled down into the swollen, weeping bearded face beneath him. "Saboor."

GHOLAN DAEI wasn't amused. "This is a joke."

Azimi and Khahari wrung their hands. It was Khahari who held up a DVD. "I assure it is not. The safehouse outside Islamabad was attacked."

Daei loaded the disk into his laptop. Every safehouse he used was wired for sight and sound. The disk itself was proof that the safehouse had been attacked and what was recorded on a daily basis had been transmitted. The chance of the transmission being traced was infinitesimal, and even if U.S. spy satellites had picked up on the encrypted transmission and located the receiver site, all they would find would be a gutted and abandoned room clear on the other side of the capital. Even that assumed that they would receive military and police permission and assistance in the investigation.

Daei had spread immense sums of money throughout the capital to prevent such assistance. He frowned as he watched the men guarding the front and back doors be taken. He raised an eyebrow as he realized three men and a woman were taking the house. "Keller."

"Yes, great one," Azimi agreed.

Daei raised an eyebrow as the feed covered the assault from room to room. "Scarface Babar."

Khahari nodded. "Yes."

Daei had initially suspected that "Scarface" Babar might have been the Mighty One. All doubt on that score was erased as Daei watched a tall, forbidding man lope through the safehouse like a wolf; that was when he wasn't striding through the building as though he owned it. Daei had heard that a true master of anything showed it in everything he did. Even in a grainy, black-and-white surveillance tape, the man's room-clearing tactics and situational awareness were something to see if one knew what one was looking at. "The Mighty One."

"We think it can be no other."

Daei's knuckles creaked. Once again he wanted to lay his hands on the Mighty One. Once again they were in the same city. Once more they were almost within arm's reach. "Copies of this have been sent to the appropriate people?"

"I thought you might wish to see it first."

Daei nodded. Despite the movement's unity, it pleased Daei that his minions first loyalty was to him. "Send the copies."

"As you wish."

"Leave me now, I need to make a phone call," Daei ordered.

Khahari tarried a moment. "Great One?"

Daei tolerated the question. "You are concerned."

"The Americans, they have Saboor," Khahari stated.

"It is most unfortunate," Daei conceded.

"But won't they…" Khahari left the implication hanging between them.

"Tell me, young brother. Why is it that we shall win?"

Khahari stood straighter. "Because we are strong, and our enemies are weak."

"Why is that?"

"Because our enemies worship life, and we worship death."

"How can this be?"

"Our enemies will fight to preserve their corrupt way of life. We will die to spread the True Faith."

"That is correct."

Khahari nodded. "They cannot break him."

Daei gazed upon his young suicide soldier. "All men can be broken. Always remember that. It comes down to the nature of our enemy. We are stronger than they are. We are willing to do what they are not." Daei folded his arms across his massive chest, "The Americans have neither the will nor the wherewithal to do what it would take to break Saboor. Even if they try to succeed with the methods the United States Military can stomach, it will take far too long, and they will be too late."

CHAPTER EIGHTEEN

Federally Administered Tribal Area

Bolan shoved Saboor out of the helicopter. The man shrieked in a most unmartyrlike fashion under his hood as he toppled into empty space. His wrists were zip-tied to his belt, his ankles bound. Saboor spasmed against his bonds and did the worm as he tumbled through the ethers. He neither wormed nor tumbled far. The helicopter was hovering only four feet above the ground. The scream of terror tearing out of Saboor's lungs ended abruptly with a splash as he landed in about six inches of water and hit the mud of the drying creek. Bolan hopped out. When it came to psychological warfare the "throw them out of the chopper" routine was an old one, but a good one. It struck Bolan as a good way to open the bidding. He helped Ous out of the aircraft, and Babar jumped to join them. The three warriors gazed down at the bound and hooded terrorist.

Saboor had wet himself.

The whirlwind of the rotor wash prevented Saboor from hearing the crowd of judges, jurors and executioners in front of him. It was very clear by his body language that Saboor knew something was terribly wrong. Bolan clicked open his tactical knife. Babar gave the pilot the thumbs-up, and the helicopter rose out of the canyon. Bolan dragged Saboor to dry ground. He yanked the terrorist to his knees and ripped off his hood for the big reveal.

Bilal, Ali and the rest of the village down to the smallest child stood assembled in an arc in front of Saboor. Behind them much of the village was still blasted and burned from the attack the man had orchestrated.

Saboor spasmed backward. Bolan held him firmly in place and spoke in English. "Bilal says he has met you before, Saboor. He didn't love you then, and I fear he loves you less now."

Saboor's jaw worked but not much sound came out.

"These people granted Ous and me *nanawatai*," Bolan continued, "right in the teeth of your attack. I owe them my life, Saboor. I owe them you."

The women of the village were assembled behind the men. All now wore headscarves and veils. Their eyes flashed pure hatred out of the black khol they had lined their lids with. The women began to ululate. It wasn't the typical sound of celebration, or the all too often heard wail of lament. The tone of the women trilling their voices up and down held an ominous note, and it bounced off the canyon walls in an unsettling fashion. It was the sound of hatred. It was a call for revenge, and it was growing in power. Saboor shook. The Western ideal of women's rights was nearly unknown in South Asia, but every woman in the FATA owned a dagger.

The women wore them openly now.

Saboor shuddered. He knew what was going to happen to him. Bolan told him anyway. "You're going to meet death without your sexual organs. You're going to meet God without a head. Your mutilated body will be left as feast for hawks, and your children will not know where the dogs have scattered your bones."

Saboor sobbed.

Bolan was beginning to think his read on Saboor was correct. He cut the man's left wrist free and coldly paraphrased Rudyard Kipling. "When you're wounded and left on Pakistan's plains, and the women come out to cut up what remains, just pick up your rifle and blow out your brains, and go face God like a soldier."

The women rippled like a wave as they leaned back and forth. The ululating took on a fever pitch as they worked themselves into a killing frenzy.

Saboor moaned.

Bolan took out the Pakistani army automatic pistol Babar had loaned him and popped the clip. Saboor stared as Bolan cocked the pistol on the single round in the chamber and tossed it to the ground in front of him. Bolan turned away.

Bolan heard Saboor pick up the gun, heard the hiss of approximately seventy daggers leave their sheaths. The Executioner looked up and waved at the orbiting helicopter. For a moment he waited, and then he heard the hammer falling on the dud round in the chamber as Saboor pulled the trigger again and again. Suicide was a sin in Islam, and Saboor was a martyr sworn to take unbelievers with him to his grave. Bolan turned, knowing what he would find.

Saboor fell to his hands wretching as he pulled the gun out of his own mouth.

The reaction of the villagers was mixed. Some stared in amazement. Some spit in disgust. Others looked away uncomfortably. Saboor's shame was incalculable. Bolan had read his quarry right. Saboor was an organizer, a planner and a recruiter. He was a brave man who was willing to shoot it out with his enemies. He might even have been willing to strap on a suicide vest and blow himself up for the cause, but he knew the old stories, and in the FATA the old stories were everyday life. Bolan had handed Saboor over to the death that even the bravest of South Asian warriors feared.

The male villagers turned their backs and began walking toward the gate.

Bolan turned away.

The women and girls flowed through the male ranks and raised their daggers overhead. Saboor screamed and grabbed Bolan's ankle. "Anything!"

Bolan toed Saboor onto his back and stepped over him. The seventy-plus veiled and kholed eyes popped in surprise. The soldier shot out one open hand to halt them. He gave it fifty-fifty whether the women would stop or roll over him and his captive like an avalanche of cube-steaking machines. The women stopped for the Mighty One, but it was a near thing. They stood in an angry, chest-heaving, dagger-wielding arc surrounding him.

The Executioner raised his voice. "Bilal!"

The menfolk turned.

Ous translated for Bolan exactly. "Bilal, this man has information I need. He is yours, but if you are willing, I wish to purchase his life."

"This dog has betrayed his faith in God. I have no use for such a creature. If the Mighty One can find both mercy and a use for the wretch, then the Mighty One is a far better man than I."

Bilal and the menfolk turned once more. The majority of the women lifted their heads haughtily and turned away, as well. A few shot Bolan looks of jilted bloodlust, but no one stabbed Bolan in an effort to claim any of Saboor's ears, eyes or other significant organs. He rolled Saboor over and rehooded and bound him.

Saboor lay weeping, as soft as a boned fish during the process. The helicopter dropped down and Bolan put a foot on the skid as the Pakistani door gunner grinned and gave him an arm inside. Saboor had never seen or heard Keller where she sat in the copilot seat during the flight.

The NCIS agent gave Bolan a grim but admiring look. "Nice work. So we get Saboor back to base and get an interrogation team on him."

"Forget Saboor."

Keller drew a blank look. "What?"

"They know we have him. They're already doing damage control."

"Yeah, but—"

"We send him back, make a fuss over him at base, let everyone know he's being interrogated. He broke himself, but it will still take time to sweat everything out of him."

Keller's hazel eyes got that predatory gleam. "Saboor is a feint."

"That's right. I'm betting he's high enough up that his capture is causing some shifting around, and they still don't know how we took him," Bolan said.

"So...?"

"So put together your strike team."

"And?"

"And I activate the RFID in my phone."

Islamabad, industrial district

GHOLAM DAEI STRODE through the warehouse. The little technician, Afdar, struggled to keep up. He was visibly upset. His friend, business partner and the man who had recruited him to the cause had been captured along with Saboor during the Mighty One's raid. Daei tried to calm him.

"Listen to me, your friend Jamshed has been captured by Americans. He is in a clean room, with a bed and clean sheets. He has been given a prayer rug and a Koran, and is receiving three meals a day that adhere to Islamic dietary law. On top of this, what authority do the Americans have in Pakistan? I have already put the machinery in place to have his release demanded."

Afdar seemed unconsoled. "As you say."

Daei wasn't as certain as he made out. He had his spies among the Americans. Rumor had it that despite his predictions, Saboor had been broken in short order, though none of his assets were high enough up in the food chain to know how. Daei also had it on good authority that Jamshed's right hand had been blown off before he could complete the deletion of all files and that his computer had left the country by courier jet to an unknown destination. Soon, if not at this moment, the CIA or the NSA would be putting their best people on the decryption of Jamshed's files. Things weren't going according to plan.

Daei knew that the Mighty One was in desperate need of killing.

"I am perturbed that Saboor was found so quickly."

Afdar shook his head. "I do not believe he was found."

Daei stopped. "And what do you mean by that?"

"There was no way to find him. Tell me how! Who would talk? Who would know to talk? Who would know whom to talk to?"

Daei began to get a cold feeling. It wasn't a feeling he was used to, and he didn't care for it. "What are you saying, Afdar?"

"Saboor could not have been found. He was traced."

"It is your supposition that somehow the American or Ous planted a tracking device on Saboor?"

"It is the only thing that makes sense."

"I find this very hard to believe," Daei stated.

"Did Saboor take anything from either the American or Ous?"

"Saboor recovered his rifle."

"He kept it?" Afdar pressed.

"Yes, he said that despite its outward appearance it was in excellent condition. He said the Russian scope body was actually camouflage for a laser range-finding scope."

Afdar gaped. "This...laser range-finding telescope. It is a digital device?"

Daei's cold feeling turned icy. "I suppose it would be..."

"The phone!" The little technician broke into a sprint for his lab, followed by Daei. Afdar's mind whirled. The phone's processor had been most cleverly devised, but he had found the secret encryption within it. His computer was busily cracking the code. He had disabled the phone's ability to make or receive calls, and he had scanned it for bugs. However if a bug was inactive, it was inert. If the enemy had somehow implanted a bug into the phone that he had missed, and if a frequency he hadn't already bombarded the phone with was being transmitted by satellite...

Afdar flew through the door to his lab and skidded to a halt in front of his workstation. The American's phone lay on a cloth like a frog on a dissecting table. The pistol barrel and its round of ammo lay off to one side. The antenna was disconnected. A few of its components were still connected by wires. Others were connected to devices of Afdar's own devising that were working away to break the underwritten encryption in the phone's small but surprisingly powerful processor. Afdar's jaw opened in slow horror as he stared at one of his monitors. A small window on the screen had popped up. It displayed a frequency wave pattern that rose and fell in a regular pattern of spikes and valley like a heart-rate monitor.

The phone was transmitting a signal.

THE CHOPPER THUNDERED across the rooftops. The late-afternoon sun lay low and waning in the west. Night raids were always preferable, but the window of opportunity was too narrow. There simply was no time. They were going in, and in broad daylight. Bolan sat next to Babar. Eight handpicked Black Storks in full raid gear sat stone-faced on the benches. The military, and particularly the special forces of Pakistan, was staunchly secular. It didn't appreciate religious extremists misbehaving in the FATA. Pakistan wouldn't allow the United States to run independent operations in her sovereign territory, but Subedar Babar had given his superiors a full report, and his superiors weren't pleased with the situation. Babar was in command, but the Americans would be allowed to "observe."

Aaron Kurtzman had gotten a full war load delivered to the Islamabad CIA station, and Bolan was armed with state-of-the-art equipment.

Ous had insisted on coming along, but the old warrior had been forced to admit that he had never fast-roped out of a helicopter and was in no shape to do so. However, he, Keller and four more Black Storks were deploying on the street around the warehouse.

The copilot spoke across the secure channel. "One minute to target!" The door gunners racked the actions on their weapons and armed their electric triggers. Bolan and his adopted team checked their weapons and gear one final time. Two air crewmen prepped the fast ropes. The helicopter slewed around in a circle over the warehouse. Babar looked at Bolan, who nodded.

The Pakistani cut his hand through the air. "Now! Full saturation!"

The starboard door gunner leaned out in his chicken straps and pointed his Mk 19 grenade launcher straight down. The gunner pushed his trigger and began walking a line of tear-gas grenades through the warehouse skylights. He didn't stop until his 32-round can of ammo was empty. "Gas deployed!"

"Reload with less than lethal! Everyone! Masks on!"

Bolan pulled his gas mask down over his balaclava. He checked the seal and strapped his helmet tight.

"Ropes!" Babar called.

The air crewmen released the ropes on either side of the fuselage and they spilled down to the cracked and shattered skylights.

Babar grinned savagely through the lines and craters of scar tissue marring his face. "Go with God!"

Bolan was taking point.

"Go! Go! Go!"

The Executioner pushed off the safety on the rifle strapped to his chest. He took the thick strand of fast-rope between his gloved hands and stepped into empty air. His descent speed was just short of suicidal, but he had men behind him and they needed to penetrate the warehouse instantly. Bolan's boots crunched through broken skylight glass. The rope hitched for just a moment, and then the rest of the coil dropped to the warehouse floor, which was a maze of mounded textiles on pallets. When the soldier touched down, he found himself in a fog of tear gas and the fog of war.

He took three rounds in the chest.

Bolan slapped leather for his thigh holsters and filled his hands. The Beretta 93-R's 3-round burst sent his opponent stumbling backward. A single round from the .50-caliber Desert Eagle took off everything above the terrorist's eyebrows.

Two more Black Storks crashed through the skylights and descended the fast ropes like spiders. A man with an AK-47 manifested himself through the gas concentration. He coughed and wheezed and raised his rifle to shoot the Pakistani operators off their ropes. Bolan's weapons snarled and boomed. A triburst made the man drop his rifle, and a .50-caliber skull-crusher punched the man to the floor.

Subedar Babar came crashing down through the glass. Good leaders always lead from the front. The exception was jumping out of airplanes and helicopters. Then their job was to make sure their team got down safe, and as last man out, surprise had long since been lost and they were a prime target. Babar's boots hit the floor. "Team away!"

The pilot shouted back through the radio. "Black Wing One, resuming station!" The helicopter rose to circle the warehouse and put its support weapons to bear where needed.

Bolan linked up with Babar. "Teams! Two by two! Begin sweep!" The Black Storks broke into two-man fire teams and began sweeping the warehouse. The soldier and his ally took their sector. The teams began reporting back.

"Team Three! Sector clear!"

"Team Two! Sector—!" The interior of the warehouse thundered.

Bolan and Babar swept in. A Black Stork clutched his bleeding arm and jerked his head at the door to the office suite. There was a surveillance camera over the lintel and a pattern of buckshot through the door. The Pakistani operative grimaced. "The woman! She is in there!"

Bolan put a 3-round burst into the camera, holstered his pistols and unclipped his rifle. The Black Storks were armed with sound-suppressed MP-5s. The Executioner aimed his SCAR rifle, which had a grenade launcher mounted beneath it, and fired a CS tear gas canister through the door. Two blasts of buckshot answered in return. Bolan loaded a fresh grenade and kicked the door.

Na'ama Shushan's flat, dead, sociopathic shark eyes had been replaced by orbs of burning, red-veined hatred. She had tossed aside her shotgun and like any good, well-trained Mossad agent, she raised her .22-caliber Beretta and drilled three rounds in Bolan's chest. She snapped her aim up, and Bolan lowered his head as two bullets lit up his helmet like a boxer's jab. He slid around the trigger of his grenade launcher and fired from the hip. The less-than-lethal round blasted out forty-eight, .48-caliber submunitions. The rubber buckshot rounds hit Shushan in a cloud. She shuddered beneath the mass flailing and fell.

Bolan stalked into the room. Shushan was in bad shape. It looked like her left eye had been pulped. There was no room for mercy in this place. He drove the butt of his rifle into her guts and saw her cringe into a fetal position. "Prisoner! Zip her! Stabilize her and extract her!"

Black Stork Team 3 ran into the room. One man began to pat her down for weapons while the other examined her eye and took out zip restraints and called in extraction.

"All street units converge," Bolan ordered.

Bolan kicked over the desk and looked for hidden hatches. "They had tunnels in Afghanistan."

"Then every pile of fabric is a possible cover," Babar said. "All units, look beneath the pallets! We are looking for a hidden—"

One of the piles blew sky-high, sending fabric ribboning in all directions and two Black Stork's pinwheeling into the piles. Babar began blaspheming in Urdu as the radio was alive with queries. Bolan frowned at the smoking hole in the warehouse floor. The Pakistani soldiers were lucky. The explosion's main task was to seal the tunnel, not take out trespassers. The charge had done its job. It would take an hour to dig out the concrete and rebar filling the coffin-size crater.

"We have an unknown number of targets escaping through a tunnel," Bolan said into his transceiver. "I need sentries in the sewers."

It was a gamble. The soldier didn't have much in the way of reserves, and the tunnel could easily lead to another building or alternate escape route; but if you were digging escape tunnels in a major metropolis, the sewers would be your quickest easiest bet.

"Copy that, pulling up the grid, sending units down," Agent Farkas reported.

Bolan turned at the sound of a scream behind him, and broke into a sprint as it was joined by a second. He skidded back into the office suite. One Black Stork was clutching his hyperextended elbow. The other was rolling around on his back, clutching his damaged knee. The window behind the lab station was smashed out. "She got away!"

The Executioner saved recriminations for later. He tossed away his rifle and vaulted to the desktop and dived out the window. Bolan knew how to take a high fall but, the concrete still hit him with brutal impact. He slapped out of the fall and rolled to his feet, ripping off his gas mask and breaking into a run.

Shushan sprinted down the alley. Despite being gassed and losing an eye, the assassin was very spry. Being a maniac had its advantages. "I got Shushan outside the perimeter! North side! Heading for the boulevard!"

"Copy that!" Keller confirmed. "Intercepting!"

"I want her alive!"

"Copy that!"

Shushan sprinted down the street. A very pregnant woman in an aqua-blue burka stepped into her line of escape. The pregnant woman screamed and raised her hands. Shushan kept running, and Bolan became very aware she was running for a manhole thirty yards ahead. The pregnant woman plastered herself against the wall as Shushan approached.

Agent Keller's burka was a CIA special.

The azure modesty garment tore away, revealing Agent Keller in sweat-soaked digital camouflage BDUs covered by the breasts and belly of a pregnancy simulation suit. Shushan missed the comical effect as Keller hurled the wad of fabric in a cotton cloud into the assassin's path. Shushan flailed as the burka enveloped her and broke her stride. Keller threw a round kick that folded the woman in two and sent her sprawling. The NCIS agent stripped the weighted poncho away from her body with both hands.

Keller began beating Shushan's shrouded, struggling form with thirty pounds of pregnancy armor. The second the assassin's struggles weakened Keller put a knee in her chest and went to work with her right hand. A palm strike to the mandible left the assassin limp.

"Hook her and book her!" the soldier called.

"What about you?"

Bolan ran past her, heading for the manhole. "I'm going down!"

CHAPTER NINETEEN

Dank and Stank came to mind as Bolan descended into the Islamabad sewer system. It was modern by most standards. The city had been built almost from the ground up, and the sewer system had been designed in the 1950s by Greek consultants. That didn't keep it from reeking like a goat rotting by the side of the road under the summertime sun. Bolan ignored the stench. He removed the folding foregrip on the Beretta and clicked a tactical light in its place. Keller's voice came from above.

"Cooper! I'm coming down!"

"Clear."

Keller descended the iron rungs and her boots hit the filthy water. She unslung her carbine and nodded. "Babar confirms the tunnel leads to the sewers."

"I thought it was going to take his men an hour to dig through."

"He says they can tell by the smell," Keller said.

"Fair enough."

"He's mobilizing local and federal police, as well as army units, to drop men down every manhole and cover every storm drain, but it's going to take time."

"Time we don't have." Bolan took out his phone and tapped an application. The phone began peeping hysterically. He handed the phone to Keller. "Here."

"Your phone doesn't like you."

"It doesn't like tear gas and by its sensors I'm inundated with it," Bolan stated.

"Your phone has a sniffer?"

"No, but the built-in flashlight has a photoacoustic infrared spectroscopic application."

"And every chemical agent has its own infrared pattern." Keller gave Bolan a smile of supreme approval. "You didn't just use the gas to subdue the bad guys, you used it to mark them."

"Yeah, but any CS particulate still clinging to them or their clothes is dispersing by the second."

"So let's go see who else stinks down here."

"You're going to have to take point or I'll be lighting up that sensor like a sun."

Keller took point. "Not a problem."

Bolan drew his Desert Eagle and took rear guard position. The NCIS agent swept the sewer section ahead of them with the invisible infrared beam. The graph lines on the screen rose and fell slightly. "If I'm reading this right we are getting minor traces of CS in this sewer section, parts per million are— Jesus!"

The graph lines on the phone spiked into the red.

Bolan and Keller advanced to a sewer junction. A body lay on the lip of the raised walkway. The soldier dropped to a knee beside the corpse and recognized the man. "It's Afdar, the intelligence operative our prisoner, Jamshed, gave up."

"Looks like someone gave Afdar a hard time. One of his buddies cut his throat."

Bolan shone his tactical light on the victim. Afdar's head had just about been removed from his body. "This was done with a sword."

Keller's eyes narrowed. This was a part of the narrative

she was still having problems with. "Great. So, we have a ninja down in the sewer with us?"

"Looks that way."

The woman looked both ways. "So, you like, brought a sword with you, right?"

"No."

"So why hasn't he shot us already?" Keller asked.

"I think he's waiting for us to walk into him. We hit the warehouse hard and fast. We achieved genuine surprise. I don't think he has his rifle. If I had to bet, he has a silenced pistol of some kind. Probably a .22. We're armored, and there are two of us. He'll want to do it close."

"Good to know," Keller stated.

"Then again, if he's feeling his roots, he might pull the old ninja, 'toss the smoke bomb, come in slashing through the smog' routine."

"Do you have some kind of countermeasure for that?"

Bolan frowned. "You don't have a gas mask."

"Unfortunately no. I was holding the perimeter up top with Ous, remember?"

"You might want to stay back a bit."

Bolan holstered his Desert Eagle and pulled a gas grenade from his belt.

"You know, I can take a little tear gas. Bet you a ninja can take more."

The soldier removed the pin. "It's not tear gas." He pulled down his gas mask and glanced around the junction. "Which way does the CS trace start again?"

Keller pointed the phone down the three paths one by one and stopped on the northern section. "That one."

"Go ahead, but slow."

Keller slowly advanced down the sewer section. "It's getting stronger..." One by one the graph lines began crawling up into the red. "Stronger..."

The smoke bomb came hurtling out of the darkness.

Bolan threw himself in front of Keller. "Back! Back! Back!"

A frag grenade would have served the assassin far better. But in a concrete tube where the roof nearly scraped your head it was hard to throw a grenade far enough to keep yourself out of the lethal radius; and smoke bombs were much lighter than frag grenades or concussion weapons.

Black smoke enveloped Bolan and expanded to fill the section. The nice thing about the dark smoke in a dark sewer was that it obscured his response, which out in the daylight would have been a pleasing canary yellow. The cotter pin pinged away, and the soldier moved rapidly backward as his own cloud expanded. He fired bursts from his Beretta into the bank of gas and smoke because the ninja would be expecting him to.

He doubted the ninja would be holding his breath. He would be creeping in slowly, depending on the fabric over his mouth and a good squint to protect him from the sting of his own smoke long enough for two swift beheadings.

The ninja was wrong on both counts.

Bolan knew he was right when he caught the sound of someone sneezing in rapid fire. The sound was suddenly eclipsed by a noise like a wolverine being killed in the snow. Keller spoke across the radio. "What the hell?"

"Stay back," Bolan cautioned. "Well back."

Keller didn't need to be told twice. Bolan kept slowly backing up. The sound of coughing, choking, sneezing and yawning followed him. The stagger and scrape of footsteps was more like a man dying on his feet than the catlike step of a ninja. The soldier stepped back and found himself out of the gas and smoke cloud. The horrific noises followed. Keller was right. Tear gas wouldn't stop a ninja. Diphenyl-

aminechlorarsine would. Technically it was called DM, or
sometimes Adamsite, after the chemist Roger Adams.

Colloquially it was called nausea gas.

It was said every person had his or her breaking point.

The ninja staggered out of the smoke and gas. He was
wearing civvies. Only the sword drooping in his hand like
a reed and the sand-colored hood covering everything
except his eyes and the bridge of his nose identified him
as a Japanese assassin from ancient lineage. Adamsite hit a
victim in a rolling wave. First it acted like tear gas, affect-
ing the eyes and esophagus, producing tears and coughing.
Then on top of that, it triggered uncontrollable sneezing.
The ninja tore away his crusted cowl as another wave of
vomiting threatened to drown him. The tip of his sword
struck sparks as he stabbed it down to keep himself from
falling.

Bolan advanced.

The ninja's sword swing was weak and wild. Bolan
dodged it. He stepped in and pistol-whipped the man
with the slide of his Beretta forehand and back. The ninja
rubbernecked and dropped to his knees, slumping as his
bowels released. Severe irritation of the bowels and bladder was a secondary symptom of Adamsite poisoning. Another symptom was occasional death. The ninja had taken
a massive concentration of DM in an enclosed space. He
needed fresh air, his nasal and throat passages flushed, and
immediate medical attention.

Bolan threw the filth-encrusted ninja over his shoulder
in a fireman's carry and was glad he was still wearing his
mask. "Keller, go ahead. Fast, I need an ambulance and a
HAZMAT unit if Babar can scare it up."

"On it!"

The Executioner trudged through the muck. The aesthetics had gotten a little ugly, but the fact was he'd caught two ninjas in one week.

Not bad.

Secure Communications Room, CIA Station, Islamabad

"Two NINJAS in one week?" Kurtzman whistled. "Incredible."

Bolan nodded. "It's got to be some kind of record."

"Yeah, well, if there was an old record you were the one holding it anyway."

Bolan shrugged modestly.

Kurtzman got back to business. "So, you lost your giant."

"The infrared chemical indexing spectrometer in the phone was fantastic, but it has its limitations. The smoke and Adamsite concentrations overwhelmed it. It's going to have to be recalibrated before I use it again. Unless Babar's subterranean sweep picks him up, he's long gone."

"So what do you intend to do?"

"We have Shushan back in custody," Bolan said.

Kurtzman considered everything he knew about the rogue Israeli assassin. "Good luck with that."

"She's been turned once. I hear it gets easier every time."

"Well, that would be a genuine tiger by the tail."

"More like the devil on a leash," Bolan mused. "I just need to figure out the appropriate carrot and stick."

"Well, let's see, she's a sociopathic assassin who likes sleeping with her targets before killing them," Kurtzman offered.

"That narrows it down a bit. Don't forget that I have two ninjas."

"Thought they were supposed to be inscrutable—"

Kurtzmann frowned "—and would rather die than betray their mission."

"They don't make ninjas like they used to."

"What are you going to do, make them an offer they can't refuse?"

"Something like that."

Kurtzman leaned into the camera. "Can I watch?"

"We'll set up a camera for you."

BOLAN ROLLED ninja number two across the well-guarded med ward. The man had survived his experience with Adamsite gas. There was an aura of weariness around his eyes that even the stone-faced inscrutability of a ninja couldn't quite hide. He was handcuffed hand and foot to the wheelchair. Bolan had taken the extra precaution of bundling him into a heavy canvas motor-pool coverall backward and epoxy resining him into the chair from the middle of his back to the hems of his sleeves and pant legs. The soldier had been hoping to watch the assassin try to ninja himself and his tender orifices out of the chair. So far the assassin hadn't summoned the strength.

Soldiers in the ward nodded at Bolan and gazed at the prisoner with a mixture of hatred and interest. Rumors had spread, and it wasn't every day you got to see a real live ninja. Unlike Syed, this man was clearly Japanese in appearance. His mission had been clandestine rather than covert. He and Ninja number two had been used as lurkers and assassins and, in a sugarcoated bit of misuse of precious assets, whoever was employing the ninjas had decided to deploy them as shock troops against Bilal's village. The ninja hadn't spoken a word since Bolan had dragged him up out of the Islamabad sewer system.

Bolan rolled Ninja number two into Ninja number one's private room.

One was in bed. He was awake and slightly elevated with all four limbs in casts. Two went rigid in the chair. An expert in reading body language would have read all sorts of conflicting emotions passing across the supine ninja's face. Bolan had left instructions to keep One well under the influence of morphine to loosen him up.

The Executioner tossed the opening ball. "So, you two know each other. Good to know."

The ninjas simultaneously became as blank-faced as a stone Buddha.

"Listen, you two aren't Iga or Koga clan. If you were, I never would have taken you alive. I suspect you're from one of the splinter groups that were hastily trained and developed during World War II and after. It explains your sloppy technique and lack of discipline."

One visibly bridled from his bed. Bolan chalked it up to the morphine. The soldier wouldn't have thought it possible, but Two grew even more rigid in the wheelchair. Bolan rolled him over by the bedside and pushed a rolling table between the two men so they could both see. He flipped open the file on the table.

"This man passed himself off as an ethnic Hazara. His cover name was Syed." Bolan flipped to a picture of the Israeli assassin. "This is Na'ama Shushan." He flipped another page to a sketch of the giant. "We believe this man is in control of the operation, at least locally."

Two gave Bolan a very hard look. "We are enemy combatants. Captured in uniform. We submit ourselves to the United States Military justice and demand all rights and protections under the Geneva Convention and Protocols."

Two had made the first cardinal mistake during an interrogation. He'd opened his mouth.

Bolan returned his stare for long moments. "Now your buddy, Syed, as he was calling himself, was chosen and trained to be an operative in Central Asia because of his general appearance. Probably had too much Mongol ancestry in him than was good for him." Bolan stroked his chin in meditation. "But like I was telling a friend of mine recently, despite everything you see in the movies, ninety-nine percent of the time a ninja's job is to pass himself off as someone he isn't, rather than doing gymnastics in pajamas."

The ninjas stared at Bolan as if he were a snake in their midst.

"Now, these days, it's just so much easier to buy yourself a local asset than insert your own people. Then again, sometimes, particularly if the job is important enough, you just have to go in and do it hands-on."

The two Japanese waited silently for the rub.

"During World War II, the Office of Strategic Services determined that approximately ten percent of Japanese could pass for Chinese and vice versa." Bolan pointed his finger at the ninja in the chair. "You're one of those ten percent." The man in the chair was taller than the average Japanese, and despite being green around the gills from Adamsite exposure, with the right accent he could pass for someone from Manchuria. "I suspect you've operated more than once in Mainland China."

The ninja stopped short of flinching.

"I'll make you a deal. I won't ask you to betray your organization or any connections you may have with Japanese Intelligence. What I demand is that you tell me everything you know about the operation that you're currently engaged in."

The ninja on the bed spoke for the first time. "And if we don't? What is it you think you are threatening us with? As you surmise, we are not Koga or Iga clan. Failure in our… association is not punished with death. What is it that you think the U.S. Naval Criminal Investigative Service will do to us? Turn us over to the Justice Department?"

The ninja stopped just short of smiling at Bolan. They both knew that the day he got off his crutches it would only be a matter of time before he escaped from the authorities and be sipping drinks topped with tiny umbrellas on the Caribbean beach of his choice. There was only one problem with that theory.

"Your problem is that you aren't a prisoner of NCIS or any other United States government entity."

"And whose prisoners are we?"

"Mine." The look that passed between the ninjas was priceless. Bolan continued. "I can do anything I want to you. I can put rock salt in your catheter or take you back to the village like I did Saboor and let the women geld you."

"I am not sure I believe you would do that."

"You're right. I'm not that kind of guy. If you won't talk, you're useless to me."

"And so?"

"And I don't think you'll walk out of Qincheng Prison alive."

Bolan watched that one hit home. He leaned in close to One. "If you don't talk to me, I'll trade you to Chinese Intelligence. The PRC would give a whole hell of a lot to get their hands on the two of you. You won't escape from them. They'll rebreak your limbs every six weeks and you will talk to them. Now, you want to talk to me? Or is 'I am not sure I believe you would do that' your final answer?"

CHAPTER TWENTY

CIA Station, Islamabad

"Pretty impressive interrogation," Keller conceded. "I'm gonna have to call you the ninja whisperer from now on."

The ninjas had talked, but much of what they had said wasn't useful. They'd given their first names, which were probably false. Sota and Mu had been extensively briefed on their targets and objectives, but their employers and their masters had deliberately kept them on a need-to-know basis. They knew almost nothing about the big picture, and knew nothing about whose service they were in.

Keller flipped through the file. "Still can't believe you let them go. I can't believe I actually put them on a plane to Japan."

"I made a deal."

"You don't think old Sota and Mu'll come back and try to kill you? And me for that matter?"

"Oh, no doubt. I gave them and their organization an affront that can't be ignored, and you by association."

"So now we have to worry about them on a personal vendetta as well as what the bad guys are up to?" Keller shook her head, "You know, Coop? You are one tough read sometimes."

"I get that a lot, but don't worry about ninjas."

"I never worried about ninjas until I met you."

Bolan shrugged.

"And now that I worry about them, why should I stop?"

"Because Sota and Mu have their own asses to worry about," Bolan said.

"I thought you said ninjas killing their own as the price of failure was only in the movies."

"Yeah, but technically they're not real ninjas. They talked about their organization rather than their clan. Those boys are like foreign troops who get sent to Fort Benning for Ranger training. They get their bad-ass badge, but they're still not the real deal."

"Real enough to walk through our security like ghosts, and you still haven't told me why I don't need to worry about them."

"Because I sent their files to someone I know at PSIA."

For a moment wheels turned behind Agent Keller's eyes as she checked her mental random access files. "Public Security Investigations Agency." A slow smile broke across Keller's face. "Japanese Intelligence."

Bolan nodded. "And?"

"And, well, PSIA can't arrest them, and even if they did they would probably escape, so…"

"You're almost there," Bolan urged.

"They'll see that the file gets to…" Once again the expression on Keller's face said she couldn't believe what she was saying. "To the, *real,* ninjas?"

"The modern shinobi I've dealt with have been real bad-asses, but even at their most twisted and psycho they're still all about serving the Land of the Rising Sun. There have always been rumors that the clans occasionally do wet work for the Japanese government."

Keller's bemusement continued unabated. "Shinobi?"

"It's the term they use for themselves. The jackasses we've dealt with have gone rogue. God only knows who they're serving, but it's not Japan and they're doing it for money, or worse reasons. The old clans up in the mountains won't like that."

"Iga or Koga?"

"Or clans I've never heard of. Regardless, there are rules. I think they've been broken, and if I'm right, there'll be a reckoning."

"Like decapitated heads and stuff?" Keller asked.

"At least two I can think of," Bolan confirmed. "Probably trunkfuls."

"You know, it's like you came out of a comic book or something."

"More like a graphic novel."

Keller smirked. "So what do you make of what they told us?"

"It fits the MO. We have off-the-rack and ready-made assassins spreading terror."

Keller frowned. "You still believe the hit on Attaché Millard in Helmand Province was a feint?"

Bolan gave the NCIS agent a frank look. "If I hadn't taken this job you'd still be investigating it, using traditional methods, and believing the Taliban was behind it."

Keller rolled her eyes. "Yeah, yeah, I know, and we wouldn't have found out about the fun going on in the FATA, much less Persian assassins and nonsanctioned ninjas or anything else. Don't rub it in."

"Millard's killing wasn't random. It helps their cause, but killing U.S. diplomats or U.S. personnel isn't their goal. Their attacks on us have been more subtle. Think about it. What's easier, attacking a U.S. Marine base or blackmailing the servicemen on it?"

"You're right, but it still begs the question of who they are and what they are really up to," Keller stated.

"The obvious answer is to destabilize the region."

"I wouldn't exactly call the region stable now."

"No," Bolan admitted, "but right now the West has co-operation, or at least some degree of it, with the Pakistan and Afghan governments. We also have a base in Kyrgyz-stan they've threatened to close on occasion that's pretty central to our mission here."

"So the kettle is already whistling and someone wants to kick it over," Keller concluded.

"Someone wants to burn down the kitchen if not the whole house."

"So what do we do about it?"

"Sota and Mu were debriefed in India," Bolan said.

"India? Whoever briefed them is long gone."

"Maybe, but our only other lead is to go back to the FATA and start to operate illegally in Pakistan, go to war with the Taliban on the ground and hope some of the real bad guys show their faces."

"Right. Sucky plan. So what do we do in India?" Keller queried.

"Stick our heads out."

Keller groaned. "And hope someone takes a swipe at cutting them off."

"Yeah, and we have one wild card up our sleeve."

"You know, it's like I don't want to know, but I can't help myself. Do tell."

Bolan leaned back in his chair. "Those files I sent to the PSIA that with luck will reach the real ninjas?"

"Yes…"

"I left a message saying where you and I were going in India," Bolan said.

"Oh my God!"

"Pack your bags. I'll tell Ous and Babar. We're hopping a courier jet to Kolkata in an hour."

CIA Station, Kolkata, India

"KOLKATA WAS sweltering. The CIA station wasn't large. It took up a modest Victorian building, but had all the modern appurtenances, including a secure communications room and a surprisingly large armory. Bolan and Ous shared a room. Keller shared one with a female intelligence analyst. It was day three in India, and they had been cooling their jets. Keller and Ous were both chafing for some action. Bolan had taken the opportunity to fly in the CIA groomer and have the rest of his disguise removed. There was bruising from where the threads of fake scar tissue had been removed from under his skin and the dyes removed, but now he looked like a man who had been in a fistfight and possibly won rather than the horribly scarred victim of a war crime.

Bolan sat in dining room of the old mansion drinking beer and eating tandoori chicken wings with Ous, Babar and Keller. The NCIS agent gnawed a bone and gave the soldier a pointed look. "Not that I don't like beer and chicken wings, and I've always wanted to see India, but how much longer are we going to wait here?"

The big American cracked a fresh beer. "As long as I think it's productive."

Keller sighed. "Pass me a beer."

A CIA agent ran into the room breathlessly. "Mr. Cooper!"

"Yes, Mr. Todd?"

Mr. Todd seemed flustered. "You have a guest!"

"Oh?" Bolan asked. "Who?"

"Sir!" The analyst gathered himself and stood straight

as he delivered news he didn't feel comfortable delivering. "I don't know. He just...appeared."

"Appeared?"

"Inside the foyer."

Bolan began to gather where this was going. "I gather no one checked him in at the gate?"

Todd stood even straighter. "Sir?"

"Yes, Mr. Todd?"

"He pretty much, just, manifested himself in the foyer."

"Manifested himself?" Bolan probed.

"Yes, Mr. Cooper." Todd was a little shamefaced. "Then security noticed him."

"Our guest wouldn't happen be of Japanese descent, would he?"

"As far as I can tell, yes, sir. I believe he is."

"Show him in, if you would be so kind," Bolan directed.

"Yes, sir!"

Todd faded back. Bolan rose as his guest appeared in the doorway. The ninja looked like any other Japanese businessman, except that his shoulders were broader than most and his posture was both utterly relaxed and perfect. Despite the heat and the suit, he wasn't sweating. He was immaculate. He wore glasses, but Bolan doubted he needed them. The force of the man rang through the room like a sonar array actively pinging.

Bolan and the ninja stared at each other for several moments. The ninja bowed. "Cooper-san."

The Executioner exactly matched the ninja's bow. *"Bushi-sama."*

Bushi was the Japanese word for warrior. *Sama* was the second highest honorific in the Japanese language. Among Japanese, it was used to acknowledge someone of higher status than one's self. Coming from a Westerner, it was simply the height of good manners. The ninja bowed again. "Kengo."

Bolan bowed once more in return and used the name given him. "Kengo-san, may I introduce NCIS Agent Keller."

Kengo bowed. Keller took Bolan's cue and bowed exactly as deeply.

"And my good friend Mr. Ous and our ally Subedar Babar."

Ous and Babar inclined their heads. Kengo nodded and turned his slightly disturbing attention on Bolan. Except for using the *san* honorific, his English was devoid of any accent. "Cooper-san, the current situation is unacceptable."

"I agree completely," Bolan agreed.

"All aspects of Japanese involvement in this situation must be erased."

Bolan nodded. "I do not believe my mission can be achieved without your assistance."

Kengo gave Bolan a distinctly noninscrutable look. "A man who matches your—" Kengo spent a moment choosing his words "—operational behavior, is, rumored to have operated in Japan on more than one occasion."

Bolan simply bowed. He figured it was fifty-fifty whether Kengo had been sent to kill him or to die if necessary in assisting him.

"Whatever is happening in Central Asia must be stopped."

"We are in complete agreement," Kengo said.

"How may I be of assistance to you?"

"My things are outside. I paid a boy to watch them. I must speak with my superiors, and in the meantime I will accept any living space available," Kengo stated.

"Todd," Bolan said, "show Kengo-san to his quarters and bring in his belongings."

Kengo bowed. "This evening we must talk."

"I look forward to working with you."

Kengo bowed once more. He followed Todd and then stopped for a moment and looked back at Bolan. "You will be interested to know that Sota and Mu are no longer a factor in your investigation."

Bolan nodded. Kengo returned the nod and left the room.

"So...that's a *real* ninja?" Keller asked.

"The real deal."

Ous lit his pipe. "He looks nothing like the ninjas Chuck Norris has defeated."

Babar nodded.

Every once in a while Bolan forgot that even in the second decade of the twenty-first century, Chuck Norris was considered nearly a god in many countries.

"He won't like that, until it's time to look like that. And when he does look like that—" Bolan shook his head "—you'll never see him."

Ous took a tug on his pipe. "That man is extremely dangerous."

"We need him."

Analyst Todd came back in with two suitcases. "I told Mr. Kengo we couldn't bring in his belongings without examining them."

"And?" Bolan probed.

"He bowed."

"Put them on the table."

Keller and Ous both stood curiously. Bolan flipped open the cases. The first simply contained a number of changes of clothes and personal effects. One corner of Bolan's mouth quirked upward. Ous smiled. One of those changes was the ninja black pajamas and hood of movies and yore. The second case caught the attention of everyone in the room.

Kengo-san was loaded for bear.

The second case was loaded with weapons. The ninja had a pair of Glocks. One was chambered in .357 SIG with a ported barrel and custom combat sights. The closest thing to a death-ray that a human could hold in one hand was a .357 Magnum revolver loaded with 125-grain hollowpoint rounds. The Swiss engineers at SIG had done everything in their power to replicate that round's performance and make it feed reliably through a semiautomatic. Kengo's Glock was the weapon of a gunfighter.

The other Glock was a Jonathon Arthur Cienar .22-caliber conversion, and the barrel was threaded for the sound suppressor packed in foam next to it. He'd also packed a tactical stock and scope mount with optics. This Glock was the weapon of an assassin. The case also contained several electronic devices that Bolan had to admit he couldn't immediately identify. He took out the one "ninja" weapon the case contained. The curved Tanto dagger was sixteen inches long, but it was a modern weapon rather than an ancient samurai heirloom. The handle was kraton plastic rather than wood, ray-skin and silk. The Velcro tabs on the Kydex scabbard clearly allowed the weapon to be worn in a shoulder holster or several other configurations. Bolan drew the dagger and his eyes narrowed at what he saw.

Nearly all samurai weapons—katanas, short swords, daggers and pole arms—were curved to allow a deep, slicing saberlike cut. Kengo's weapon was disturbingly sharpened on the inside of the curve like a sickle. The outer curve of the blade was abnormally thick for strength and leverage. Keller pointed an accusing finger at the rather menacing curve of steel. "That's messed up."

"It's a *kubikiri*," Bolan confirmed.

"And what does that mean?"

"Roughly translated from the Japanese—" Bolan sheathed the weapon "—it means *head cutter*."

"And Sota and Mu are no longer a factor in our investigation," Ous said.

"Like I said, probably trunkfuls."

Ous raised an eyebrow. "Trunkfuls of heads?"

"Kengo's clan wants all traces of Japanese involvement in whatever is going on erased," Bolan placed the blade back in its packing. "And he wants to send a very clear message to whoever is orchestrating this—don't play with ninjas and don't ever involve the Land of the Rising Sun."

Ous nodded, took a tug on his pipe and blew a smoke ring. "I like him."

CHAPTER TWENTY-ONE

"He just doesn't look like a ninja," Keller muttered.

Kengo came down the stairs wearing sports sandals, khaki cargo shorts, a vintage Hawaiian aloha shirt and a pair of Wayfarer sunglasses. A battered, Hokkaido Nippon-Ham Fighters ball cap completed his look. Except for the fact that he had forearms and calves like bowling pins he looked like a Japanese tourist who had come to see one of the big festivals. It was an excellent tailoring job. Only an eye as practiced as Bolan's would detect the man was well armed. He gave Bolan and his team a big grin. "Good morning!"

"Morning, Kengo-san."

"Oh, call me Ken. All my western friends do."

It wasn't lost on Bolan that "Ken" in Japanese was another word for sword. Bolan eyed Kengo's cap. "Fighter fan, huh?"

Kengo's grin turned rueful. Since 1947, the Hokkaido Nippon-Ham Fighters had been just about the most losing team in Japanese professional baseball, and the least popular. They called themselves "The Fighters," but their full name with their parent Nippon-Ham organization made them sound like some strange brand of ritual Japanese meat gladiators. They were a source of never-ending fun for sports commentators and fans of other teams. "I was born into a Nippon-Ham Fighter fan family." He shook his head sadly. "It is a burden that must be borne."

"I know people who are Oakland Raiders fans," Bolan said consolingly. "It doesn't necessarily make them bad people."

Kengo grunted in amusement.

Bolan found himself liking the ninja. That was good because Kengo and whatever clan he represented were just about the only card he was holding anymore, and it was a wild card. He was depending on the hope that Kengo and his clan had spent the intervening seventy-two hours before Kengo's arrival doing some very brutal cleanup back in Japan, and in the process had generated some new leads. Bolan's biggest concern was that they had, but wouldn't be big on sharing information.

That didn't seem to be a problem for Kengo. "We have taken control of Sota and Mu's organization."

"Who were they?"

"They were not a true clan. As the Second World War expanded, and particularly as Japan started to know defeat, martial artists, Yakuza, soldiers and others were recruited, given as much training as possible and put into operation by clans, including my own, as an emergency measure. They were not true Shinobi. Their clansmen did not train them from birth. Nor were they used as Shinobi. All too often they were used as little more than clandestine shock troops. Most of these ad-hoc Shinobi units were ground up and died as the American fleet rolled up the Pacific and the Chinese rose in their hordes to repel the Imperial Japanese Army. Nevertheless, some groups survived. After the war they continued to operate, using their unit designations. They often sold their services in battles between rival Yakuza syndicates. Japan has many enemies, and sometimes they were used against them. So for the most part the clans tolerated their activities."

Kengo's story jibed with most of what Bolan knew. "Sota and Mu's unit went rogue."

"Sota and Mu were third-generation Whispering Pines, and despite that unit's brave and noble service during the war, they have strayed far from the path in the modern era."

"What's the status of the Whispering Pine now?"

"In the past four days they have undergone what might be described as a hostile takeover and reorganization."

Keller grinned. "Tell me the bad guys don't know this has happened."

"This action took place under the auspices of my clan. We were most thorough. However, the Whispering Pine, to their credit, did not lie down quietly. Many of them were killed, including much of their hierarchy. This has left us with an incomplete picture of who exactly contracted them and what the true ambitions of this unknown agency may be. This is why my clan has ordered me to cooperate with you. We must pool our resources to resolve this problem.

"And it is our current assessment that the takeover happened without our enemy's knowledge, and we still have a line of communication with them."

Ous blew a smoke ring. "Our enemy will believe that you are Whispering Pine ninjas, and work for them."

"That is our sincere hope, Mr. Ous. However, there is a very real possibility that the enemy knows something is terribly wrong and setting us up for an ambush."

Babar scratched his scar-divided beard. "I am not sure I can pass for Japanese."

Kengo laughed. "No, and neither can Ous. Even if I had the time and resources to remake you, I do not believe your accents and mannerisms could be suppressed, and we will only have one shot at this."

"What about me? You gonna Geisha me up?" Keller quirked an eyebrow at Bolan. "He put me in a burka."

"I believe it would be best if you take the role of command and control, and along with Mr. Ous and Subedar Babar be our strike team if we require reinforcement."

Ous tugged on his pipe and peered at Bolan. "Am I to believe that you are going to turn our friend Japanese?"

Everyone in the room looked at Bolan. Kengo fold his arms across his chest in confidence and smiled. "I believe he will make a fine ninja."

BOLAN REMEMBERED his mother once said that one had to suffer for beauty. Ninja beauty school had a harsh headmistress. Upon Bolan's acquiescence to the transformation, a crate had miraculously manifested itself outside the CIA station's gate and Kengo had gone to work. The soldier was six-three, and 220 pounds of solid muscle. Nothing could be done about his size. Everything else appeared to be fair game. Like all skin colors, Asian skin tone was mostly determined by melanin and sun exposure. Kengo chemically peeled away Bolan's saddle-leather "Mighty One" sun damage, and then used his own, self-described "midtone Asian" coloring as a template. Asians also tended to have significantly smaller skin pores than Caucasians, which had led many Westerners historically to describe the Asian complexion of having a "porcelain" look.

Kengo deep-cleansed Bolan's pores and temporarily contracted them chemically. The effect was very subtle but the before-and-after difference was huge.

Kengo didn't stop there. He sculpted Bolan's eyebrows and took his self-inflicted number-four shag and clipped it down to a three. Kengo thickened and coarsened Bolan's hair so that it looked like it was one step away from the "hedge-hog" look that a lot of Asians got when they started to grow out their hair. He stripped away nearly all of Bolan's body hair above and below the waist. Keller was all giggles during the process. "Give him the bikini wax, Ken! I want him to taste the pain!"

Both warriors declined on either inflicting it or enduring it.

The eyes were where he did his best work. Bolan received a number of injections. Kengo insisted it wasn't Botox. The process wouldn't involve the nerve enervation of a Botox injection, and he insisted it would work much faster and the effects would wear off over a period of a week or two. He also insisted that unlike Botox, the effects could be chemically reversed in a matter of hours.

Whatever cosmetic concoction Kengo injected into the soldier's face, Bolan thought it burned like fire.

Bolan spent the night feeling like a runner who had hit the lactic acid threshold, except he felt the burning and cramping in the muscles around his eyes rather than in his legs. Only one in several million Asians sported baby-blues like Bolan's. Very dark brown, almost black extended-wear contact lenses took care of that. The soldier put them in and went downstairs to the library for his big reveal.

For a moment stunned silence gripped Bolan's team. Keller was the first to speak. "Oh…my…God."

Kengo nodded. "I am very pleased."

Bolan looked at himself in the library's full mirror. Whatever Kengo had injected him with had pulled the corners of his eyes up, the inner corners slightly down. The process hadn't only changed the shape of his eyes but narrowed them. The same process had slightly lifted the outer corners of his eyebrows and again slightly drawn the inner corners down. The effect was an almost permanent though mild look of disdain for everything he saw, like a haughty Mongolian conqueror. Bolan's new "hawklike" gaze would have given the ninja Syed a run for his money. The Executioner had done a few quick draw drills in his room before coming down and was pleased to find the alterations hadn't affected his peripheral vision. Short of radical plastic surgery, which Bolan had undergone more than once in his War Everlasting, he had to admit even to himself that this was the most unrecognizable he had ever seen himself. It literally felt like he was wearing a mask, and talking and eating tended to tug on it uncomfortably.

There was nothing to be done about Bolan's nose, cheekbones or chin. He didn't specifically look Japanese. Indeed he looked like a man of mixed ancestries. Adding in his size and build, what Bolan did look like was the kind of man rogue ninjas would send to clean up someone else's mess.

He looked like a killing machine of Asian manufacture.

Babar grinned and ran his fingers across the railroad tracks of scarring across his face. "I wish to be next!"

"Quite remarkable," Ous agreed, "Unless you spoke, I would not recognize you on the street."

"Speaking of that," Kengo said. "I am pleased that I cannot detect what part of the United States you are from by your accent. I will speak to our contacts in English at all times. You will do the same. I do not claim any command or seniority over you, but ninjas often work in pairs, so publically I will be *sempai*."

Sempai meant senior and often mentor. Bolan nodded, "And I'm *kohai*, your protégé or assistant."

"Correct. However, if for any reason you feel the need to speak, please do so. By necessity my people have a somewhat relaxed attitude about these things, particularly in the field."

"Got it."

"However, should someone besides myself speak to you

in Japanese, simply turn to me. I will sort the situation out."

"And what do you suggest if you're not around?"

"Kill them instantly. Whoever it is will not be a friend of ours."

Bolan ran a hand over his tingling, tightened and tinted face. "I've never been a ninja before. Any special equipment needs?"

"We have little in the way of specific issue weapons. We only don the traditional dress and use swords when we wish to terrorize our opponents, and deliberately let them know whom it is they are dealing with."

Keller gave Kengo a dry look. "What about that head sickle you're packing?"

Kengo sighed tolerantly. "Agent Keller, taking off a grown man or woman's head quickly and cleanly, even with a sword or an ax, is far more difficult than you may have been lead to believe. In fact swords and axes designed to decapitate are usually useless for any other activity. In feudal Japan the taking of heads as trophies in battle was commonplace. The *kubikiri* was designed to be the most efficient tool to remove a head that a warrior could easily carry along with the rest of his weapons and equipment. Despite modern advances in forensic science, in my profession we still believe that the presentation of the head provides the absolute most positive proof that we have succeeded in our mission."

Keller looked askance at Kengo. "Got it."

Kengo turned to Bolan. "To answer your question, I would recommend whatever easily concealable weapons rig you feel most comfortable with." He gave Bolan a sly look of challenge. "I can provide you with a kubikiri if you wish."

"Definitely," Bolan replied. "When's our meet?"

"Tonight, and until then I recommend you eat soft food and rest your face." The ninja grinned happily. "It may be a long night."

Kolkata Station, Secure Communications Room

"HOLY CRAP!" It took a great deal to startle Aaron Kurtzman. Bolan's new look coming across the streaming satellite link was up to the task. It was even more rare to see the man utterly dumbfounded. "Stricker, you're…"

"Yes?"

"You're Japanese."

"That was the plan," Bolan stated.

"Or some…unreasonable facsimile thereof. What did they do to you?"

"Secret ninja techniques," Bolan replied.

"Really?" Kurtzman blinked. He leaned into the camera. "How does it feel?"

"Hurts like hell."

"So what's the plan?" Kurtzman asked, getting down to business.

"Kengo says the information his clan got out of the Whispering Pine massacre was incomplete. We don't know much about the enemy. Kengo's clan does have an open line of communication. His clan has set up a meet. Ous and I did some real damage to the Whispering Pine contingent in the FATA. It's natural that they would want answers and payback. The plan is to pass ourselves off as genuine Whispering Pines, be employed as assets and break open the investigation."

"Tall order." Kurtzman shook his head. "Then again, look at you. Just look at you."

"We'll pass along some nonessential data on NCIS and

the state of its investigation. Though I think our best opening bid might be the Shushan woman."

"You're going to offer to ninja her out of captivity?"

"With Keller and Farkas orchestrating it from behind the scenes," Bolan told him. "They got her out once. That tells me they have something big planned for her. I think they just might want her out again."

"And have you figured a way to ensure her loyalty?"

"Not yet."

"So what are you going to do?" Kurtzman asked.

"Tonight?" Bolan checked his watch. "Go take a meeting."

CHAPTER TWENTY-TWO

Bolan drove. The CIA had slicked up the Hindustan Motors Contessa. The vehicle had been manufactured in the nineties and had the appearance of a U.S. seventies muscle car. The slicking up had all been on the inside. The exterior was scratched and dinged. The faded paint that had once been "ox-blood" red could now be described charitably as rusted-out brown, and that was where the primer wasn't showing through. On the other hand the suspension was tip-top and as tight as a drum for a car of its age, much less one that'd had always had the reputation of being soft in the rear. The rumble and clank of the engine told Bolan that someone had taken out the old 4-cylinder gasoline engine and dropped in a highly modified Isuzu 6-cylinder turbo-diesel. He had liked the car on sight and had a vague urge to put the pedal down to see what the old girl could really do.

The soldier rolled along the west bank of the River Hooghly. He and Kengo both had their windows open to catch the evening breeze off the river. North Kolkata was the oldest part of the city. Nineteenth century architecture sat surrounded by mazes of narrow alleyways. It was the oldest part of the ancient city and also one of the poorest. Kengo watched slums, sweatshops, ancient temples and relics of the British raj pass by. He made a circular gesture with his hand that encompassed the city and Bolan's driving.

"You have operated in Kolkata before."

Bolan didn't deny it.

"May I ask you a question?" Kengo asked.

"Sure."

"What are you thinking about?"

Kengo was the most unninjalike person Bolan had ever met. More and more it convinced him that Kengo was indeed the very real deal. The man had been utterly forthright with every question asked of him. Bolan saw no reason not to return the favor. "Assassins."

Kengo stared at Bolan for a moment. "Interesting subject."

"My investigation started in Afghanistan. There was evidence there that we were dealing with the Persian *Hashasheen*."

"The Ismaili Assassins. I have heard of them."

"I've had dealings with them before," Bolan stated.

"Really?"

"Then I came to Pakistan and discovered ninjas."

"Well…" Kengo laughed. "That is to your credit."

"Oh?"

"Oh yes. Most people do not discover ninjas," Kengo said. "Usually in these kinds of situations ninjas discover them, and then they are never heard from again."

Once more Bolan found himself liking Kengo. "Now I'm in India, and I think of another breed of assassins."

Kengo nodded thoughtfully. "You speak of the Thuggees of Kali."

"I've opposed them before."

"I believe you."

"When I last dealt with them, I thought I had destroyed them. At the time they could turn invisible and had stolen three Pakistani nuclear warheads."

Kengo internalized this. "You are a very interesting person."

"It goes back to my original theory," Bolan said.

"Off-the-rack assassins, yes, and thank you for sharing your file with me. You suspected elements of the Persian Assassins. Tell me, did you destroy them, as well?"

"All who opposed me."

Kengo took a moment to take that in, as well. "And now you suspect that perhaps you were not thorough enough in your destruction of the Thuggees."

"Perhaps."

Kengo chewed that over. "There is a saying in Japan, that when one stamps upon a nest of snakes it is not always certain that some few may have wriggled away among all the wriggling."

"Not bad."

Kengo gave Bolan a curious look. "Could they truly turn themselves invisible?"

"You're a ninja," Bolan countered. "Can't you?"

"It is said that a ninja can walk through walls. Listened for, he cannot be heard. Looked for, he cannot be seen. Felt, he cannot be touched."

It hurt Bolan's face but he smiled. "You stole that from *Kung Fu*."

Kengo laughed. "That was a good show."

"It was."

Kengo verbally diverted. "How does your face feel?"

"It's starting to go numb."

"That is normal. You will be able to make facial expressions, but you will have to make them deliberately."

Bolan glanced in the rearview mirror. He deliberately smiled at his reflection. He frowned with effort, and it took two seconds of conscious effort to raise his eyebrows out of the V Kengo had given him to match. He stopped trying, and his face fell back into the predatory scowl.

Kengo shrugged. "There are worse things for a ninja than having a battle mask for a face." Bolan pulled the car over by the banks of Hooghly. Kengo glanced at him questioningly. "Yes?"

"You've been extremely helpful."

"Within limits, I have been ordered to be so," Kengo said.

"Since we're going in together, I figured one good turn deserved another."

Kengo considered this. "Thank you?"

"I told you when I fought the Thuggees they could turn invisible."

"Yes, I found this very intriguing."

"They were using light-transfer technology," Bolan stated.

"Fiber-optic receptors." Kengo nodded to himself. "Transferring light from one side of an object to another."

"It was crude. They hadn't figured out how to make it into armor or clothing. They were pretty much hiding under fiber-optic bed comforters, but when they weren't moving, you didn't see them. You saw what was behind them. All you saw was the room or the landscape," Bolan explained.

"I will tell you that my people have been very interested in this for some time, but I find it hard to believe that India has developed this technology."

"Why's that?" the soldier probed.

"Because if they had, we would already have stolen it from them."

"It was the Thuggees of Kali who stole it from a Silicon Valley start-up they had infiltrated in California."

Kengo eyes narrowed. "I see."

"Like I said, it was crude. If they moved, or if there was a light source behind them, you could see distortions. But in an ambush, or an assassination situation, it gave them a terrible advantage, and they were as practiced as their forebears with their strangling cords."

Kengo mentally revisited his knowledge of assassin cults from around the world and their methods. "The rumal. Thank you Cooper-san. I will be vigilant."

"We brainstormed about how to fight invisible opponents using this technology. We came up with a number of solutions. They varied from bursting sacks of flour in the air to paint ball rifles and grenades."

"I am very grateful you have shared this information with me."

"One more thing."

Kengo cocked his head and grinned disarmingly. "Oh?"

"A woman I know locked on to the fact that the light transfer technology transferred incoming light and sent it along the fibers to the receptors behind you."

Kengo frowned. "That is the accepted view of how this technology works."

"So she figured out that if you couldn't carry sacks of flour, paint weapons, or get the overhead sprinklers to come on and reveal your opponent's shape, there was another, even better alternative."

Kengo leaned forward like a hungry man presented with a steak. "And?"

"The transfer of light from one side of the fabric to the other isn't instantaneous. The break takes place in millionths of a second. The human eye would never notice it, but it wasn't fast enough to beat a laser. Lasers are coherent light. They move at the speed of light, and when a laser hit the fabric there was a few milliseconds break when it hit and was transferred to the back."

"And even the crudest laser range-finding device would detect that break!"

"Our girl rigged up weapon-mounted lasers for us. Their main modification was that they had an audio alarm that would peep if the laser struck something that registered millisecond breaks instead of instantaneous bounce back like they would if they had hit a solid object," Bolan said.

"And you blasted anything in the direction that peeped! Simple, brilliant, perfect!"

Bolan reached into the kit between his feet and pulled out two, laser-aiming modules that had the John "Cowboy" Kissinger's genius all over it. "When I knew I was going to come to India I had a bad feeling. I had a number of laser aiming-light transferal detecting devices worked up by my organization and sent to the CIA safehouse. I noticed your Glocks had accessory rails. These are for you. If no nonfactory modifications have been done to your Glocks' lower frames, these should be properly zeroed out to twenty-five yards. If you have any rifles, carbines, shotguns, or PDWs with Picatinny rails, I have several units for them, as well."

Kengo was the most friendly, forthright, unassuming, nontraditional Japanese, much less ninja, that Bolan had ever met. Now the man's face became stone as he took the sighting units in his cupped hands, turned and bowed so low in his seat that his nose nearly brushed the upholstery. "Cooper-san, from the moment I met you, I knew you would be a gallant and honorable ally. Now it is my privilege to know you as a friend."

Bolan returned the bow. "Kengo-san, let's kick this pig."

Kengo slid the laser onto his .22-caliber Glock's accessory rail and took out a Swiss Army knife to tighten the screws. "Definitely."

New Town

"WE'RE HERE." Kengo checked his loads. Bolan pulled the Contessa and onto the construction site. "We go in as if we own the place."

New Town was one of the first modern, urban-planned parts of the city. Farmers had worked the alluvial flood plain since time out of mind. Now skyscrapers, town houses and housing developments rose like shining glass-and-steel mountains, forming a new skyline. The meeting place was a high-rise whose top seven floors still had no windows. Bare girders stuck up into the sky from the top-most floor like a crown of spikes. Construction equipment and materials littered the ground all around the high-rise in a sea of planned chaos. A chain-link fence surrounded the site, but the gate was open. The lone security shack was dark and empty.

Bolan drove through the gate and followed the gravel path down into the pitch-black parking garage. The sub-terranean level was a sea of pallets, bundled pipes and industrial-size wiring spools. He pulled to a stop. As per the arrangement, the soldier blinked his lights twice and cut the engine. For a moment the two men sat in utter darkness.

A small LED white light blinked three times ahead and off to the right. Bolan had taken a mental snapshot of his surroundings before cutting the lights. The light was coming from cover between two pallets of cable. A single row of orange emergency lights in the ceiling blinked on, throwing the underground garage into a very Halloween-like sea of dim glow and dark shadows. Bolan and Kengo stepped out of the car. A small Indian emerged from be-tween the two huge spools of cable. He barely cracked five feet tall and wore a sparkling white dhoti and an oxford shirt. A white turban topped him off, and at first glance he looked ridiculous. He pressed his hands together and bowed. "I am V."

Bolan immediately smelled the danger radiating from the man in waves. His small stature and comic relief in a Bollywood movie look were his passport for killing the unsuspecting. Kengo gave the bare minimum of a bow. "I am Ken."

The Executioner couldn't feel his face, but he knew it was set in a permanent scowl like a water buffalo and he left it that way. "I am Mas."

"You are expected, honored guests."

"We are extremely disturbed by the recent events in the FATA," Kengo said.

"As are we, Sahab-Ji." V. bowed again as he used the big Hindi honorific. "We understand that two of your men were captured. We were given to understand such a thing was impossible. We are also given to understand that the Americans released them. This, too, we find quite baffling."

Kengo was good. He managed to radiate a barely controlled rage while at the same time speaking politely. "You will be pleased to know, V.-san, that Sota and Mu are no longer of any concern."

"I see. Very well. Please accompany me." V. gestured back the way he had come. "There is someone you should meet."

Kengo and Bolan stepped forward.

The rumal whipped out from V.'s hand like a snake, striking for Kengo's throat. The ninja's blade was an orange flash in the subterranean lights. The coin in the rumal's fold, which gave the weapon striking weight and compressed the trachea once the strangle was established, sailed across the parking level. V. stared for a startled moment at the remaining six inches of cotton hanging limply in his hand. Kengo seized V.'s fingers, bones breaking as the ninja squeezed. He yanked V.'s arm straight, and the blade of the *kubikiri* chopped between the bones of V.'s wrist. Kengo twisted the blade and pulled. The ninja took off the Thuggee's hand like a butcher going through a joint of lamb.

V. gasped and sat, clutching his stump.

Bolan's pistol cleared its holster as Kengo suddenly did a remarkable imitation of man doing the limbo beneath an invisible pole. Kengo clutched at his throat and tried to stab backward with his blade, but his unseen opponent had him. Despite all of Kengo's training his enemy had all the leverage.

"Drop!" Bolan roared.

Kengo dropped. He fell completely into the strangle and forced the Thuggee to take his whole body weight. Veins pulsed across Kengo's face as the strangle sank in accompanied by his body weight. Only his training and the tensed muscles of his neck kept his trachea from cracking. Bolan was already utilizing the laser. He pointed the Beretta a foot above Kengo's head, and the aiming module peeped in rapid alarm. The soldier squeezed off three bursts from the Beretta as rapidly as he could pull the trigger. Kengo fell to the ground, gasping and coughing as his assassin released him.

Bolan spun and lased. "Back to back!"

Kengo bounced up off the floor like a slightly malfunctioning jumping jack and his Glock cleared leather. He tottered to Bolan's side and turned so that the two warriors could face all comers. They had two advantages. Every kill the Thuggees made was a ritual sacrifice to the goddess Kali. For that sacrifice to be pure, the killing had to be done without the shedding of blood.

The second advantage was that Bolan was pretty sure they didn't know about the aiming module trick.

Kengo's Glock peeped. He fired off three quick double taps.

Bolan kept scanning behind them. "Back to back, move with me." The two warriors walked in the direction of Kengo's shots. In the dull orange light the blood staining the garage floor looked black. Bolan eyed a path of drops that stopped about two yards away. He lased the end of the blood trail and the module peeped. He raised his sights a foot and fired off two quick bursts. The shadows where the blood ended imperceptibly pulsed. "Watch my back."

The soldier strode past the blood trail and crouched. His hand hit something solid, and he grabbed a handful of something that didn't appear to be there. He yanked the fabric away and found a man who could have been V.'s twin. The man wore one of Kengo's double-taps to his abdomen and six of Bolan's bullets in his chest. "Back the way we came."

Bolan and Kengo returned to the battle's starting point. The Executioner dropped to a knee beside V. as the little man moaned and rocked back and forth, holding his wrist. He reached into the man's pocket and snatched out his spare *rumal*. "How many more?"

V. clamped his jaw shut.

Bolan drew his new *kubikiri*. "Tell me what I want to know, or I'll cut off your other hand."

"Three!" V. gasped. "We were thought sufficient to deal with two."

"Is there someone in the back we need to talk to?"

"No. Since the massacre in the FATA, the involvement of your people was deemed a liability. I was ordered to see to your deaths."

"Let me explain the situation to you. We are profoundly

disturbed by what happened in the FATA. Finishing the mission, and revenging ourselves upon the Americans is now a matter of honor for us. If you do not cooperate with us in this, then revenging ourselves upon you and your people will be a matter of honor for us, as well. It is important that you explain this to your people so that they can make an informed decision about what they wish to do next. Do you understand?"

V. nodded.

"Good. As a gesture of goodwill, you may inform your superiors that we are willing to once again remove the woman from U.S. custody." Bolan tucked the rumal back in the man's pocket like an afterthought. He went over to the two dead Thuggees and took their light-transferring shrouds. "We expect you to contact us within twenty-four hours."

Bolan and Kengo returned to the car. The soldier threw the shrouds and their power packs in the trunk and locked it. Kengo didn't speak until they were back out along the river. "This was the same MO used by the Thuggees you fought before."

"Yeah. A few of them in India or Pakistan may have survived our purge and made off with some of the shrouds."

"How could they possibly be connected with the Nizari Ismaili Assassins?"

Bolan had been giving that a great deal of thought. "When I fought them before, they were modern incarnations of the ancient sects. Revivalist movements. Despite religious fundamentalism being key to their movements, both the Ismailis and the Thuggees were remarkable for being able to adapt their religious doctrine and behavior to meet changing needs, whether suddenly having to survive the Mongols or dealing with the British Raj. On top of that, the largest, modern surviving population of Ismailis is located in India."

"But the Ismailis are Muslims. The Thuggees are Hindu and worship idols. You would not think they could work together," Kengo observed.

"Like I said, both sects were famous for their ability to change with the times, and terrorism makes for strange bedfellows."

"Interesting." Kengo grew quiet. Bolan waited for the rub and it came. "Cooper-san, I will require one of the light-transfer units."

Bolan shook his head. "No."

The car got very quiet. "What if I require it for there to be any more cooperation between the two of us?"

Bolan had been waiting for that, too. "What if I said that after this mission, assuming it's successful, I would send one example to Japanese Intelligence."

Kengo considered this long and hard. "I might trust you to do this, Cooper-san, but I am not sure your government would adhere to the bargain."

"You're not dealing with my government. You're dealing with me. There's a difference."

Kengo gave this more, long moments of consideration. "Do you know, I had not thought it possible to strangle a ninja."

"I once heard a martial-arts master say that it wasn't the number of techniques that made a master, but his utter mastery of those he knew. Thuggees pretty much do one thing, that's strangle people, and they've been developing their technique for God only knows how long."

"You consistently say profound things, Cooper-san." Kengo glanced back the way they had come. "Do you believe V. will contact us?"

"I give it a fifty percent chance."

"Given the circumstances and what is at stake, those are not particularly good odds."

"Yeah, but we have a backup plan," Bolan stated.

"I would dearly love to hear it."

"I slipped a RFID in V.'s rumal. Since you cut off his hand, I doubt he'll be using it again in the next twenty-four hours, much less even taking it out of his pocket."

Kengo clapped his hands and his smile lit up the car. "Cooper-san, we are going to have to make you an honorary ninja."

CHAPTER TWENTY-THREE

"We seem to have angered the ninjas." The little man gazed sadly out of the panoramic apartment window and took in the lights of Kolkata below. Gholam Daei sipped almond honey milk as he gazed upon Sreenath Tendulkar. The two men couldn't have been a greater study in opposites. Daei could easily have passed, indeed, on more than one occasion he had been compared, to heroes out of Persian mythology. The man in front of him was short, pear-shaped, balding, bandy-armed and bow-legged. He could be charitably described as somewhat dopey-looking. Daei had absolutely no doubts whatsoever that the day Sreenath snuck up behind him with a twisted handkerchief in his hands would be the day that Gholam Daei died on his knees with his eyes bugging out of his face. "And," the man continued, "I have not only lost a brother but also lost the skills of not one but two of our greatest brethren."

V. Tendulkar sat unhappily at the breakfast bar in a haze of painkillers with his arm bound across his chest. He would never wield the rumal again. Tendulkar's third brother, Harbajan, and his accomplice Suresh still lay dead on the floor of the subterranean garage. Their bodies would be retrieved, sanctified and given proper burial when it was certain their extraction wouldn't be observed.

For Sreenath Tendulkar the night of the ninjas had been a triple blow. His identical triplet, Harbajan, was dead. V. the youngest of the trio by forty-seven minutes, was maimed. Sreenath Tendulkar was the secular leader of an ancient death cult that specialized in widespread murder, and in the current era, assassination. The ability to seemingly be in two if not three places at the same time had been an asset beyond price. "What are we to make of this turn of events?"

"The behavior of the ninjas is quite startling."

V. turned from the window. "Perhaps the problem is that the ninjas sell their souls for bowls of silver, while we commend ours to the service of a higher power."

Daei kept his discomfort with the comparison off his face. The overwhelming majority of Muslim imams would say that Daei's faith had strayed far from the tenants of Islam. Many would describe it as outright heresy. However he considered himself a devout Muslim. There was only one true god. Allah was his name, and Mohammed was his prophet. Only infidels bound for hell's flames worshipped idols.

Sreenath Tendulkar prayed at the sacred flame of a naked, four-armed goddess of Death who wore garlands of human skulls.

Gholam Daei was on total jihad. It was his purpose to bring about the global caliphate. He fully realized once this Garden of Eden was established that there might not be a place for a man like himself in it. That didn't matter. His place in Paradise was assured. From what Daei could gather, Sreenath wished to fully awaken the sleeping abomination he worshipped. Every human life extinguished by the squeeze of the rumal brought the goddess one infinitesimal step closer to awakening and performing her dance of destruction that would end the world.

The Tendulkars and their people seemed to believe the growing global jihad was an excellent step in the right direction toward the orgy of Armageddon they awaited, and they were happy to help.

"I do not want a war with a clan of ninjas," Daei said. "It would be a very dangerous and costly distraction from what must be done. If the ninjas are compelled by honor to slaughter our enemies, then I say we let them do it, and indeed, even employ them further."

"Our opponents are now aware of the involvement of ninjas," V. said.

"Indeed, and when we left our daggers as calling cards in Afghanistan, the American found out he was dealing with Ismaili Assassins. He found out about the ninjas in the FATA. This night he has learned of the Thuggees."

V. once more. "It was a terrible failure."

Daei waved the thought away. "Assassins, ninjas, Thuggees. I tell you, to almost anyone on Earth it would sound like something out of an extremely bad Hollywood film. Who would believe such a thing? Can this American truly convince his President of such a thing? Can he then convince the imams and the Revolutionary Guards of Iran, the governments of Pakistan, Afghanistan and India that three groups, whom most presume to be mythological or at best extinct, could form such a cabal? And even if our American friend is that convincing, I put it to you, V. Tendulkar, can he do it in time?"

"Which means he must try to stop us himself." V. joined Daei once more in looking out over the lights of India's City of Joy. "I fear that will force him to ever increasingly dangerous and desperate acts."

CIA Station, Islamabad, Detention Room

THE MOSSAD ASSASSIN sat in the corner of the bare room. She had been stripped and searched, then issued a pair of men's sweats that were probably seven sizes too big for her, and no shoes. The sweatpants had no drawstring, so she would have to hold them up with one hand. It was an old Russian technique. Detainees often had a hard time escaping when they had to hold up their pants with one hand. Bolan thought it was a useless countermeasure. He was pretty sure Na'ama Shushan would gleefully skip through the CIA station and the streets of Islamabad naked as the day she was born, killing anyone in her path until she found some clothes that fit.

The killer couldn't stop staring at Bolan's transformation. Her remaining eye continually scanned his changed appearance. "Remarkable." She gave Kengo a long look, as well. "And you're different from the others."

Kengo shrugged.

Shushan stretched in her shackles and made of show of looking bored. "While you have been pretending to be a ninja, Agent Farkas interrogated me. I will tell you that there is nothing that the United States government can threaten me with that I am afraid of." Her eye roved Bolan once more. "And I do not believe you are capable of doing what would be physically required to make me talk."

"No doubt," Bolan agreed.

Shushan registered a vague curiosity. "So why are you here?"

"To offer you a choice."

The woman rolled her single eye. "You are boring me again. As I have said, you cannot bribe me, and you cannot threaten me."

"I didn't come here to threaten you or to bribe you. I'm here to make you an offer."

Shushan blew a stray lock of hair off her brow. "Then at the risk of further boredom, what exactly are you offering me?"

"Do you want to be operational again or not?" Bolan was pleased by the stunned silence that met the offer. "I know you're not afraid of incarceration or death. We both also know I'm not going to carve the cooperation I need out of you. I need more than just information. I need your willing participation in the mission. Are you in or out?"

Wheels turned behind Shushan's single eye. She ran her tongue across her teeth. "And what exactly is it you wish of me again?"

"I'm going to find out whatever is going on, and stop it. To do that I need to infiltrate the group perpetrating it. You're one of my keys to getting in."

"So, you are going to ostensibly break me out of U.S. custody again, posing as ninjas, and trade me back as a gift?"

"I'm not trading anything. You're joining my team, and you're going to do everything in your power to help me get in, maintain my cover, help me discover exactly what is going on, and you're going to help me stop it. If I'm killed, I expect you to continue the mission to the end."

Shushan smiled. Despite the massive bruising on her face, the eye-patch and the fact that she was criminally insane, she was an excruciatingly beautiful woman. "Do I get a gun?"

Keller scowled. "We all know you can get anything you want as soon as you're back in the bosom of your assassin buddies. You're thinking about escaping."

Shushan gave Keller an icy look. Bolan got the impression that the beautiful Israeli assassin didn't care much for other women. "She's thinking about her initial return, and the fact that she might be perceived as damaged goods. When we go in, we could be walking into another kill zone just like we did in Kolkata." Bolan shrugged. "And, yeah, she's thinking about escaping."

"And I want to help you because...?"

Bolan glanced around the room. CIA stations didn't have prison cells, but due to the nature of the business most CIA stations had a room or two that a person of interest would have a very hard time getting out of. "This is about as nice as it's going to get. You're best-case scenario is that I give you over to Agent Keller."

Keller gave Shushan a sunny smile.

Bolan continued. "She'll turn you over to the Navy. You'll be tried as a terrorist by a naval military tribunal or in the Federal courts. You'll very likely spend the rest of your life in jail, or leave it as a very old woman. Personally, I suspect your life behind bars will be short. Once you're incarcerated, I think we both know there are people out there who will move heaven and earth to see you killed."

Shushan smirked. "And that is the best-case scenario if I do not cooperate?"

"Yeah."

"And what would be the worst?" she asked.

"I wash my hands of you and turn you over to the Mossad."

That shut Shushan up for a few seconds. She cocked her head and gave Bolan a very curious look. "You are telling me, that if I assist you, we succeed, and I survive, you will give me my freedom?"

"Well, those are three pretty big ifs," Bolan conceded. "But yeah, a reasonable facsimile of freedom."

Keller just barely restrained herself from interjecting.

The assassin lifted her chin in challenge. "And just what does a reasonable facsimile of freedom mean?"

"I'll be watching you," Bolan said. "You seem to enjoy two things in life—sleeping with men, and then killing them. If you get out of this alive, I suggest you stick with the former and keep the latter a happy memory."

"And if I should fall back upon my wicked, black-widow ways?"

"I'll hunt you down and kill you. If by some chance I take you alive, you tell the director I said hi when you get to the detention center outside Tel Aviv. The offer is simple. You're going into the field one more time. The man running the mission is me, and when it's over, you're retired. I'll use my influence to protect you from Israeli Intelligence. Any other enemies you've made will be your problem."

Shushan considered this for a few heartbeats. "I will require a small, compact .22-caliber semiautomatic pistol."

The ghost of a smile passed across Bolan's face. Shushan had been trained in the Israeli old school methods.

"It does not have to be a Beretta 70 or 71," she continued, "but it must be accurate out to twenty-five meters. It must be reliable, and loaded with the highest velocity ammunition available. If possible, it must be threaded for a silencer and be reliable with subsonic ammunition, as well."

Bolan nodded. "Done."

Keller made a disgusted noise.

Shushan ignored the NCIS agent and kept her eye on Bolan. "I want two of them. With spare magazines, and I want a knife."

"Done. Anything else you require besides clothes?"

"That will be sufficient." The assassin's eye roved over Bolan's frame in open speculation. "For the moment."

CHAPTER TWENTY-FOUR

Bolan whipped the sword overhead in a high guard. He stood in the courtyard stripped to the waist. Kengo had given him a sword and said he didn't expect the soldier to have to use it, but there might be situations where he would need to wear it. Bolan put the sword through its paces. Unless he needed rest, downtime was training time. He knew he was no master of the sword, but the Executioner took the blade through one of the kenjutsu katas he knew. It was extremely simple. He raised the sword overhead, took three steps forward and cut, he took one step back and defended. It contained only three cuts, high, middle, center and one thrust. The retreat contained three defenses, high, low and center. These were the absolute playground basics of Japanese swordsmanship. Sweat pinpricked Bolan's chest and back as he hit one hundred repetitions for each technique and started again.

He should have been sweating buckets.

Kengo's pore-tightening technique left Bolan unable to sweat normally, and he felt himself starting to overheat. He doubted he could reach five hundred repetitions of the kata without suffering heat exhaustion. It was something he would have to keep in mind while he operated in Central Asia in high summer.

Bolan knew he held a true ninja sword. It bore a slightly longer blade than a normal *wakizashi* short-sword blade mounted on a slightly longer than normal *katana* longsword hilt. The short blade was carried in a long scabbard. In ancient days it would give a ninja a heartbeat-quicker draw than a samurai carrying a *katana* of regular length and weight. The combination of a long hilt and a short blade gave the weapon a great deal of leverage, and optimized it for close-quarters combat. Bolan knew the kata he was running wasn't quite correct for the blade he wielded, but he wanted to get a feel for the weapon. He raised the blade overhead in the high-guard once more.

It felt good.

Bolan cut, recovered and stopped as he became aware of Na'ama Shushan behind him. He lowered the blade and turned. "Good morning."

"Good morning."

Shushan shook her head as she took in Bolan's appearance. He was getting that a lot. "How did you detect me?"

"Smelled you," Bolan said.

"Oh."

"It's a nice smell."

"Thank you." Shushan's eye flicked to the gleaming curve of steel in Bolan's hands. "You are very skilled."

"It's basic kata number one."

"You can never practice your basics enough," Shushan stated.

Bolan sheathed the blade and laid it on the wrought-iron patio table. "True that. How are your weapons? Up to spec?"

Shushan had gotten her guns. One call to John Kissinger had produced a pair of German HK-4 pistols personally tuned and accessorized by the master smith himself. They'd been put on a courier jet to Islamabad within twenty-four hours. "I prefer single-action automatic to double, but I could not have asked for more beautiful weapons. The attention that has been paid to them would be obvious to an amateur. Thank you."

"You're welcome." Bolan remembered Shushan's other request and reached into his pocket. "Here." He handed her his personal Mikov switchblade. "I want this back."

The soldier couldn't tell what was moving behind the assassin's remaining violet eye, but her lips smiled as she took the knife. "Thank you. I will give it back."

Bolan gave it fifty-fifty that she tried to return it to him in the back, thirteen or fourteen times.

She gave Bolan another curious look. "I have never met a man like you."

Na'ama Shushan was a black widow. She slept with men and killed them. Telling a man what he wanted to hear was her first step in setting him up for the big, fat kill. Then again she was a murderer and a sociopath. She might very well fall under the rule that if you wanted her respect you had to beat it out of her. Bolan had defeated her in hand-to-hand combat, captured her twice and blown out her left eye with rubber buckshot. He didn't suffer from the sin of pride, but neither did he put any stock in false humility.

There just weren't a whole lot of human beings walking the Earth with his résumé.

"Thanks. How are you feeling?"

Shushan raised one graceful hand to her eye-patch. One violet orb grew reproachful. "It still hurts. I get headaches."

"That's to be expected. The optic nerve is one of the most sensitive, and it has the shortest route to the brain."

Shushan scowled.

"It could be worse."

The assassin quirked one corner of her mouth. "What, you could have blown out both my eyes?"

"My other option was lead."

Shushan's gaze ran up and down Bolan again. "I don't normally go for Asian guys."

Bolan laughed.

Shushan joined him. He thought her laugh was beautiful. It was the kind of laugh a man might do anything to hear. "We should go upstairs."

"That's a really bad idea."

"I want you to make love to me," the woman said.

"I've read the obituaries of men who've made love to you."

Shushan walked up to Bolan and lifted her chin a few inches from his face. Kengo's face-changing techniques had done nothing to Bolan's nose. He did smell Na'ama Shushan, and she smelled good. She was a master assassin, and a master seductress. He could feel himself responding and was glad that Kengo's work had left his face an unresponsive mask.

Shushan whispered, her lips inches from Bolan's. "Their leader is a giant named Daei. The strangler I met was only known as V. You told me you broke him, but the V. that I met would never break simply by severing his hand. The man I met would willingly die for his cause. It would take horrific torture to make him talk. I saw the sketch your CIA artist made of V. It is identical to the man I met. He has a double."

"I know. I killed him."

Shushan ran her finger down Bolan's chest. "You and I should go upstairs."

"No."

Shushan gave Bolan an insane grin. "When we insert, I am going to tell the giant and the strangler I am sleeping with you. I am going to tell them that you have betrayed your ninja training because you are obsessed with me. They will believe this because they have files on some of the men I have broken. I will tell them you are half-caste, and that while you are a brutal, dangerous fixer for them, your mixed heritage has nevertheless left you as something of an outcast. You are bitter about this. I am going to tell them I am pumping you for information, but you are ninja, and I must be very subtle. It will be in your interest of your cover to comply. They will think this will give them leverage over you. They may well try to actively recruit you and bring you deeper into the mission if they think I can sexually control you."

"And if I say no?" Bolan asked.

"If you refuse now, the mission is over. Turn me over to Agent Keller." Shushan leaned in even closer. "If you refuse midmission, I will betray the mission, you and Kengo."

"I'm going to have to get back to you on that one."

Shushan's assassin-seductress smile stayed painted on her face. "Don't wait too long."

Floatel, Kolkata Millennium Plaza

V. REGARDED THE NINJAS with visible trepidation. His remaining hand shook as he drank his iced chai. The Thuggee had changed into an expensive taupe business suit. His arm lay in a sling like a tennis injury. Bolan himself would have included a lump for the hand, but it would take a sharp eye to detect anything amiss. It was V.'s demeanor that drew question. A lovely breeze blew off the Hooghly River. V.'s brow sweated as much as his chilled glass. Bolan and Kengo ignored their mutilated, strangler host and drank lagers and enjoyed the view. The Floatel was literally what it sounded like, India's only floating hotel. Permanently docked in Millennium Plaza, it offered spectacular views of the river and the city. The promotional literature described it as having a vacation on the Thames or the Seine. Bolan considered it more spectacular.

He idly wondered who was debriefing Shushan and whether they would leave the charming, open-air bar alive.

He and Kengo had allowed themselves to be disarmed out on the plaza. A single mutual slide of the eyes upon boarding the Floatel had them agree on diving over the side if things went south. The strangler, the ninja and the warrior waited while fates were decided in a stateroom below. V. spoke quietly over the sound of Bollywood dance music coming from the stereo inside and the hoot and call of river traffic on the Hooghly. "It is quite remarkable that you were able to wrest the woman from U.S. custody not once, but twice. May I ask how such a thing was accomplished?"

Kengo deigned to look at the little killer. "The same way you will strangle in the future. With great difficulty."

V.'s eyes widened in shock. His hand flew reflexively to his stump.

Bolan took up the good cop mantle. "Nevertheless, you came within a heartbeat of being the first man in history to ever strangle a ninja. Your technique was breathtaking. It is regretful to have damaged an artisan like yourself, V.-san."

Kengo got up and walked over to the bar with a scowl. Bolan gazed back out over the Hooghly. "One of your compatriots took that honor. My clansman would have died beneath the rumal had I not aided him. There is some shame in this."

V. gulped chai. "You are kind."

"May I ask you an honest question?" Bolan said.

"Of course."

He looked pointedly at V.'s maimed appendage. "Is this an insult that can be forgiven?"

V. stared at his stump. "I was trained not to think in such a fashion, yet…" V. shook. "I yearn to cast the rumal one last time upon him." He gave Bolan a shy smile. "Hopefully when you are not around."

A powerful-looking Sikh in turban, tunic and trousers moved directly to the table. He pressed ham-size hands together in respect at V. "Greetings, Holy One."

V. couldn't return the gesture, but he brought one hand edge-on to his chest and nodded.

The Sikh gave Bolan a bow. "Greetings, Mas-san."

Traditionally, Thuggees were Hindu, but historically there were anecdotes of both Muslims and Sikhs having been indoctrinated into the ranks. Bolan nodded back. "Greetings, Singh-san."

Every male Sikh's last name was Singh, which meant "Lion."

Singh bowed once more. "Singh is all the honorific I require, honored guest. Will you and Kengo-san accompany me?"

Kengo watched from the bar. Bolan rose, and the two men fell in behind Singh, followed by V. V. might have been missing a hand, but Bolan still didn't like having the little strangler behind him. They walked down the plushly appointed hallway to a conference room. Bolan was struck again by the venue. The hotel had only one entrance and that was the docking bridge. If the bad guys were willing to shoot up the Floatel, it would be one hell of a shooting gallery.

Two Indian men who looked like private security stood outside the door. They nodded to Singh and opened the door. Bolan and Kengo followed. One guard came in and the other stayed outside. It was a typical business conference room. A long teak table dominated the room. A vast plasma screen for audio-visual presentations hung on the far wall. A bowl of fresh fruit and flowers formed a bright centerpiece. Bolan and Kengo's gear bags and suitcases were in the corner. Na'ama Shushan sat at the right-hand side of the table, and next to her sat a man Bolan didn't recognize. Like a lot of killers, at first glance he didn't look like much. Average height, build and features. To Bolan's eye he looked Persian, but he had very little about him that would stand out anywhere from Egypt to India. The man gave Bolan a very long look, but then again the soldier knew he was pretty striking-looking at the moment. He knew his instincts were right when the man spoke with the accent of man whose first language was Farsi.

"Please, be welcome. Be seated." He gestured at a sideboard. "Would you care for bottled water? Juice?"

Bolan and Kengo spoke in unison. "Beer."

Bolan and Kengo sat, with V. taking a seat next to the big American. The guard went to fetch beer.

"Kengo-san, Mas-san, the incident in New Town was most regrettable."

"Regrettable," Bolan responded, "but not absolutely unforgivable, given the circumstances."

The guard reappeared with an ice bucket containing a six-pack of beer. The Persian waited while Bolan and Kengo opened their beverages and then opened a bottle of water. "Cheers."

Bolan and Kengo inclined their heads and toasted.

The Persian put down his water and sighed. "That is very reasonable of you. However, the maiming of V. is considered unacceptable."

V. flinched.

"He was at your mercy, and you mutilated him. This was costly in several ways to friends of ours."

Singh folded his mighty arms across his chest.

The meeting had just turned into a poker game. The

stakes were life and death. It was time to pull a mutually agreed upon wild card. Bolan and Kengo looked at each other for long moments. Kengo nodded, and the soldier rose.

"There is a dagger in my bag." The Persian blinked. Bolan jerked his head at the security man, who looked at the Persian. The Persian nodded. Singh's hand went under his tunic. The guard went and rummaged through Bolan's bag, returning with the *kubikiri*. Bolan took the blade with a slight bow and unsheathed it. For a clean cut Bolan laid his outstretched little finger on the table. He placed the edge of the blade on the third knuckle of his finger and locked his gaze with V.

V. gasped.

The Persian looked at Bolan askance.

Shushan was positively glowing.

Bolan gave V. a single nod. "Forgive us."

Kengo rose. "No, the offense was mine." He took the dagger and put the first knuckle length of his left little finger on the table. "I will require the use of my hand for the duration of the mission. You may have the rest of the finger when our business is concluded." Kengo sheared off the tip of his middle finger with a single cut. He took a napkin from the fruit plate, wrapped the fingertip with origami-like precision and placed it in front of V. with a bow.

Bolan took out his pocket square, snapped it and handed it to Kengo. He arranged his features into an even more powerful scowl. "Let us return to business."

The Persian leaned back in his chair and appeared to be reevaluating the ninjas. "I believe our business for this evening is finished. We will contact you in the morning."

Bolan had a deep suspicion the Persian desperately wanted to contact his superiors. The Executioner and

Kengo both bowed. The big American produced a card. "We are staying here. Please have our things delivered there at your most immediate convenience." They turned on their heels and walked out of the Floatel as bold as brass. They passed one of the outdoor cafés. Omar Ous sat sipping coffee and reading an English copy of the *Times of India*. He snapped it and turned the page by way of acknowledgment.

The two men walked out of Millennium Plaza. Bolan broke the silence as he hailed a cab. "How's your hand?"

"It hurts like hell. Goddamn Yakuza. They set a precedent for asking forgiveness the rest of us have to live with."

"The good news?"

Kengo shook his head. "I am desperate to hear the good news."

"I'm pretty sure we passed the second audition."

CHAPTER TWENTY-FIVE

Kolkata, safehouse

Shushan's perfume preceded her. She placed a pistol on the bedstand and slid into Bolan's bed. He slid his own weapon back under his pillow, sighing in the dark. "You got past my ninja."

Shushan spooned in. "Not without a rather thorough check for a wire."

"I told him I didn't want to be disturbed unless it was an emergency."

"Ken-san also believes it is to our advantage to have the enemy think we are sleeping together, and I thought you would like a briefing on what went on at the Floatel."

Shushan laid her head on Bolan's chest. He lay equally naked beneath the sheets. She placed a very familiar hand low on the soldier's stomach. "They were impressed. I personally found the whole performance somewhat theatrical. Then again, in my experience, Thuggees and Ismaili Assassins are somewhat predictable."

"You have a lot of experience with them?"

"Perhaps not as much as you..." Shushan countered. "But Ismailis are Muslim. Thuggees worship Kali. Distorted as their versions of their religions have become, they are fanatics and their religions predicate their actions. Ninjas? Who knows what a ninja might do? Your behavior dovetailed with all of their preconceived notions."

"Who's the Persian?"

"The only name I have is Karrar. I believe he is an Is-maili."

"And the Sikh?"

"I believe Singh is a Thuggee."

"Isn't that a little unusual?"

"Thuggees are Hindu worshippers of Kali, and yet it was not unknown to have Muslim and even Sikh converts. The Thuggees have their ways."

Bolan knew from very hard personal experience about Thuggee conversion methods.

"Oh, by the way," she added. "V. is in love with you."

"Who isn't?"

Shushan laughed.

"Tell me about the giant."

"You are right. He is not in love with you."

"Tell me about him."

"He is very interesting. I have worked closely with him. He is an Ismaili, and Persian. I have heard others refer to Daei as 'Tiractur' in private."

"Tractor?"

"That is the corruption of the word in the Middle East. The man has spent many long years training in the *Zurkhaneh*."

Bolan knew the word. It was Persian and it meant "House of Strength." It was the house where traditional Persian martial arts were performed with a heavy emphasis on wrestling and strength-building.

"His strength is inhuman. Even Ken-san would be in a great deal of trouble if he came within arm's reach of Daei. I will tell you something else. He hates you and wishes to lay his hands upon you. Your disguise is magnificent, but Daei is as suspicious as he is strong, and do not underestimate his intelligence. He is a master planner. I would be very careful around him. If you find yourself in his presence, I would let Ken-san do all the talking."

"What more can you tell me about their real mission?" Bolan asked.

"This resurrected branch of the Ismailis have embraced jihad against the West. The Thuggees want the end of the world. Ninjas work for money or their own inscrutable objectives."

Bolan smiled in the dark. "Ismailis, Thuggees and ninjas…"

"Oh my," Shushan finished. "What are you thinking?"

"Afghanistan, Pakistan."

"You think these actions were a ruse?" Shushan shook her head. "All of their targets seemed legitimate."

"I agree, breaking up the peace process in Afghanistan, emplacing blackmail rings in our military bases, stirring up the FATA and getting their hands in the Mid-East heroin trade—all of that furthers their aims."

Shushan searched for the thread. "Useful feints?"

"You've been too busy enjoying your job rather than thinking about it."

Shushan made an amused noise. "There may be some truth in that. So what are you saying these activities represent?"

Bolan let out a long breath. "Prep work, for what's to come."

"For a global caliphate?" Shushan's tone made it clear she didn't lend much credence to the idea. "Really?"

"At least it's prep work for the kick-off party."

"And what do you believe this kick-off party will be?"

"Ismailis, Thuggees, Ninjas, even you. You all have one thing in common."

Shushan lifted her head, and Bolan felt her one eye upon him in the dark. "We are assassins."

"I think they intend to assassinate somebody."

"Who?"

"What would constitute the biggest assassination of all time?"

"That is easy," Shushan said. "A standing American President."

"And the President of the United States is currently in Australia," Bolan stated.

"And according to the schedule of his diplomatic tour, your President will be in India at the end of the week."

Bolan rolled the waman aside and rose. "I need to make a phone call."

AARON KURTZMAN stared across the link. Hal Brognola, the Farm's director and link to the White House, sat in a chair in his home on an inset window, glowering. Bolan wasn't surprised to see him on the link.

"You're telling me Ismaili Assassins, Thuggees and ninjas want to take out the President?" Brognola asked.

"The Assassins and the Thuggees do." Bolan nodded toward Kengo. "Us ninjas are just the hired help."

"Yeah, and what about renegade Mossad assassins?"

Bolan glanced at Shushan. "They're doing it for love."

Shushan's mouth quirked in amusement.

Brognola wasn't amused. "How exactly do you want me to put that to the President, again?"

"I'd try the truth. You tell him that when he comes to India an attempt is going to be made on his life, and it's going to be made by ringers with thousands of years of cumulative practice."

Kengo sat across the table beside Shushan. They could hear Aaron Kurtzman and Brognola through the laptop speakers, but from their position couldn't see their faces. Kengo nodded. "Sir, I'm surprised by this theory, as well, but I have to admit it makes as much sense as anything. The target is certainly big enough, and the effects certainly politically destabilizing."

The big Fed stopped short of gnashing his teeth. He always got a little more irked than usual when his boss's life was threatened. "Very well, Mr.... Ninja?"

"Ken-san."

"Well, tell you what, Ken-san. You're the ninja. The President is going to be surrounded by a small army of Secret Service agents, not to mention a small army of Indian army personnel. Given that scenario, how would you snuff him?"

Kengo considered the question. "For me, as a ninja, this would be a suicide mission. This is generally not in our purview. For a ninja to be caught or identified during his mission is a disaster, for himself, the mission and his clan. Ninjas only engage in suicide missions in extreme situations."

"Extreme situations..." Brognola scoffed. "Seems like a pretty vague distinction to me. Things seem pretty extreme as it is. Of course, I'm just a civil servant. How about maybe a ninja defines 'extreme' for me, particularly given the current circumstances?"

Kengo appeared to take no offense. "Of course. For example, no ninja would accept a mission to kill the President of the United States unless our nations were at war. Such an action would bring about the destruction of his clan and be a blow to the State of Japan from which it might never recover."

"Nice." Brognola still wasn't impressed. "But what about these Whispering Pine ninjas?"

"Ninjas only in name, and that, sir, is the answer to your question. The Whispering Pine collective, through their shameless behavior, have implicated the ninja clans and the State of Japan in an attempt to destabilize the Middle East and Central Asia and possibly an assassination attempt on the President of the United States. That is your extreme situation. My clan has ordered me to erase this threat. I am completely willing to die should circumstances require it to fulfill this mission. Last night I cut off the tip of my finger. The rest of that digit is promised. Had the enemy required me to rip my belly, I would have done so to maintain Cooper-san's cover. I am on a suicide mission. I do not expect to leave India alive."

It was hard to be flip in the face of such selfless resolve. "I appreciate that, but my question stands. How would you do it?"

"Ninjas wouldn't. Particularly in India, it is the Thuggees and the Ismailis who would stand the best chance. Thuggees will only use the rumal. It is hard for me to imagine a situation where they could get close enough to the President to employ them, much less do so without your Secret Service cutting them to shreds while they tried."

Aaron Kurtzman chimed in. "I've been doing research. The Ismailis were famous for infiltrating a group or community, killing their target with a dagger when the time was right, and then calmly waiting for the authorities. The President will be meeting, greeting and glad-handing hundreds of Indian businessmen, politicians, military brass and local glitterati. I think they're your best-threat scenario. The Ismailis may have been embedding operatives in India for years for just such an opportunity."

Bolan agreed. "The President is coming to Kolkata."

"Yeah, as a matter of fact he is."

"Is the first lady coming?" Bolan asked.

Brognola began to drum his fingers on his tabletop. "Yeah."

"I think you should get ready to tell him to cancel the

India leg, and be ready to do so at the last second. I need you to give me as much time as possible to get inside these guys and their plan."

"I don't have to tell you that news like that is going to go over like a French kiss at a family reunion," Brognola said. The President is counting on coming back with a new round of trade agreements with India."

"I know."

"He needs a win. America needs a win. India needs a win. Cancelling at the very last second is going to be taken as lack of faith and commitment by the Indians. Not to mention a grave insult. The Indian prime minister wants his photo op."

"I know. He's in danger, too."

Brognola stabbed a finger at the camera on his side of the link. "Listen, I'm not complaining. I agree with you. I want to cancel the trip right now. This is just a sample of the ear-screwing I'm going to get!"

"I know," Bolan repeated.

"You've met the Man. Even if I can get your 'ninjas and Thuggees and Ismalis, oh my' mantra through his head, I give you ten to one odds he just ups security and says the United States of America does not alter its course or abandon its strategic partners in the face of possible threats. He'll say that's what the enemy wants, and if he cancels they win."

"If he cancels they lose," Bolan stated.

"Not on the world stage."

"Better than POTUS and FLOTUS being strangled or gutted like fish. We've faced the Ismaili Assassins before, Hal. Their daggers are like ninja's swords. Mostly for tradition and terrorizing people. They don't have any religious prohibitions against automatic weapons or explosives. The method of attack could be conventional or unconventional, and given the nature of the players involved, expect the attack to be layered." Bolan gave the big Fed a frank look across the link. "You really need to talk to the President."

BOLAN GAVE KELLER the pertinent details. He and Kengo were about as deep undercover as it got, so there was no way they could afford a clandestine meeting with Keller, Ous, Babar or Farkas. The members of Bolan's ad hoc strike team were cooling their heels and getting cabin fever in the CIA Kolkata station. Agent Keller's glower across the link rivaled Brognola's but she was whole lot prettier doing it. Keller was U.S. Navy and she didn't respond well to her commander in chief being threatened. "The President."

"It's the only thing that makes sense."

"Well, he's going to be here in a few days. What are you and Ken going to do about it?"

"Ken-san and I agree that there's only one choice. We need to make ourselves indispensable to their mission."

"Listen, your disguise is fantastic, but you and Ken are still Whispering Pine flunkies. I mean, you're ninjas, and that's groovy, but like you said, you're the hired help. How do you propose to make yourselves integral to the mission?"

"Easy. We need to goose them, freak them out so they panic and make some mistakes. At the same time we need to screw up their operation so badly that they can't complete their operation without us. That gets us on the inside to stop it, but, at the same time, we have to do all that without them knowing it was Ken-san and I who did it. Oh, and I want to pull Daei out of the shadows. He's the highest up player we know. We need to engineer a hands-on Daei intervention."

Keller glanced from side to side as if she was waiting for the rub. "And you engineer that how?"

"We're going to have to engineer a slaughter," Bolan said.

"A slaughter?"

"Right, among their ranks."

"And how are you going to avoid the blame for that and get Daei to put his ass on the line?" Keller asked.

"There's only one guy I know who can do all that."

Keller made a face. "Okay, I give up. Who?"

"Why…" Bolan cracked his knuckles. "The Mighty One."

CHAPTER TWENTY-SIX

Kolkata

Bolan and Kengo followed Singh through the maze of catacombs. They didn't know how sophisticated the enemy's countersurveillance was. Electronics weren't part of Shushan's purview, but she had described what she had seen so far as "top of the line." It put them at a disadvantage, but Bolan and Kengo had decided the risks outweighed the benefits.

Keller and the team had followed in a loose tail as they had driven out into the sticks. Once Singh had taken them into an old office building and led them down into the earth, Bolan and Kengo had lost any hope of backup.

They had been trudging through the muck for about half an hour.

Bolan glanced at the foulness both old and new creeping down the walls. That and the ankle-deep water told him they were very close to the Hooghly. Bolan gave it a good chance they might actually be underneath one of the tributaries of the dark and ancient river. The Hooghly was a holy river, often called *Ma Ganga*, or "Mother Ganges" by the locals. The same population who worshipped it didn't blink an eye about dumping their sewage into it. Industrial cities farther north dumped chemical waste into the river in breathtaking tonnages.

The smell in the catacombs was horrific.

By the glare of the flashlights, the crumbling walls looked ancient. The tunnels were extensive. They weren't British Raj–era sewers or some ancient Indian irrigation system. Someone had dug these tunnels long ago for their own purpose, and Bolan suspected only the Death Goddess Kali and her worshippers knew why.

A phalanx of Ismaili Assassins flanked Bolan and Kengo, four in front and four in back. It was a strange-looking troop of very dangerous men in casual wear and duck-waders trudging through the muck. The only thing that would have completed the picture would have been if they were carrying torches. Bolan doubted you could get a torch to burn in the miasma of fumes beneath the earth. That, or one spark would detonate the catacombs like a gas main.

Bolan slid a glance at Kengo. The ninja slitted his eyes slightly in agreement. The two men stopped in place. The Assassins behind them nearly toppled like bowling pins trying to avoid bumping into the ninjas. Singh looked back at the commotion. "What is happening?"

"Where are we going?" Bolan asked.

The Sikh smiled through his beard. "To a place you need to see."

The Executioner turned his chemically mutated face upon the big Sikh. "That is suitably vague."

"The Whispering Pine have served most bravely," Singh said, "but you are neither of my brethren nor the Ismailis. You are mercenaries, of admirable dedication, but you serve for bowls of silver."

Bolan willed his numb face into a glower. It was enough to almost make Singh take a step back. The soldier put his faith in Kengo and ignored the Ismailis around him putting hands to weapons and took a step forward. "This is no longer a matter of silver crossing palms. This is a matter of the honor of my clan. We are prepared to die."

Singh took a step back. Bolan gave him space and didn't follow. Singh held up a placating hand. "You must understand. The time of the harrowing is now, and you are outsiders."

"Time of the harrowing" sat cold and ugly in Bolan's craw. "If Kengo-san and I are to be effective, we must know what our responsibilities will be so that we can make the appropriate preparations."

Singh bowed and spread his hands. "I urge you, please follow me a little bit farther. Much will be made clear to you."

Bolan and Kengo looked at each other and nodded in unison. "Very well."

The warrior and the ninja followed the killers deeper into the tunnels. The water was just about knee level when they came to a vertical shaft. The shaft was more recent construction. By the condition of the concrete and the iron rungs forming the ladder upward, Bolan made the construction from some time in the last century.

Singh led the way upward. Sunlight scorched down the shaft as the man opened the hatch. Bolan slid on his shoes and climbed up into the fresh air.

The hatch opened on a little island with a single tree. That told Bolan the island was solid rather than one of the ever-shifting sandbars. Kengo emerged and looked around. Singh took a deep breath of the breeze off the water and sighed. "When the time comes," he said, "we will be met here. Then the final leg of the mission will begin."

Bolan looked around the little island. They weren't on the main Hooghly, but one of its smaller branches. There was little on the banks other than a few huts on stilts. To the north Bolan could see the high-rises of the old downtown and farther north the taller spires of New Town. "Who will we be meeting?"

Singh swelled with pride. "Destiny."

Besides the single tree, the little island was nothing but tall reeds. From the Hooghly's banks the island would look like nothing. The reeds on the southern edge of the island had been crushed in a swathe that ran right up to the hatch. The Hooghly was a deep river and had a tidal bore. Bolan suspected that the little island spent at least part of each day under water. It made the swathe of grassy destruction difficult to read. There were no tracks left in the mud, but the grinding and tearing of the stalks gave Bolan a firm impression.

Whatever had rolled up on the island had done so on treads rather than wheels.

He was beginning to get a very bad feeling. "How shall destiny manifest itself?"

"Kali shall stir in her slumber. The Great Satan shall be dealt a terrible blow. The mission your clan was commissioned to perform shall be accomplished, and those who gave your clan offense shall be cleansed from the Earth."

"And how is this to be accomplished?"

"I cannot speak of it to you just yet," Singh's eyes blazed with the fire of the fanatic. "But I can tell you this, Mas-san. When the time comes, my people wish you and Kengo-san to be a form of insurance. You shall be the safeguard of all accomplishment."

"Insurance." Kengo grunted. "I am not sure my clan will be appeased by such a role."

"Oh, do not think you will be hanging back in the shadows. It would be more appropriate to think of your role as the third tine of the trident that we shall drive into the heart of our enemy, and your hands will be upon the torch that will light the greatest fire in human history."

Bolan looked northward toward the city. "You can tell us nothing more?"

"Not until tomorrow."

The President of the United States was arriving in India the next day. It was pretty clear that Singh knew far more about the mission than he was telling. "Why have you brought us here?"

"Can you not guess?"

"You have revealed that part of the mission is to be amphibious."

Singh smiled. "Are you and Kengo-san accomplished at such things?"

"I would venture to say we are far more accomplished at such things than you."

"Tomorrow your role will be made known to you."

"And if we are told tomorrow and we believe our participation in this mission will compromise our clan or the State of Japan?"

"I believe I can say with absolute certainty that once the plan is set in motion, the State of Japan will be the least thing on anyone's mind. However, if you do feel it necessary to refuse, all we ask is that you not interfere. Return to Japan. When all is said and done the Land of the Rising Sun, and your clan, may well find a host of new opportunities." Singh gave Bolan a very strange look. "And perhaps a measure of vengeance for past atrocities committed against you."

"Can you tell me nothing more?" Bolan pressed.

"No, not until tomorrow."

Harrowing, cleansing and revenge for past atrocities against the State of Japan sealed the deal for Bolan. There would be no waiting for the next day. Singh blinked as Bolan drew his Desert Eagle and his Beretta 93-R from the cross-draw and small-of-the-back holsters beneath his shirt.

"Surrender immediately."

Singh gave Bolan a fatalistic smile he didn't care for. "Kill them."

It all happened very fast. Bolan snap-kicked Singh in the groin. He turned as an Ismaili brought up an MP-5. The soldier fired, a .50-caliber bullet blowing out the man's sternum, lung and spine. Bolan's Beretta 93-R let loose a triburst that blasted an Assassin into the tall weeds. Kengo produced a pair of .45 Colt Government Model pistols and shot without looking, like some cyborg that had already marked his target's positions. Assassins fell. Bolan spun, firing, and a .50-caliber bullet burst a brain. A 9 mm triburst sent another Assassin in a screaming splash into the shallows. Kengo's .45s jackhammered in his hands. As an Assassin produced an Uzi, Bolan put both front sights onto the Ismaili's chest and slammed the front of his rib cage to splinters.

Bolan swung as Kengo made a noise.

Singh had managed to rumal the ninja. Kengo pointed both .45s over his shoulders at the man, who held the strangle in place with his left hand. He stabbed the dagger in his right hand up underneath Kengo's left shoulder blade. The ninja gasped and both of his shots missed. The 3-round burst from Bolan's Beretta sent Singh's turban ribboning away along with a good portion of the top of his skull.

The island was suddenly still except for the flocks of river birds that had burst from their perches and squawked in consternation into the sky. Bolan dropped his Desert Eagle and caught Kengo as he folded and took him to one knee. "I'm going to leave the knife in for a second."

Kengo nodded. "That is probably best."

Bolan kept the ninja upright as he scanned the island.

Eight Ismaili's and one Thuggee lay in the mud or bobbed in the shallows. "We won."

Kengo nodded again. "Good."

"We killed all of our suspects."

"I never liked them."

Bolan smiled. "You're okay, Kengo."

"Thank you. You are—" Kengo gasped as Bolan pulled the dagger free. A few words in Japanese that sizzled broke out between Kengo's clenched teeth and he collapsed in Bolan's arms.

Bolan packed his handkerchief into Kengo's wound. "The son of a bitch stabbed you."

"I am aware of this," Kengo said.

"He's a Thuggee. They don't spill blood."

Kengo grimaced and took a knee. He regarded Singh. "It is anomalous."

"If he brought us here, I think he's the best of their best."

Kengo put a fist into the mud to keep himself upright. "Do you realize that you never have anything encouraging to say?"

Bolan picked up the knife. There was nothing Persian or Indian about it. It was a thoroughly modern weapon. It looked a lot like a stunted filet knife, like something that was made to slide between bones. Bolan didn't care for the three flutes on both sides of the blade that had sucked up tiny rivulets of Kengo's blood. "I am going to have this sent to my people."

"You do that."

Kengo fell face-first into the mud.

Kolkata safehouse

BOLAN STAGGERED through the door. Kengo was large for a Japanese, and every last ounce of him was either muscle or bone. Shushan grabbed an arm and helped lay the ninja facedown on the couch. "He's been stabbed?"

"Yeah. Get the med kit."

She disappeared and came back with the trauma bag the Farm had sent. The stab wound itself wasn't very big, but it bled out of all proportion to its size. Bolan figured the knife's design had something to do with that. Shushan pursed her lips as she watched Bolan's ministrations. "They went for the heart. That's an awkward blow."

Bolan nodded at the rag he wrapped the knife in. Shushan unwrapped it. "This blade looks like it was built for feeling around inside people." She ran the clinical eye of a professional killer over the curved, whisper-thin blade. "A real rib tickler."

"Go into my room. In my smaller bag I have some diplomatic courier pouches. In the side pocket are some sterile sleeves for medical samples."

"Right."

Kengo let out a long sigh. "I passed out."

"You lost a lot of blood."

"I would like to sit up." Kengo grimaced as Bolan got him upright on the couch. "What happened?"

Bolan's eyes narrowed slightly. "Singh stabbed you."

"Ah yes, I remember."

The Executioner cocked his head at the ninja in interest. "Doesn't that bother you?"

Kengo cocked his head in return. "Yes, I am often very bothered by being stabbed. I am quite annoyed with Singh and I thank you for killing him for me."

"No, I mean he's a Thuggee. Thuggee stranglers don't shed blood."

"Perhaps he is not a very good Thuggee."

Bolan rolled his eyes.

"He's certainly not a very good Sikh," Kengo tried.

"You know, you're the only ninja I've ever met with a discernable sense of humor."

"I'll have you know ninjas are renowned for their sense of humor. You know, more and more I am beginning to believe that I may be the only real one you have ever met." Kengo frowned at the knife on the table. "You are implying that Singh did not stab me with the intent to kill me. Thus, in his view of the world the act did not constitute a sacrifice to Kali, and thus shedding my blood would not constitute a transgression against his beliefs."

"Yeah."

"You realize he was strangling me at the time."

"That was so he could stab you. Stabbing ninjas is an uncertain business even under the best of circumstances."

"Then why would he stab me the way he did? I can tell you that internally I am aware of the fact that the tip of his knife came very close to my cardiac tissue. If his beliefs allowed him to disable me without killing me, there are many far more effective and less risky places to strike with a knife."

"Right, but Singh wanted you to genuinely believe he had tried to kill you."

Kengo gave Bolan another wry look. "You are familiar with Occam's Razor?"

"Yes, the law of parsimony. The simplest explanation is most likely the correct one. It applies here. Singh is a Thuggee. Thuggees do not shed the blood of their sacrifices. He didn't stab you to kill or disable you. He stabbed you because he wanted to put a knife in your body."

Shushan laughed as she entered the room. "That is the traditional reason for stabbing someone."

Kengo wasn't laughing anymore. "You are implying there is something on the knife."

"Yes."

Kengo frowned. "I'm a ninja."

"I know."

"It is traditional for us to develop a great deal of resistance to many poisons."

"How about psychotropic drugs?"

"What are you implying?"

"I've fought the Thuggees before. They initiate new members into their ranks with some very powerful hallucinogenics. It's called 'The Sweetness of Kali.' They say once you've tasted it, you're hers forever."

"And?"

"And they also use it to recruit people against their will, and compromise them."

"How do you know this?"

"They compromised my team, and they came about an inch away from recruiting me."

Shushan looked at Kengo with interest. Her hand casually slid toward the pistol tucked in her waistband. "The ninja has been compromised?"

Kengo contemplated this. "I do not feel like I have been drugged."

"Even when I had metabolized the drug, later on they were able to induce a flashback."

"Since I have never been exposed, and do not seem to feel any effects, that might indicate a binary drug. One that will not produce its effects until the victim is exposed to the other half of it."

Shushan seemed more bemused than alarmed. "The ninja is a psychedelic bomb waiting for a trigger."

"Possibly. Keep an eye on him." Bolan put the knife in the sleeve and sealed the diplomatic pouch. He wrote down the coded address that would get it sent straight to the Farm. "Na'ama, I need you to get this to the international airport, then get back here and keep an eye on Ken."

   "Where are you going?"
   "I need to file an after-action report with Karrar. With
any luck, we just became indispensable."

CHAPTER TWENTY-SEVEN

Floatel, conference room

"The American is here." Bolan's words sent shock waves around the room. Karrar's jaw dropped. V. spoke tremulously. "Where is Singh?"

"Dead."

Karrar gave Bolan a very hard look. "And those we sent with him?"

"Dead."

The half-dozen Ismaili gunmen standing behind Karrar put hands to weapons.

"Where is Kengo?" Karrar inquired.

"Wounded. He is back at our safehouse. The Shushan woman is tending his wounds."

"How do you know it was the American?" Karrar asked.

"I saw him. I shot at him."

"Did you hit him?"

"No."

"Who else was there?"

"The Pakistani soldier, Scarface Babar. Omar Ous. Agent Keller, along with several Americans who are either operatives or agents. Agent Keller and Ous are dead."

"How do you know?"

"I killed them," Bolan replied.

Karrar relaxed slightly. "What about the rest of the Americans?"

"Two escaped."

"And Babar?"

"He fled in a different direction. He appeared to be wounded. He is a Pakistani special forces soldier operating illegally in India. I do not believe he presents a threat anymore. With Keller dead, that leaves only the junior agent, Farkas, in India with a great deal of explaining to do. Their investigation is broken."

"Keller...and Babar," Karrar mused. "I see you did not bring us any heads."

"All of the bodies are dismembered and at the bottom of the Hooghly. I decided trying to evacuate Ken-san through the streets of Kolkata while at the same time carrying a bag of bloody heads would be impractical."

"How were you discovered?"

"We were not discovered. Ken-san and I came from Japan. There is no one who could be aware of us or tracking our movements outside your organization." Bolan let his voice grow cold. "One or more of your people were being tracked or are traitors."

This information went over like a lead balloon. V. unconsciously put a hand to his stump. "You have contacted your people?"

"My clan has been apprised of the current state of affairs."

Karrar looked at V., who nodded.

Karrar looked back at Bolan. "What are your orders?"

"The honor of the Whispering Pine must be avenged. To that effect I am willing to do anything that redeems the death of my clansmen and kills or causes harm to those responsible, specifically the Americans."

Karrar and V. exchanged another look.

"Specifically," Bolan concluded, "we are prepared to help you assassinate the President of the United States."

Guns were drawn. The Executioner stared down the several weapons pointed at his face impassively. "He arrives in India within hours. It is not a great stretch of the imagination to assume he is your goal."

Karrar held up a calming hand to the gunmen. "Assuming such a startling turn of events were true, why would you wish to assist us? Indeed, why might you not want to stop us?"

"If I wished to stop this, I would simply have killed every man in this room except you and V. and then tortured all pertinent information out of you."

"So why would you wish to assist?" V. queried.

"The simplest reason is that my people have a code. We have taken payment. We must finish our task. There is also the honor of the clan and revenge."

"Is that truly enough to motivate you into assisting in the assassination of an American President?"

"Normally I would agree. The State of Japan is not at war with the United States. The killing of the American President would serve no purpose but to endanger Japan. However, the killing will take place in India." Bolan looked to Karrar. "I assume the shadow of blame will fall on Pakistan?"

Karrar shrugged. "You fascinate me, go on."

"War between India and Pakistan would be far more than enough to destabilize the region. With the death of an American President the United States would be drawn in. This of course would embroil China. The council of clans believes that such a destabilization would be exactly the sort of motivation the State of Japan would need to reclaim its former martial spirit, both militarily and economically."

"Yet, you do not fear discovery of Japanese involvement?"

"Few believe in Thuggees or Ismaili Assassins anymore." Bolan arranged his face into a smile. "No one believes in ninjas."

"There is your physical presence," V. suggested.

Bolan kept the smile on his face. "You would be shocked to the extent that I can change my physical appearance."

Karrar and V. exchanged another look.

"What is the plan?" Bolan asked.

Karrar shook his head. "That will be made clear tomorrow."

"That is what Singh told me. Now he is dead and the mission is in jeopardy."

"The mission is not in jeopardy. We have several alternatives."

"The traitors?"

"Alarming," Karrar allowed. "However, they are of too low a level to make a difference. Had they been true insiders, the total mission would already have been compromised. Somehow the Americans got a tracking device on one of our men in a previous encounter, or someone within our group alerted them that a group of men were going out. Both lines of inquiry are being ruthlessly pursued."

Bolan knew he wasn't going to get any more information without pushing too far. "Very well."

Howrah, waterfront district

SUBEDAR BABAR wasn't pleased. He and Bolan drank chai and watched the heavy traffic over the Hooghly Bridge between Kolkata and her satellite city Howrah. The Executioner gave Babar his briefing about the current situation. Babar was maintaining his cover as a Pakistani special forces operator on a nonsanctioned mission and on the run in India. "This meeting is dangerous."

"Right now I trust you, Keller and Ous. That's it."

"What about Ken?"

"I like him, but he's a wildcard, a ninja. I trust him to do what he believes is best for his clan and the State of Japan. If that suddenly means cutting off our heads, he'll do it without blinking. Plus, between you, me and the lamppost, he may have been chemically compromised."

Babar's face revealed his confusion. "I do not know what that means."

"It means he may have been drugged. He's aware of it."

"So you trust no one."

"I trust you."

"Thank you, and I thank you for the briefing. However, I do not believe you risked a face-to-face just to update me. There is something you wish to say that is for my ears alone."

"That's right. I don't think assassinating the President is big enough."

This was met by incredulous silence. "Well, what are you willing to settle for, Armageddon?"

"Like I said a while ago, I think whatever is going to happen is going to be the kick-off, and, what the hell, let's call it Armageddon."

"You do not believe assassinating the President of the United States on Indian soil will be a big enough…kick-off?"

"No."

"Pray tell, what would you consider a suitable kick-off to the end of the world?"

"Can I ask you a professional question, as a subedar of the Pakistani Special Service Group?"

Babar's eyes went a little cold through his mass of scars and facial hair. "I will answer any question within reason, depending upon its pertinence to this mission."

"I need to know something about the Black Storks and their primary mission."

Subedar Babar rattled off the Pakistani SSG standard talking points. "The SSG has six stated national defense missions. We conduct unconventional warfare, we engage in foreign internal defense, special reconnaissance, direct action, hostage rescue and counterterrorism."

"Yeah, but could you tell me something about your nuclear responsibilities?"

Babar's facial expression blanked. "That is classified."

"I understand, but theoretically, if Pakistani National Command Authority put out the call, 'broken arrow,' would the Black Storks be involved?"

"Theoretically, the retrieval of a lost or stolen nuclear device would most likely involve the deployment of some assets of the SSG." Babar began to look distinctly uncomfortable. "Why do you ask?"

"Have you ever had any contact with anyone in authority, within the National Command Authority?"

Babar's expression grew evermore suspicious. Pakistani National Command Authority was in direct control of Pakistan's nuclear arsenal.

"Let me put it this way," Bolan added. "If I asked you to, would you contact the highest person up the chain of command of the National Command Authority you can manage and ask them if they're missing any nukes?"

It was the first time he had seen the brick-hard Pakistani out of sorts. "I need to make a phone call."

GHOLAM DAEI WATCHED the video of the ninjas' debriefing for the third time. His dark eyes stared long and hard at the image on his laptop as he took in every nuance of the conversation. There was something about the stone-faced, half-breed ninja that he didn't care for. Perhaps it was the ninja having discovered their objective so easily. Perhaps it was that so many good men had died and this ninja stood untouched. His imperious manner certainly had something to do with it, but that wasn't it. There was something about the ninja Daei didn't care for at all.

V. looked at the giant anxiously. "You do not trust the ninjas?"

Daei sighed. He trusted his instincts implicitly, but whatever suspicion was scratching at the back of his mind about the ninja eluded him. "It is not necessarily a matter of trust. The Whispering Pine proved themselves invaluable in Afghanistan and Pakistan. They were able to walk in and out of U.S. military bases with impunity, and they laid the seeds of terror in the FATA that we will need in the second phase of the operation. The ninjas possess a set of skills almost unknown and unmatched in the modern world, and they have melded it with modern technology. However, the fact remains that neither my people nor yours ever intended upon their involvement at this level of the operation."

Karrar frowned. "So what is to be the ninjas' role?"

"It is not so much that they have a role to fulfill at this juncture, it is simply that I do not believe we can afford a war with the ninja clans by denying them one. Tomorrow is but the first step. In fact we may indeed wish to employ the Whispering Pine again. It is best to stay on their good side, and give them what they want. It costs us nothing, and they may still prove instrumental."

V. asked the question they were all thinking. "And what of what the ninja said of traitors walking among us?"

"It is hard to imagine such a thing," The giant stared holes through the image of the ninja on the screen. "Hard to imagine a traitor among their ranks, either. I find myself believing more in his other theory that somehow the enemy had a way to track us. Nevertheless, it is only we among the upper echelon who know the final plan and its permutations. The American has almost no resources do draw upon now. He will watch helplessly as we drive our dagger into the heart of the world."

"He is still in Kolkata. He will still be trying to stop us to the last."

"Then the dagger shall take his life, as well."

"Perhaps we should send one or both of the ninjas after him," Karrar suggested. "It would give them something to do, get them out of our way, and I think the Mighty One would look better without a head."

"I had considered that, but this Mas-san has guessed our objective."

"Our objective, but not our method."

"No, but they are Japanese and ninja. They seek glory now. I do not think they will be denied the final objective."

"So," Karrar said again. "What is to be their role?"

Daei clicked his laptop shut. He had made his decision. Perhaps the next ninja the Whispering Pine sent would have a better attitude. "I am going to allow them to die for the honor of their clan, their emperor and the State of Japan."

CHAPTER TWENTY-EIGHT

"The president has landed," Hal Brognola confirmed.

Bolan stared into the camera and shook his head at the big Fed. "Put him back on the plane."

"Do you realize what that would look like to the Indians?"

"Better than the Man and his lady being blown into their component atoms."

Brognola was caught flat-footed. "What?"

"Much less Kolkata being fused into glass," Bolan stated.

"Let me be clear about this. You're saying the bad guys have a nuke?"

"I'm saying they might."

"And what the hell is that supposed to mean!" the big Fed demanded.

"I think I'll let the subedar explain." Bolan nodded at Babar.

"Sir, I have been given clearance to share certain information with you and your government. Mr. Cooper asked me to contact the Pakistani National Command Authority and ask them if we were missing any warheads, which, with some trepidation, I did."

"So...how was your conversation?" Brognola asked.

"Short," Babar replied, "and not what I expected."

"And just what were you expecting?"

"I fully expected to be dressed down, told I was insane

and possibly demoted. I assure you the National Command Authority is not known for its sense of humor."

"What did they say?"

"The gentleman I spoke to, who shall remain nameless, asked me, very confidentially, why I was asking."

"And?" the big Fed probed.

Babar looked at Bolan. "I told him."

"And?"

"I was summoned to National Command Authority to report immediately to the Director-General of the Strategic Plans Division."

"Uh-huh, and you're still there in India because why?"

"Because given the scope of Cooper's suspicions and the American President's imminent arrival, I told the Director-General that I did not believe there was time for a face-to-face conference."

"So what did the Director-General tell you?"

Babar stopped short of squirming in his seat. "This is somewhat, embarrassing, for my country."

"Subedar, with all due respect, are your people missing a nuke or not?"

"We do not know."

"Jesus." Brognola looked fit to be tied. "Last I heard, the Pentagon estimates your military has between eighty to one hundred and twenty operational nuclear warheads. That's a two- to three-digit number at most, Subedar. How goddamn hard can it be to keep track of them?"

Babar pulled himself up with as much dignity as he could muster. "Harder than you might imagine. Some of our weapons are loaded on ballistic missiles in hardened silos. Others are deliverable by truck-mounted mobile rocket systems. We recently developed cruise missiles capable of delivering a nuclear weapon, and for that matter, a preponderance of our stockpile is still designed to be 'toss-bombed' the old-fashioned way by strike fighters. The fact is, we do not have all our warheads in the same place. Indeed, that would be foolish. The Pakistani military is staunchly secular. We are always afraid of fundamentalist Muslims trying to grab a weapon for an act of terror. We have multiple, redundant levels of secrecy and cutouts."

"So what happened?" Brognola probed.

"A virus was introduced in the computer system of our Strategic Arms Division. A very sophisticated virus, a worm as you call it. The SAD is now receiving conflicting reports as to the inventory and disposition of our warheads. All nuclear-armed facilities are now in lockdown. Every missile and rocket warhead must be checked by hand. All stockpiles must be visually verified. It beggars belief that this was not at least in some way an inside job. If the SAD has been compromised from the inside, then the National Command Authority must have absolute confidence in those doing the confirming, and even then their results independently verified. The fact of the matter is, my government does not know if it is missing a nuclear weapon yet, and I cannot guarantee whether we will within the next twenty-four hours."

"Well, thanks a hell of lot for telling us now!"

The subedar sighed. "If your government thought it might be missing a nuclear warhead would you contact mine?"

"We would if your President was coming the next day!"

"Would you?" Babar countered. "Would you really?"

"Well, hell, maybe not," Brognola muttered. "So what are your orders, Subedar?"

"If a Pakistani nuclear weapon detonates in Kolkata, there is every reason to believe that India will respond and there will be a full nuclear exchange. My government has considered sending a strike team into Kolkata. I responded that Cooper and Ken have generated the only real lead we have. We do not know where the missing weapon is. A raid or a strike against the enemies we have identified in the Floatel or the New Town tower would be no guarantee of success. Cooper and Ken continuing their infiltration is the only sure way to secure the weapon, if it is indeed missing. My orders are to continue to assist the current mission. If the enemy has a Pakistani weapon, then I am to secure it at all costs and see that it is returned to my country, ideally without the Indian government being the wiser."

Brognola could see Babar, but Babar couldn't see him. The big Fed gave Bolan a plaintive look. "And you say Kengo is wounded and possibly chemically compromised?"

"If we get into a situation and the Kali drug goes active in his system, I can't vouch for his behavior."

"This just doesn't sound like a recipe for success."

"So get the Man on a plane."

"The President has made it abundantly clear that he will not alter his agenda to terrorist threats."

"Even nuclear ones on foreign soil?" Bolan probed.

"He'll want confirmation, and even with the subedar's report, we have no proof the virus introduced into the Pakistani Strategic Arms Division is related to this situation."

"I'm telling you it is," Bolan said.

"That's good enough for me. You know that. But it won't be enough for him."

"Then the mission stands the way it is."

"So what do you have? A tunnel complex and some tracks in the mud?" Brognola asked.

"The tide erased the tracks in the mud," the Executioner replied.

"Oh, I forgot, we're going with crushed weeds."

Babar did some math. "The Indian army fields several armored vehicles with amphibious capability."

The same thought had occurred to Bolan. "From what Keller told me, the President is giving two speeches in Kolkata. Both are open-air and near the Hooghly. No matter how much security the President has, no one is expecting an armored vehicle and none of the Secret Service agents are hiding antitank rockets in their shoulder holsters. Neither is Indian security. The Kolkata police have some patrol boats, but nothing that can take on an amphibious tank or armored personnel carrier. If they have a nuke, all they have to do is to roll it ashore so that they get a nice ground burst without the Hooghly River's water and mud sucking up any of the detonation. It could be detonated from miles away. No one has anything in place to stop it."

Babar sighed heavily. "I agree with this assessment."

"So we should ask the Indian military if they're missing any amphibious tanks or armored vehicles?"

"No, we'd never get an answer in time, and it would only most likely let the enemy know we're on to them. We can't afford to let them scrub the mission and try again later," Bolan said.

"So you and a compromised Kengo are going in ninja?"

"That's the long and the short of it," the Executioner acknowledged, "Meantime, I need you to arrange a boat for Keller and her team, with as many heavy weapons as you can arrange in Kolkata. We need tank killers. The Hooghly River averages two hundred feet in depth, in some parts nearly twice that. If we can sink whatever vehicle they're using to the bottom, that would absorb one whole hell of a lot of the blast. A few yards of water could make all the difference."

Brognola came to the last question. "So, any suggestions on exactly what we do or don't tell the Indians?"

"I agree with the subedar," Bolan said. "It'll be best if they never know. If we tell them now they'll go berserk, and our bad guys and the weapon will pull the big fade into an uncertain future."

Babar looked infinitely relieved. "I will do everything in my power to assist you."

"Babar, Keller and Ous will be our boat team. We can't afford to be sending out any kind of signal, so they're going to have to deploy on the Hooghly early and wait. Farkas will be running control from the safehouse. If and when we can, Kengo and I will either radio, use our cells or text for backup or extraction and vector in Keller's team. Meanwhile, slave as many satellites as you can to scan the Hooghly River. A swimming armored vehicle will be slow moving and distinctive."

"So that's the plan? You and Kengo go in blind while Team Keller waits for your call?"

"Pretty much," Bolan agreed.

"I'll tell the President."

"You do that."

Floatel, dawn

BOLAN, KENGO and Shushan stood naked in front of the giant. V. gave the big American an apologetic look as he ran a wand over Bolan's body. "You will forgive the security measures." It wasn't weapons being searched for. V. turned to the giant. "They are clean." The trio carried no electronic devices either internally or externally. If they wanted to send out a call, they were going to have to appropriate someone else's phone. Karrar ran a wand over the swords and the H&K silenced PDWs in the gear bags Bolan and Kengo had brought with them. He shoved the wand into Shushan's purse and shrugged. "Nothing here."

Bolan nodded. "We are completely committed."

Daei nodded in return. "I have absolute faith in it. You may dress."

Bolan and Kengo donned black technical turtlenecks and dark cargo pants. They were raid suits until they donned their sports jackets. Shushan was wearing a little white cotton sundress for Armageddon. Her .22-caliber pistol slid into a thigh holster. Gholam Daei strode through the back door of the conference room. "Come with me."

The Executioner got a bad feeling as he followed the big man down the emergency stairs. They left the top deck and descended floor by floor. There were no boats currently docked to the Floatel. Bolan had severe doubts about an amphibious tank or armored personnel carrier paddling up to the side of the floating luxury hotel by the dawn's early light. His worst fears were confirmed as the giant opened a door that opened out onto the Hooghly. A green awning covered the emergency exit area.

Beneath the awning was the sail and open hatch of a submarine.

Bolan had seen the model before. It was a Russian minisub. Their construction had been a cottage industry during the cold war. They were tiny, cramped and slightly on the suicidal side. Their most promising feature was the fact that they had tank tracks that let them crawl along the bottom along enemy coastlines. Their main purposes were probing enemy coastal defenses and the deployment and extraction of espionage agents or special forces teams.

The Farm's satellite surveillance would be useless. Unless Keller or Babar had spontaneously thought to equip their makeshift attack boat with depth charges, they would have no countermeasure against it, much less ever detect it. How the enemy had gotten hold of a Russian minisub was a moot point. Except for weapons straight out of their

nuclear stockpiles, the Russians were willing to sell just
about anything to anybody who had the cold hard currency
to pay for it.

The giant leaped lightly into the sail and squeezed his
frame down the hatch. Bolan, Kengo, Shushan, Karrar, V.
and a pair of Ismaili Assassins followed. The minisub's
main cabin was a spare barrel of steel with folding benches
on both sides. "Make yourselves as comfortable as you can.
Our journey is not long, but it is close and tedious. Once we
seal the hatch it will be unpleasant." Bolan and Kengo sat
together. Shushan sat across from them. The giant dropped
to one knee on the steel deck and unfolded a map. "Listen
carefully."

Shushan pulled an air pistol from her purse and shot
Kengo in the chest.

Half a dozen pistols stared Bolan in the face. Kengo's
hand shook as it reached up and pulled out the dart. Sweat
literally burst from his brow. White foam oozed from the
corners of the ninja's mouth as his eyes rolled back in his
head. Kengo fell onto the deck in violent convulsions.

V. literally waggled his eyebrows at Bolan. "We are to
understand you are aware of the Sweetness of Kali."

Bolan was well aware of it. He had once had the
drug coursing through his veins. In the proper amount
the Sweetness of Kali was a trip to Nirvana that heroin
couldn't hold a candle to. Kengo had been given a hotshot,
just like Bolan had once, and that was a trip straight to hell.

"Indeed, if our information is correct, you have tasted
her sweetness."

Shushan gave Bolan a happy smile. "I told you you
should have slept with me."

Bolan ignored her and glanced down the barrel of Karrar's Glock. "Shut up and do it."

The giant laughed. "Do it, O Mighty One?" He measured Kengo. "He is not Whispering Pine. He is—how do you say it?—the real deal. When he wakes from his ordeal, if he wakes, he will tell us many fascinating things."

"Ninjas don't break."

"Not under torture." Daei nodded. "But after one, two, three tastes of Kali's sweetness? I am told that much like an LSD trip, it is best to have a guide. Kengo-san will be led out of his third or fourth nightmare, and that journey will unlock his mind."

V. gave Bolan a happy smile. "Is it true, brother? You have tasted her sweetness? What shall happen to you when you taste it again?"

Only the chemicals Kengo had put in Bolan's face kept his expression neutral. The last time he had fought the Thuggees had taken him to his limits.

Daei nodded as he saw through Bolan's mask. "I am very interested to learn of your relationship to the United States government." He nodded to an Ismaili. "I wish to keep their swords as souvenirs. Other than that, I wish no unsecured weapons."

The Ismaili took the ninja blades and stored them in a locker beneath the bench. He took Bolan's and Kengo's H&K PDWs and heaved them out of the hatch into the Hooghly. Daei produced a pair of handcuffs and shackles, and slid them across the deck to Bolan. "Restrain yourself."

There was no recourse except to stay alive and conscious as long as possible and hope opportunity presented itself. Bolan manacled himself. "How did you find out?"

"Seal the hatch. Rig for silent running." An Ismaili closed the hatch and spun the wheel. The cabin throbbed as the screws began to turn.

"Your face," Daei said. "Tell me about it. I can see the Mighty One in the FATA, but this is quite spectacular."

Bolan saw no reason to lie. "Call it secret ninja magic."

"That is one reason why Kengo-san still lives. We will learn this."

"How'd you learn about me?" Bolan repeated.

"Can you not guess?"

Bolan could. "Farkas."

V. smiled. "Yes, you took him and his family from beneath the knives of the Assassins." The giant Ismaili scowled. V. gave him a bow. "So I arranged, with the help of the Whispering Pine, that Agent Farkas taste the Sweetness of Kali. He tasted deeply, and, I will tell you, he is a most sweet, devoted slave of the goddess. When ordered, he will vector Keller's team into an ambush where they shall be slaughtered."

Bolan ran his eyes around the cabin. "I never figured Assassins and Thuggees as suicide troopers. Figured you'd get others to do that for you. We're just going to roll up out of the weeds and fuse yourselves and everything else for ten miles into glass?"

V. and Karrar looked to the immense Ismaili. Gholam Daei scratched his beard bemusedly. "We have a few moments to spare, so I will tell you. We are prepared to die, but we are not suicidal. Our goal is not martyrdom. Our goal is victory, and I fear your friend Babar did not tell you everything about his nation's nuclear secrets."

Bolan had thought the sinking feeling in his guts couldn't sink any lower.

"Pakistan and India have fought before. Arguably, it can be said that Pakistan has won most of these engagements, but facts are facts. These engagements were limited in scope and took place in remote corners like Kashmir and what was to become Bangladesh. The fact is, the Indian army, navy and air force are all twice as large or larger than Pakistan's. India is a far larger and richer country. They have been rapidly expanding their armed forces and the sophistication of the weapons they wield. Come the day of a real war between these countries, all that separates most of India from Pakistan is the Great Indian Desert. Most of it is flat. How to stop the endless hordes of Indian infantry and armor divisions?"

Bolan knew the answer. "Enhanced radiation weapons."

"Neutron bombs, yes."

"The Pakistanis don't have any."

"Not yet, but the Chinese do. I know this because I happen to have one of their warheads in my possession."

"A Chinese weapon delivered by the Pakistanis that kills the U.S. and Indian presidents." It wasn't quite Armageddon, but Bolan knew it was a damn good start. "Kolkata gets irradiated rather than blasted into a smoking crater, and you sail away with two hundred feet of water between you and the radiation wave."

V. nodded happily. "Kolkata is Kali's city. When she wishes it destroyed, it is she who shall turn the City of Joy into the joyous burning ground."

Bolan shot a look at Kengo. He was really hoping the man might pull some ninja power out of nowhere and equalize the situation. Kengo continued to lie on the deck eye-rolling and frothing.

The sub's pilot called back from his station. "Estimated time to target one hour."

CHAPTER TWENTY-NINE

Computer Room, the Farm Annex

"They've been in that floating funhouse for over an hour," Hal Brognola growled. "Something's wrong." Aaron Kurtzman sat at his workstation. The big Fed's unsmiling face on one screen took up about one-sixteenth of his attention. The multiple, high-intensity imaging satellite feeds had the rest. Brognola was right. Bolan, Kengo and Shushan had walked into the Floatel more than an hour ago. No one had come out. The only people who had left the "floating funhouse" appeared to be guests, and all had exited the premises across the footbridge. No boats had come or gone. Certainly no amphibious armored vehicles.

Something was wrong.

Kurtzman adjusted the grain on the thermal satellite image. The heat of the Floatel's generator and her kitchens were globs of glow on his screen. He continued to dial down, easily making out patrons on the restaurant deck taking their breakfasts as steam and migratory birds rose from the water as the sun rose. The satellite could even penetrate to the deck below, but from there the images began to become confusing as different thicknesses of superstructure and smaller heat sources changed the images into smears and ghosts.

Kurtzman touched a key. "Agent Keller, what have you got on the ground?"

Keller came back from their makeshift patrol-attack boat. "I've got nothing. No movement."

He hit another key. "Farkas, is there anything you can think of on your end?" The computer expert frowned and tapped the key a little harder. "Farkas?"

"Yes! I mean no! I mean, I'm here."

Brognola snarled across the link. "Get your shit together, Agent. I think we have a problem."

"No, I mean yes, sir! Understood!"

Kurtzman's finger hovered over a key. The NCIS agents weren't allowed to see Farm personnel other than Bolan. Hal Brognola openly worked for the DOJ, but his role with Mack Bolan and the Farm was a closely guarded secret. Kurtzman's and Brognola's video feeds were blocked to all on a need-to-know basis. Any time you opened a feed on someone, you left open the possibility the enemy could detect it and peek back. The computer wizard decided to take a slight risk. He had spoken with Farkas on several occasions. There was something in the NCIS agent's tone that Kurtzman didn't care for, and it was something more than nerves on the morning of Armageddon. He punched his key decisively. There was a chance that Farkas's computer would inform him that his video camera had just turned on. Agent Farkas's face appeared in a window on his screen.

The NCIS agent was shaking and sweating like a malaria victim.

"Agent Farkas, are you all right?"

Farkas jumped. "What? I mean— What do you mean?"

Kurtzman hit another key, and back in Washington Brognola began to receive the same video stream. It took the big Fed about a heartbeat to put two and two together.

"Son, you look like hell. Tell me what's going on."

Farkas's head whipped around the CIA secure communications room as if he were looking for the invisible men spying on him. His eyes suddenly focused directly on the camera lens of his computer monitor. "Oh God... Oh God... Oh God..."

"Son, what's going on? You need to tell me. If it's your family, I know exactly where they are, and I can get you a live video link to them in thirty seconds."

"Oh...God..."

Brognola didn't like what he was seeing. "Agent Farkas, think about your duty. Think about your oath. All I'm asking you to do is talk to me."

Farkas suddenly went disturbingly calm. "Sir, I'm so sorry."

"Agent, listen to me. I'm here to help. All I—"

Farkas stuck the muzzle of his .40-caliber SIG-Sauer service pistol beneath his chin. Brognola and Kurtzman shouted at the same time. "Farkas!"

NCIS Agent Farkas blew out his brains live on video. He slumped forward in his chair and disappeared from the monitor camera view.

The big Fed spoke first. "This isn't good."

"No."

"Suggestions?"

"Where is the President now?"

Brognola checked the President's itinerary. "Finishing breakfast with the Indian president. Then they're going to drive together to the concourse to deliver a speech and field questions from the international press."

"My best guess? Whether Mack is dead or not, the bad guys are still game on."

"How?" Kurtzman replied by focusing the lens of a camera over a mile up in the air on the rear of the Floatel. He highlighted an awning that stretched out over the water. Brognola got it. "They're not amphibious."

"They're subaqueous," Kurtzman concluded.

"Damn it…"

The computer expert did some very rough math. "Figure your average minisub can manage about five knots. One knot equals 1.16 miles per hour. We'll call their maximum speed 5.8 knots. Of course they're trying to be quiet. Let's say they're sailing half speed, so two and half. We assume they're heading north for the concourse. If they have tracks, they'll drop down and crawl the last bit. Whatever bomb they're using, they don't want water beneath them. The blast would shove downward and a significant amount of effect could be smothered by the Hooghly. They'll want to creep out of the reeds and deploy the bomb on land. If they have a sub, this is no longer a suicide mission. They may be figuring to escape. What time is the speech on the concourse set for?"

"Half an hour."

Kurtzman opened his link with the strike team. "Agent Keller?"

"Yes, Bear?"

"Farkas has betrayed the mission. He's committed suicide. I need your team to get three miles north up the Hooghly and start slowly working your way backward. You're looking for a minisub."

Keller took the news with remarkable professionalism. "The first speech on the concourse? Thirty minutes?"

"We believe so. I'm walking our satellite imaging three miles north now and initiating a grid-by-grid walk back. If we see anything first, we will **vector you in**."

"Infiltration team status?"

"Unknown," Kurtzman replied.

Keller paused only for the briefest second. "Copy that. Strike team inbound."

THE LITTLE SUB ROCKED as it rested on the bottom of the Hooghly. Gears ground and the cabin lurched as the caterpillar tracks engaged and dug into the mud. The sub tilted as it began going up the incline of the riverbank. Daei smiled. "It was a risk to bring you and Kengo-san to the Floatel. It was a risk to bring the weapon to the Floatel. It was a risk to bring the sub there, as well, but you, my friend, ruined the catacombs for us. What is Kengo's real name, by the way?"

Bolan focused his attention stoically on Shushan's cleavage. Shushan beamed sunnily.

"What is yours?" Daei asked.

The air in the sub was hot and close. Bolan watched a rivulet of sweat battle between gravity and surface tension as it crawled down a curve of Shushan's flesh. This was probably about as good as the rest of his life was going to get.

Daei's lashed out with the back of his hand. Bolan's head rubbernecked and purple pinpricks danced across his vision. He was grateful for the numbing effect of Kengo's ninja facelift. "How you shall suffer beneath my hands," Daei rumbled.

"Periscope depth!" The pilot called. There was a pause as his copilot gave the scope a 360-degree turn. "We are clear in all directions!"

"Take us up."

The sub lumbered up the ever-increasing incline. The movement of the vessel slowed and became muddy as it lost buoyancy and climbed onto the land. "We are ashore!"

Daei cracked his knuckles and stretched. "Prepare to

deploy the bomb. Karim, Azimi stay here and watch the prisoners. Na'ama, you will stay and assist them." Dazzling light flooded into the hold as Daei flung open the hatch. He took up a rifle and clambered up into the fresh air. V. followed him awkwardly with one hand. Karrar and two Assassins brought up the rear. The pilot and copilot relaxed and lit cigarettes. Karim and Azimi looked back and forth between Bolan and Shushan and the overdosing ninja on the deck. The Executioner kept his eyes between Shushan's breasts. Shushan kept the muzzle of her weapon aimed between his legs. Bolan smiled. Shushan's single violet eye narrowed. "What?"

"Is it too late?"

Shushan cocked her head.

"Ever had sex in a minisub?"

Shushan smirked. "No."

"I have."

Karim scowled. Azimi looked interested.

Shushan glanced at the bulkhead inches over her head. "A bit cramped, a bit close."

Bolan shrugged. "I do yoga."

Karim lashed out. It wasn't quite the atomic bitch slap that Daei packed, but Bolan spit blood. The Executioner kept his eyes on Shushan. "Last chance for romance."

Karim cocked his hand. "This conversation is—"

Shushan gave Karim two .22 rounds in the temple. Before Azimi could blink, she gave him the same. The brothers slumped nearly simultaneously. The pilot and copilot leaned around to see what was happening. The pilot took two in the left eye and the copilot two in the right. Shushan dropped her smoking empty pistol to the deck. "When I learned Farkas had betrayed us, I was at something of a crossroad."

"I can imagine. How did you get them to trust you?" Bolan asked.

"I told them everything I knew. I told them I could have escaped, which was true, but that I wanted to sleep with you before I killed you, which was true, as well, and that I was much more useful to them as an insider."

"Bit of a risk."

"Everything I told them, and you, was true. After you made me lose my eye, I was really of two minds about who to side with."

"When did you make up your mind?"

"Just now." The killer picked up the brothers' fallen, silenced Beretta Tomcats pistols. They were pocket pistols, made bulky by their suppressor tubes. With only seven rounds of woefully underpowered .32 ammo, they weren't exactly Bolan's first choice of what to bring to a gunfight. Shushan added to the woe. "Daei and his men are wearing armor. I don't believe V. is a factor."

Shushan took the keys and unshackled Bolan. He rubbed his wrists and dropped to one knee beside the prostrate ninja. "Kengo-san."

Kengo moaned and shuddered in the fetal position on the deck plate. He was experiencing the mother of all bad trips.

Bolan pulled the ninja to his knees and slapped him back down. He picked him up and gave it to him forehand and back. Bolan grabbed Kengo's face in both hands and stared deeply into his eyes. "Kengo-san?"

Kengo's eyes rolled, but he muttered and gasped something in Japanese.

"Brother—" Bolan mentally tried to beam every last ounce of his personality into the chemically compromised ninja "—are you in there?"

Kengo's eyes synchronized, albeit badly, and the ninja

regarded Bolan with binocular vision, and something like recognition. "It's…bad…"

"I know." Bolan pulled Kengo back to his knees and steadied him. "Can you focus?"

Kengo slammed his hands together in front of him. His fingers began writhing in various intricate configurations as if he was playing cat's cradle with himself. The ninja grunted with strain and tried to breathe rhythmically.

Shushan sighed. "What is he doing?"

"Hand seals. They help focus internal power."

Shushan rolled her eye. "Oh…"

Bolan reached into the locker and pulled out the swords. He drew a blade and shoved it between the ninja's twining hands. "Here, focus on this." The blade shook in the ninja's grip. Kengo stared so hard at the steel his eyes crossed. Bolan took up the other sword and rose. "How's that working for you, brother?"

Kengo hissed through clenched teeth. "Brother, there are spiders…crawling all over my eyes…"

Shushan wrinkled her nose. "Eew."

The ninja shuddered. His knuckles went white on his sword hilt. "But…I can see past them."

Bolan pulled Kengo to his feet. "Take one head and we'll call it good."

"I will take one head…"

Shushan stared up the hatchway. "There are four of them, five if you count V. They have rifles. We have only two pistols. How do you wish to play it?"

Kengo shook like a leaf in the wind, but his voice was suddenly clear. "You will require a diversion. Go on my signal." Kengo climbed up into the sail. There was barely room for him and Bolan to crouch out of sight. Kengo slithered over the back of the sail and slid down the slope of the hull. Shushan came up beside Bolan. "What is he—"

Kengo's voice tore the morning quiet. *"Banzai!"*

Bolan and Shushan rose, guns leveled. The sub rested on another little island in the Hooghly. Daei, V. and the two Assassins whirled away from a conical, olive-drab casing they had unbolted from cleats on the sub's outer hull. Karrar was closest. Kengo charged as Karrar snapped up his Russian carbine. Whether it was the honor of the clans, his internal power or the fact he was hopped up out of his mind, Kengo managed to absorb half of Karrar's magazine on full-auto. Kengo's sword was a quicksilver flash in the morning sunlight. Karrar's head flew from his shoulders. The corpse collapsed, and Kengo fell on top of him.

Kengo-san had gotten his head.

Bolan shot the closer Assassin three times in the face and brought the little pistol around on Daei. Shushan carefully walked her shots up the second Assassin's chest, and her sixth and seventh shots smashed past screaming teeth. Daei got his rifle unslung and shoved it up in front of his face. Sparks flew off the carbine's magazine and action as the Executioner fired his last four rounds. He leaped the sail as Daei staggered backward with blood all over his face. Bolan tossed the spent pistol and baseball slid down the prow of the sub, whipping his sword overhead as his boots hit mud.

Daei roared and threw his damaged carbine end over end at Bolan like a six-pound tomahawk. The soldier brought his blade into a guard as the revolving rifle hit with all the power of the three-hundred-pound giant behind it. The ninja blade snapped and part of the rifle slammed into Bolan's numb face in passing. He shook his head to clear it and lunged with the six-inch shard still protruding from his hilt as Daei charged.

The giant accepted a brutal cut along his arm as he vised

one hand around Bolan's throat and slammed the other into his crotch. The soldier's vision went white. Daei pressed his adversary overhead and gorilla-slammed him into the ground.

Bolan lay in the mud gasping and staring up into the sky like a landed fish.

He still had hold of the shattered sword.

Bolan sat up.

"Now, Mighty One," Daei said, sneering. "Let us—"

Shushan's spent pistol clouted Daei in the teeth. He turned as Shushan leaped from the prow of the sub with her legs scissoring in an admirable flying butterfly kick. The giant smashed her lashing feet aside with one huge forearm and sent the woman spinning into the reeds.

Bolan rose. The remaining shard of steel slid out of the broken hilt with a metallic ring and fell into the mud. He held an empty sword hilt in his hand.

Daei exposed his bloody teeth. "Pathetic."

Bolan gestured the giant in. Daei took a step forward and nearly stumbled.

Kengo's hand grasped Daei's ankle. The giant shook his leg and nearly slid in the mud. Bolan lunged in. He drove the butt of the sword hilt into Daei's temple. The giant groaned and dropped to one knee. Bolan whipped the hilt over his opponent's head and heaved the handle back against the giant's throat. Daei tore at the soldier's arms and wrists, but his sausage-like fingers slid on muck and sweat. Bolan heaved back with all of his might. Wood, silk and skin crackled in his hands. Daei's cartilage crackled beneath the pressure. Bolan roared and gave the sword hilt a final heave.

Gholam Daei's trachea popped and broke.

The Executioner released the giant as he fell forward, gargling chunks of his larynx. Daei kicked and clutched at his throat as his face purpled. Kengo's hand still held the giant's leg in a death grip.

A rumal snaked around Bolan's throat. The soldier felt himself yanked backward, and his vision went white as a knee viciously blasted into his right kidney. The soldier tried to spin, but his opponent moved behind him like a perfectly synchronized dance partner. A second kidney blow stopped the strangulation spiral and dropped Bolan to his knees. He saw Shushan lying face up, staring sightlessly into the sky. The livid mark of the rumal encircled her throat. She had been silently strangled while Bolan and Kengo had brought down the giant. The rumal cinched tight for the kill. V. was no longer wearing a sling and he had somehow regained the use of his missing hand.

"My name is Sreenath Tendulkar," Bolan's strangler announced. "You killed my brother Harbajan." Bolan tasted copper behind teeth as Sreenath gave him another brutal knee. "You cut off my brother V.'s hand at the wrist. Surely you noticed they were twins. But it seems you were not aware we were triplets."

The Thuggee put his knee between Bolan's shoulder blades to pin him in place. "You are a fool, and you have failed in the mission. Kolkata, Kali's city, shall be Kali's burning ground. But I want you to die knowing that you are blessed, because you are truly a fit sacrifice for Kali. You will know the bliss of—" Sreenath ceased his monologue as he sensed something was wrong. He drew back to give Bolan another knee. Despite the agony trying to lock his body like tetanus, Bolan managed to twist aside from the blow and rise from his knees.

The Executioner had fought Thuggees before.

The Farm and the Future Warrior Project had come up with direct countermeasures for them. The most important thing in fighting Thuggees was the fact that they liked to strangle people. Bolan wore what looked like a common, turtle-necked raid suit, except that the collar wasn't made of cotton or wool. Carbon was a very interesting fiber. You could make it do all sorts of things. Two of the more relevant things you could make it do were to expand or contract on command. Bolan's collar was a very primitive example of a carbon fiber matrix. It didn't require electrical or chemical stimulation to function. It was stunningly simple. In effect the collar was a reverse Chinese finger trap. The harder you squeezed the collar, the more the carbon fiber material expanded and bulged back.

Bolan could still breathe with effort and blood was still more or less flowing to his brain. He twisted in the grip of the rumal as cotton strangling cord fought carbon fiber matrix and failed.

Sreenath screamed at what he saw in Bolan's eyes and released the rumal. He staggered back and pulled one of the filleting-thin, drug-delivering blades from a sheath behind his back. Bolan bent with effort and picked Kengo's sword up out of the mud. The Thuggee crossed his arms in front of his face, screaming in terror.

Bolan took a step forward and ran the Thuggee through.

Sreenath gasped as the Executioner twisted the blade. The Thuggee folded like a boned fish and fell as Bolan yanked the sword free. The soldier undraped the rumal from around his neck and wiped Kengo's blade clean. Gholam Daei had ceased his thrashing. His face was cyanotic blue from choking to death on his own broken throat. Bolan knelt beside the ninja. He had a half dozen holes in his back from where Karrar's burst had blown through him. "Kengo-san?"

Kengo whispered from his facedown position. "Cooper-san…" The ninja managed to turn his head Bolan's way. "We won?"

"We won."

"Good." Kengo's face relaxed into the mud.

There was nothing to be done. Kengo was shot to pieces. "How are you feeling?"

Kengo made a noise that might have been amusement. "The drug is very powerful, yet I found being shot in the chest twelve times was very…bracing. It focused my mind wonderfully on the task at hand."

"You saved my life, brother."

"Five opponents, and all you asked of me was one head. Brother, it was the least I could do."

Bolan brought a hand to his brutalized face. "Tell me this ninja battle mask thing is going to wear off on its own."

"Brother…you have never looked better."

Bolan held up the sword. "I have your sword. It will return to Japan." Kengo's body relaxed into the mud. His eyes glazed over as he joined his ancestors. Bolan lowered the blade. "So will the story of what you did today." The soldier glanced up at the sound of a pair of supercharged diesel engines. A cigarette boat whipped around the bend in the Hooghly, throwing up twin rooster tails in its wake. Bolan saw Keller's hair whipping in the wind behind the wheel. Ous leaned out with an M-14 rifle at the ready. Babar stood in the passenger seat with the tube of an anti-armor rocket leaned on the windshield.

Bolan raised Kengo's sword.

Keller throttled back and brought the boat to a smooth stop against the reeds. Bolan lowered the blade once more and walked over to the weapon in question. The device was very suspiciously shaped like a 130 mm artillery shell, in very common use by both China and Pakistan. The fuse in the nose had been removed and filled in. Someone had bolted a small control pad—interface onto the side of the weapon's casing. It appeared to be waterproof and consisted of a keypad, a dial and a digital readout.

Keller and Ous leaped from the boat and swept the little island in opposite directions. Babar had abandoned his anti-tank rocket and taken up a rifle. He beelined for the enhanced radiation weapon lying in the muck.

"This device belongs to the Pakistani military and as her highest ranking officer present I am taking possession of it," he announced.

"Actually I think it's Chinese, or a prototype your governments were working on together." Bolan shrugged wearily. "I never got the full story."

Babar fingered his rifle and stared at Bolan very steadily. "As agreed, I claim this device."

"All right, you take the device and load it in the boat. Head down the Hooghly about eighty miles or so and turn right at the Bay of Bengal. Just follow the coastline and sooner or later you'll hit Karachi." Babar failed to see the humor. Bolan pointed the tip of his sword at the control panel on the side of the nuclear shell.

The timer on the readout was ticking away.

"Hope you can make it in fifteen minutes or less."

"Hmm…" Babar scratched his beard. "I see."

Keller and Ous joined the group. The NCIS agent blinked at the bomb. "Shit."

Ous looked like he missed his pipe. "Can you diffuse it?"

"Not with what I have on hand."

Keller checked her watch. "The President is going on in ten minutes. Tell me you have a plan."

Bolan took a look around the tiny scrap of mud and reeds they stood on. "We load the weapon into the sub, along with all the bodies, sail it into the middle of the river and scuttle it."

Keller blinked. "You mean, we let the bomb go off. Right here where the bad guys wanted it to go off."

"It's an enhanced radiation weapon."

"A what?"

"A neutron bomb. Three feet of water will stop the radiation wave. We're going to submerge it two hundred feet below the surface. I don't know what the Chinese and Pakistani engineers are packing, but the whole point of a neutron bomb is to have a small explosion. U.S. weapons are five kilotons tops. You figure a five-kiloton blast, two hundred to three hundred feet down? People on the river will report an anomalous tidal surge. If anyone is looking in this direction when it goes off, there may be reports of one hell of a water spout."

"That's it? No mushroom cloud? No radioactive fallout?"

Bolan ran what he knew about enhanced radiation weapons with what he knew about the Hooghly. "The surviving metallic bits of the sub will give off potentially lethal secondary radiation. There won't be much of it. The Hooghly has a significant tidal bore that'll disperse it. The secondary radiation fizzles out in about twenty-four hours."

Keller turned to Babar and raised a questioning eyebrow. "It's your bomb, Subedar."

Babar looked at the weapon with the sadness of a soldier whose country was still in a nuclear arms race. "Do it."

"FIRE IN THE HOLE." Bolan pressed the firing button on the Indian army, Israeli-manufacture rocket launcher. The 82 mm rocket hissed across the rippling waters of the Hooghly and detonated against the prow of the minisub. Bolan lowered the smoking empty rocket tube. "Time."

Keller looked at her watch. "Three minutes."

All of the bodies, weapons and evidence lay in a soup

of gore in the minisub's hold. They formed a nest for the bomb in the sub's belly. The sub tipped as it began to take on water. If it didn't sink on its own within the next two minutes, Bolan was going to have to climb inside and pilot it to the bottom. He watched the Hooghly push the stricken sub downstream. "Time."

"Two minutes."

The sub sank with agonizing slowness. After an eternity, the edge of the sail dipped into the water and the Hooghly began spilling down through the open hatch and filling the sub in earnest. "Time."

"One minute ten…nine…eight…seven…"

The sub stood on its nose and slid beneath the dark waters of the Hooghly. Bolan rapped the rail with his knuckles. "Go."

"Thank God." Keller shoved the cigarette boat's throttles forward, and the craft lunged forward like a racehorse out of the gate. Bolan, Ous and Babar looked back as the boat streaked southward. They slewed through an S-curve, and the minisub's death descent was hidden from view.

"A shame," Ous said. "I liked Kengo. He was a mighty warrior."

"He was."

Babar gave Bolan a guilty look. "I am sorry about the weapon, but my nation—"

"And my nation are allies, though our national interests won't always be the same." Bolan stuck out his hand. "I've been proud to serve alongside you."

Babar actually managed to blush through the beard and scar tissue that took up most of his face. "Oh, well…" He shook Bolan's hand.

Keller throttled back the engines. "Ten…nine…eight. seven…"

Several thousand yards behind them a column of white

water rose nearly a hundred feet into the air like a rocket. The spout reached its apex and hung suspended for a heartbeat like some wizard's magical tower. The swirling white tower disintegrated as gravity pulled it back down and pulled it apart.

"Keller, we want to stay ahead of that," Bolan advised.

"My people have secured a safehouse for me in Diamond Harbour," Babar suggested. "I hear it is quite lovely, and just fifty kilometers downstream."

"Don't have to ask me twice." Agent Keller rammed the throttles forward once more. She clearly enjoyed putting the speedboat through its paces. Bolan sat in the cockpit with her.

Keller looked at his grim visage and sighed. "Cheer up, we won."

"I've fought Ismaili Assassins and Thuggees before. Ismailis always have a supreme leader. Thuggees always have a high priest. Daei and V. Tendulkar were field generals. We still have a problem."

"We still have a President, Kolkata is still lovely this time of year, and in forty minutes or less I guarantee I will have you in Diamond Harbour sitting on a veranda with a cold beer in your hand. We won today, didn't we? Tell me we won. I'll even throw in a back rub."

The way the morning had started, a back rub, a beer and a veranda in Diamond Harbour sounded one hell of a lot like victory. "Yeah." Bolan closed his eyes and leaned back in his seat. "Today we won."

* * * * *

TAKE 'EM FREE
2 action-packed novels plus a mystery bonus

NO RISK
NO OBLIGATION TO BUY